What man that sees the ever-whirling
  wheel
Of change, the which all mortal
  things doth sway,
But that thereby doth find, and
  plainly feel,
How mutability in them doth play
Her cruel sports, to many men's
  decay?

EDMUND SPENSER
BK.VII 1552(?) - 1599

Ever Whirling Wheels

Valerie M. Walland

SILVERDALE BOOKS

Ever Whirling Wheels

ISBN 0 9539567 0 9

Published by Silverdale Books
42 West Malvern Road
Malvern
WR14 4NA

Production co-ordinated by:
The Better Book Company Ltd.
Warblington Lodge
The Gardens
Warblington
nr. Havant
Hampshire PO9 2XH England
Telephone : 023 9248 1160
Facsimile : 023 9249 2819
Printed in England

Cover designed by Richard Draper

CHAPTER ONE

Reluctantly Rose woke to a new day. Stretching, and still only half awake, she hoped it had all been a bad dream. But, as she came fully awake, she knew she was not in her little room in College Road, she was in Ratcliff Court. She was fourteen and 1860 had just begun.

Should she light the candle? No, it was too cold to reach out of the bedcovers. Besides, she didn't need a candle to see the cracked ceiling; the frost-caked window; the missing panes stuffed with rags; the washstand holding her favourite basin and ewer, its painted roses reminding her of summer.

She went into her usual daydream, the one in which her father had not been killed and they still lived in their nice house. They were very happy, father, mother and Rose. Every morning she and mother waved father off to his Bank in the City. Every evening when he came home he would tell them about his day. Then they would tell him how well Rose was progressing with her reading, their walk in the park...

Thinking of the park brought her back to reality. They never went to the park now. The only outings they had were when mother managed to get work as an occasional dressmaker. Rose looked forward to these trips. They could get away from Ratcliff Court for an entire day. The houses they worked in were mostly in the new suburbs. Modest, semi-detached villas where only one or two servants were kept. Sometimes they would walk and sometimes they would take an omnibus. On arrival they would be shown to the sewing room situated on the top floor well away from the rest of the house. She did the plain sewing while mother cut out and sewed the dresses for the ladies and children of the house, the sewing machine clacking busily.

Sometimes they would be allowed to take home scraps of left-over material. Her beautiful patchwork bedcover had been made from these scraps. As she pulled it round herself she ran her hand over one particular piece of material. She had gazed at this piece so often that she could find its precise location even in the dark of a January morning. The square was covered with tiny beige flowers on a blue background and came from her favourite house which belonged to Mr and Mrs Wallace. Mrs Wallace was very kind and always told them to go down to the kitchen and get something to eat before they began work. The maid, Sarah, was very talkative and soon Rose knew all about the household.

"We used to live in the middle of London." Sarah had told them on their first day as they sat in front of the kitchen fire eating toast smothered in marmalade.

"When madam lost Master George – he was only three, poor little mite." Sarah looked across at Mrs Anderson and, lowering her voice said "Measles". Mrs Anderson nodded. Raising her voice and leaning forward Sarah continued.

"When madam became pregnant this time she got it into her head that it was the London air that was killing the babies. She had already lost two, you see." she explained "Nothing would satisfy her but we had to move out of London. It made a great deal of work I can tell you."

"The family have not lived here long then?" Mrs Anderson enquired.

"Only a few months. I don't like it very much. I prefer London. I'm thinking of getting another position."

Mrs Anderson was puzzled.

"I should have thought this was an easy position with only Mr and Mrs Wallace to look after."

"Oh, there are other children. Well, Mr John is not a child – he is the eldest and works with Mr Wallace at the factory. Miss Mary is eleven and Miss Grace is twelve. It's Miss Grace's birthday soon and Madam wants you to make some new dresses for her. Miss Grace has decided that none of her dresses are grown-up enough for a young lady of 13. When Miss Grace wants something there is no peace until she gets it."

Forestalling more gossip, Mrs Anderson got to her feet.

"Come along, Rose, we have work to do."

Rose enjoyed hearing about the inhabitants of the houses they worked in but not all servants were as friendly as Sarah nor the work as interesting. More often than not Rose and her mother had to work very hard mending acres of linen to earn their few pence. They were seldom offered refreshment and by the time they had finished it was usually late at night. When they arrived back at Ratcliff Court they were both exhausted.

Remembering these trips, Rose sighed. They were getting fewer and fewer. Rose knew that her stepfather took all the money they earned and she hated him for it. He didn't seem to earn any money although he went out in the evening, sometimes staying out all night. When her mother asked him where he had been he told her to mind her own business.

Her thoughts turned to last night. There were things she did not understand. For instance, why her mother had been so angry with her stepfather. It was not because he had come home drunk and bad-tempered. He had done that ever since they had come to live in Ratcliff Court, eighteen months ago.

Why did he have to get drunk? He had never done so while he was their lodger. Rose hadn't wanted them to have a lodger but mother had explained that father had left nothing with which to pay the bills. Taking in a lodger would mean they could still keep their heads above water. But things did not get better, only worse and they even had to dismiss the servant.

She had been shocked when her mother had announced that she was going to marry Mr Anderson. He was so unlike her gentle father. Mr Anderson was big and rough with a very loud voice and bristly side whiskers and moustache. On the day of the wedding he had made Rose kiss him and she thought it was horrible. She tried to avoid doing it again but he seemed to delight in making her, laughing at her protests. He had even tried to make her call him father but this she resolutely refused to do in spite of his threats of a beating if she did not.

The day before the wedding, Rose asked her mother why she was marrying such a horrible man. Her mother had been brisk and told her that it was the only way they could survive and she must put up with it. Then she told her that they would have to leave their nice house and sell most of their things. When Rose enquired where they would live she said she did not know. Mr Anderson had arranged everything.

The morning of the wedding came in spite of Rose's prayers. She had hoped for rain but it was a warm and sunny July day. They packed their few remaining possessions into the handcart which Anderson had managed to borrow from somewhere. Rose had some books which her father had given her. She had managed to conceal them from Anderson so far but how to get them out of the house? Finally she put them in the box containing the ewer and basin. She had had to plead very hard to be allowed to keep the ewer and basin but had won in the end. Once the cart was loaded they set out to walk from College Road to the Church. It seemed a very long way. The streets became narrower, meaner and noisier. Anderson pushed the cart along the road leaving Rose and her mother to follow as best they could. He did not look back once nor slacken his pace. Several times he was lost to sight in the crowds and they had to push their way through until he came into view again. Eventually he stopped in front of some black iron railings. A notice board informed anyone who might be interested that here was St George's-in-the-East.

Anderson looked round and, seeing a ragged boy, called him over. As Rose and her mother caught up he spoke to them for the first time since leaving the house.

"Here we are. The boy will look after the cart."

Rose remembered very little of the service. The Church was dark in spite of the bright sunshine outside. When it was over they emerged and stood blinking in the strong sunlight. Anderson gave the boy a penny and pushed the cart down the street. After a short walk he had turned down a narrow alley.

Rose had thought this a dreadful place and had shrunk closer to her mother who had put a protective arm round her. Rose had felt her shaking. They had walked past shops and public houses, pawn-shops and strange buildings which emitted pungent smells when women, carefully carrying large jugs, came out through the doors. The street had been crowded with people who all seemed to be shouting at the tops of their lungs. In the distance she had seen an enormous wall over the top of which a crowd of ships masts could be seen. They were near the river then.

Anderson had stopped and turning to them with a broad smile had said, with relish, "This is Ratcliff Highway and here," indicating a narrow entrance between two buildings, "is your new home." Rose's attention had been attracted to the building to the left of the entrance. It was a shop of sorts which seemed to be full of animals in cages. The door was propped open and the smell coming from inside made her feel sick. A sign over the door in badly faded gold lettering read "Jamrocks – Wild Beast Dealers."

Anderson had looked at her closely. "Can you read what that sign says?"

Rose had felt her mother stiffen.

"No – I can't read" she had replied.

"The other side is No 29" Anderson had informed her then, seeing her blank stare, "where the murders were committed."

In spite of herself Rose had been curious.

"Murders?"

"Four people murdered. The baby had its throat cut and..."

"Stop it!" Mrs Anderson had taken his arm and shook it as she saw Rose had gone white.

Anderson had laughed and pushed the cart through the entrance.

Rose had looked round. It did not seem possible that anything could be worse than the Highway. This had been. They stood in the middle of a square composed of three-storey terraced houses. There was hardly a window with its full share of glass. Some windows had been boarded up. Washing, a uniform grey, hung from lines secured across the corners of buildings. Each doorway had at least two ragged children sitting on the doorstep. The courtyard was paved with cobblestones greasy with filth. The smell was overpowering. A dog had come and sniffed round Anderson's feet. He had kicked it away.

It yelped. A man had sauntered out of a doorway. A woman, pulling a ragged shawl round her shoulders, had followed him.

"Anderson is it?" Anderson nodded. Digging into the pocket of his ragged trousers he had produced a large iron key.

"That one," indicating a house two-thirds of the way round the courtyard. Leaning familiarly on the man's shoulder the woman had looked them up and down but said nothing.

Anderson had nodded and taken the key, then pushed the cart to the door of the house. Handing the key to his wife, he ordered, "Get the door open and these things inside."

Mrs Anderson had recoiled.

"We can't live here!" she had protested.

"You're lucky to be living anywhere. It'll teach the pair of you not to have such superior airs. Think yourselves lucky that you have the whole house to yourselves. These houses have at least eight families in them, several them sharing one room. You have a house all to yourself. Now get the door open."

Without a word Mrs Anderson had taken the profferred key, inserted it in the lock and opened the door.

The house was very small, very dark and very smelly. The front door opened onto a small room, a rickety wooden staircase in one corner led upstairs.

Anderson sniffed.

"Needs scrubbing. There's a pump out in the courtyard. Get some water from that. I shall expect it done by the time I get back." Then he had left them.

It had taken hours to clean the house. Several slatternly women came and peered in at the downstairs window until Mrs Anderson contrived a curtain from a tablecloth.

The previous owner had left a wooden table downstairs and two beds upstairs. The upstairs room had been partitioned into two rooms. The only entrance to the second room being through the first. Rose was told to put her things into the small second room.

Life now consisted of trying to keep the place clean, food on the table and a fire in the grate. At the end of each day they fell into bed tired out. Rose's only relaxation her books, which she hid under a loose floorboard beneath her bed. In summer she could read until late but in the winter she had to be careful not to use up too much of her candle. She was certain that, although she never mentioned them, her mother knew she had managed to keep the books.

One night, about six months after they had moved to Ratcliff Court, Rose woke to find her mother sitting on the end of her bed shielding a lighted candle with her hand.

"What is it, mother?"

"Nothing, I am sorry I woke you. We will leave here one day, Rose, I promise. I have plans but it will take time. Do you think you can put up with things a little longer?"

"I will try," Rose sleepily replied.

"Good girl. Now go back to sleep."

Rose hated her stepfather. Lately she had caught him staring at her. It had made her feel uncomfortable without knowing why. Last night he had come into her room, woken her up and told her to get dressed and come downstairs. Her mother who had followed him into the room asked sharply, "What do you want with Rose?"

"She's coming out with me. I'll introduce her to a few of my friends – they'll like her with those green eyes and black hair – she could make our fortunes."

"You keep your nasty friends away from my daughter!"

"Am I the master in my own house or am I not?" He turned back to Rose who was getting out of bed.

"Hurry up! Make it quick or I shall come back and hurry you up!"

Then to Rose's relief, he left the room.

Rose hurriedly began dressing.

Speaking quickly, her mother ordered, "Stay here, Rose. When I have gone ram the chair against the door."

Rose did as she was bid and then put her ear to the door. She could hear her mother shouting. She had never heard her do that before. She could not stay here, her mother needed her. Quietly removing the chair from the door she crept through the outer room, stopped at the top of the stairs and looked down into the room below. Her mother and stepfather were confronting each other, her tiny mother glaring up into his face.

"Rose is going nowhere with you. I don't care about myself but I *do* care about my daughter."

He went purple with rage.

"The pair of you think you are so grand, don't you! Well, you have both got to earn your keep. Where *is* that girl?"

Rose watched, unable to move. As he turned to make for the stairs Rose shrank back but saw her mother snatch up the poker and go after him. He heard her and, half turning, flung up his arms to protect his face. She was aiming for his head but as she was so tiny and he was so tall she could not reach and, instead, the poker hit his left forearm. Rose heard a sound like a twig snapping then, without a sound, he fell to the floor and lay still.

Rose ran down the stairs.

"Is he dead?" she asked apprehensively.

"No, but I think his arm is badly broken. You go to bed, Rose, I can manage here." She gently shooed Rose upstairs.

Rose knew she would never sleep but she obediently got undressed and into bed. After a long time her mother came and said goodnight as if nothing had happened. Rose took one look at her face and decided against asking any questions. She had intended staying awake but she was exhausted. Now she had woken up and it was not all a dream.

She pulled back the bedclothes, got out of bed and lit the candle. It was bitterly cold. She dressed as quickly as she could but even so her hands were too numb to do up the tiny buttons on her dress. As she was struggling her mother came into the room.

"Let me do that for you, Rose," she said.

"Can't we go away, Mother?" she begged not for the first time. This time she was surprised when her mother agreed.

"Yes, I have been thinking all night and I have an idea. Get your things together and make a bundle. Then come downstairs but be very quiet."

"Stepfather?"

"He is still asleep."

After her mother had left the room Rose began to pile the things she would take with her on the bed. She would use the bedcover to carry them in. This did not take long as she was wearing her only dress. Just as she was tying up the corners of the bedcover she remembered her books. She could not go without her books! She wasn't going to leave any of them for HIM! Quickly she rescued them from their hiding place. It was then that she realized she would not be able to take her basin and ewer as they would be too heavy. She would have to make do with her books. Taking the basin and ewer off the washstand she put them on the bed, wrapped them in the bedclothes then, with tears in her eyes, took off her shoe and used it to smash them to pieces. He would not be able to sell them now!

Putting her shoe back on and grabbing up her bundle in one hand and her candle in the other, she didn't look back as she made her way down the stairs to where her mother stood at the bottom.

Neither of them looked at the body lying on the floor.

"Put out the candle and come along." Rose blew out her candle and, pulling their shawls over their heads, they let themselves out into the Court. It was barely light. The frost shone on the cobblestones. There was nobody about at this early hour. It was slippery underfoot as the filth that usually littered the slimy stones had frozen into a solid mass. They walked quickly across the courtyard and out into Ratcliff Highway.

CHAPTER TWO

The pavement was icy and Rose walked very carefully. She had never been out so early in the morning. The only sign of life was forms huddled in doorways. It was entirely different to what it was when they came back late at night after work. Then it was a frightening place. Sometimes sailors, each with a girl on his arm, would link arms and push their way down the pavement forcing people to step into the road almost under the horses' feet. There were shops emitting strange smells. Bold-looking girls with skirts above their ankles. There was a bright building with light blazing through the windows and such a tremendous noise of singing and laughing and shouting that Rose wondered how they could possibly hear what they were saying to each other.

From time to time the door would open and several people would stagger out. When she had asked her mother if they were ill she was told that they were drunk. There seemed to be a great many people who were drunk. Occasionally a man would approach them and say something to her mother who would give him such a frosty look that he would apologize and go staggering off to accost one of the bold girls. Now the Highway was quiet, waiting for the dark.

Rose was relieved when they left the Highway and came to the wide thoroughfare.

"Where are we going?" she enquired.

"To Mrs Wallace's but I am afraid that we must walk. I don't have enough money for the fare."

"Do we have a sewing job there?"

"No, but I must see her."

They said no more. Daylight began to lighten the streets. The short January day began. The street was filling with people going to their work. Men in working clothes with here and there a woman hurrying along, her shawl wrapped tightly round her. The traffic was denser here and the horses sometimes slipped on the icy road. Rose watched as a horse pulling a heavily laden farm wagon slipped to its knees. The driver jumped down from his perch and tried to get it to its feet. The traffic was halted while other drivers came to the man's assistance. Between them they managed to get the horse up. It was trembling and steaming in the cold air.

Omnibuses went rattling by full of city men going to their desks. The pavement was crowded. They were jostled and forced to slow down. As they got further from the city centre the streets became quieter and they could walk at their own pace. It was now full daylight. The streets were wider and lined with trees. First, small terraced houses and then, large detached ones. Each house had a front garden containing at least one huge tree now bare of leaves. Several omnibuses passed them as they trudged along and Rose wished that they had been able to afford the penny fare. Her feet were completely numb and her hands, one clutching her bundle and the other keeping her shawl together, were frozen. It had not seemed so far on the omnibus.

"Nearly there, Rose," her mother said encouragingly, as Rose began to drag her feet.

"Why are we going to Mrs Wallace's if there is no work and where are we going to sleep tonight?" Rose was feeling anxious.

Mrs Anderson slowed down. As they walked she explained that she had decided to ask Mrs Wallace if she would take Rose as an extra servant.

"Mrs Wallace seems kind and I am sure she will at least listen to what I have to say. The fact that she is pregnant is a point in our favour."

"But what will <u>you</u> do? Where will you go? Are you going to ask Mrs Wallace to give you a job too?"

"No, I don't think Mrs Wallace would even consider that. I want to get you settled. I am going to try and get a post as a cook and I think I know where I can do that. I have been making enquiries for some time. I knew we would have to leave some day but I was hoping it would not be necessary until the summer, when I had money put by."

"Here we are." Her mother halted in front of one of a pair of new semi-detached villas and turning to Rose she opened her shawl and unpinned her brooch from her dress "Before we go in I want to give you this." Rose knew that it was the only piece of jewellery that she had left. She had resisted all Anderson's attempts to make her sell it. It was a golden heart tendril with three pearls suspended from the centre. It had been a present from Rose's father their last Christmas together.

"But you always wear that brooch," Rose protested.

"I want you to have it, then I know that it is safe." She undid Rose's shawl and pinned the brooch to her dress.

Before Rose could answer Mrs Anderson gathered up her skirts, opened the iron gate and proceeded up the path to the main entrance of the house. Rose was very surprised. Normally they went to the kitchen door. They had never gone to the front entrance.

The entrance was, in Rose's opinion, very elegant. White marble pillars stood either side of the porch. The door was set back in a recess, the walls lined half-way up with blue and white tiles. The floor in contrast having black and white tiles. The fanlight over the door was picked out in red, green and blue glass, the clear glass lozenge in the middle painted with a black "No 13".

Mrs Anderson raised the brass doorknocker, smiled at Rose and knocked on the door.

They waited and Rose felt like running away as she was sure they would get into trouble. Sarah opened the door and looked at them in amazement.

"What are you doing here?" she peered back over her shoulder and lowered her voice.

"Madam is in a bad mood today. I don't think it will be very long now. Why didn't you go to the kitchen door?"

"I have some business I want to discuss with Mrs Wallace."

Sarah looked doubtful.

"I don't think she will want to discuss dressmaking today."

"It is not about dressmaking and it is very urgent. Please try and do something, Sarah. I have to see her."

"Come in then and let me get this door shut before she complains about the draught."

Sarah ushered them into the hall. As they had always gone to the upper floor via the back staircase Rose had never been in this part of the house before and looked round with interest.

The floor was tiled in a decorative square pattern. The walls covered with paintings. There seemed to be scarcely space between them. There was just room for an iron hallstand. One side of the hall was taken up with a carved wooden staircase which lead to a small landing before continuing to the first floor. Beyond the staircase the hall led to a heavy mahogany door. Admonishing them not to sit on the hall chairs, Sarah pulled her cap straight, approached one of the several doors lining the hall and, after knocking lightly upon it, entered. They heard a weary voice say "What is it, Sarah?" before the door was shut.

Gratefully Rose loosened her shawl in the warmth of the hall.

"What will we do if Mrs Wallace does not want me?"

"I don't think we need worry about that. I am sure that if I can persuade her to listen to me she will be only too pleased to help us."

Sarah re-appeared.

"Madam will see you, but only for a few minutes."

She stood aside for them to enter the room which was warmed by a blazing fire in the grate. A few watercolours on the walls, little tables everywhere covered with books, pieces of china and pieces of material. On a little table by the window were three miniatures. One of a little girl with blonde ringlets and rosy cheeks. The other of a rather sullen looking boy of about seven and a small chubby child who must be the boy who died aged three. All three frames were covered in black crepe. A piece of sewing had been tossed aside on to a chair. Mrs Wallace lay on a sofa drawn up in front of the fire. She was very pale and very heavily pregnant. Her blue eyes regarded them wearily.

"Thank you, Sarah, that will be all. Stay outside the door. I will ring if I need anything."

"Yes, madam."

Mrs Wallace waited until the door had closed.

"Please come and sit down, Mrs Anderson." She indicated a chair near her. "And – Rose, isn't it? Sit on this little stool by the fire. You both look frozen." After she had made sure they were comfortable Mrs Wallace asked

"Now, what is this all about?"

Taking a deep breath Mrs Anderson leaned forward in her chair.

"I am desperate, Madam. You were the only person I could think of who could help me. May I speak to you in private?"

Mrs Wallace looked surprised but said, "Certainly."

From the table beside her she picked up and rang a small bell.

Sarah appeared almost immediately.

"Take Rose to the kitchen, Sarah."

Rose looked at her mother who nodded and patted her arm.

"Off you go, Rose."

As she followed Sarah from the room she wondered why her mother needed to speak to Mrs Wallace in private. After all she, Rose, knew that she was going to ask Mrs Wallace to give her a position as a domestic of some sort. Sarah walked quickly down the hall, through the mahogany door, descended a short flight of steps and entered the kitchen.

Rose had been in the kitchen before but now she looked round with interest knowing that, if her mother was successful, this would be where she would spend most of her life. Situated in the basement it was dull on the brightest of August days but now, on a dark January morning with only feeble daylight coming from the high window, it was gloomy and would have been depressing but for the light from the twin globes of the gas chandelier. The firelight from the black leaded range threw a red glow over the tiled floor. Close to the fire on a black and red rag mat a wooden armchair was placed. A scrubbed wooden table took up much of the floor space. Nearly the whole of one wall was taken up with a large wooden dresser full of china, jelly moulds and cooking utensils.

Sarah indicated the wooden armchair and Rose sank down gratefully and held her cold feet out to the warmth.

Sitting down on one of the wooden chairs drawn up at the table and picking up a cleaning rag Sarah began polishing a silver candlestick.

"So, why are you here then?" she asked curiously.

"We have left home."

"Left home! Well I never. Why?"

"My stepfather is not very nice and..." she hesitated. She didn't want to tell Sarah about her mother hitting him with the poker. She knew that Sarah was a great gossip. "We decided to leave."

"I see – things got a bit too much did they?" Sarah asked shrewdly.

"Yes, they did. Mother decided that she had had enough and she is hoping that Mrs Wallace will take me on as extra help. She will need more help with a baby."

"*I* could certainly do with some help. Do you know I have had to do everything for the last two years? The cook left and they never bothered to get another. Mrs Wallace kept saying she would once we moved but she never has. She has been very poorly you know. I think ..."

A bell jangled. Rose and Sarah both looked up at the row of bells on the wall by the passage door. The one marked "morning room" was juddering on its spring. Sarah flung down her cloth and jumped to her feet. Rose was not sure what to do and ended up trailing along the hall behind her.

CHAPTER THREE

As they entered the sitting room Rose glanced at her mother who smiled and nodded. Mrs Wallace said, "Thank you, Sarah. Will you wait for a moment, please?"

Obediently Sarah stood by the door with her hands folded demurely in front of her. The picture of the discreet servant.

"Come here, Rose." Rose obediently walked forward to stand in front of Mrs Wallace. She folded her hands in front of her as Sarah had done.

"I have had a long talk with your mother, Rose, and I have decided to employ you as a maid-of-all-work. You are rather young but I am sure you are a hard worker and you look strong. You will be given your uniform and one afternoon off every three weeks. Your wages will be £7 per year all found. As you get older and if you give satisfaction I may pay you more. Do you attend Church?"

Rose hastened to reassure her.

"Oh yes, madam, we used to attend St. George's when we could."

"Good. You will be expected to attend morning and evening service. We attend Trinity Church."

Rose was overjoyed! She would never be going back to Ratcliff Court again! She would never have see her stepfather again!

"Thank you very much Mrs Wallace – madam." she corrected herself.

"Sarah will inform you of your duties and show you where to sleep. I hope that you will be happy here."

"Oh yes, thank you, madam," Rose managed to say.

Mrs Anderson got to her feet.

"Thank you very much, Mrs Wallace. I was sure that as a mother you would understand."

Mrs Wallace smiled.

"Please see Mrs Anderson out, Sarah."

Sarah came to life.

"Yes, madam."

Mrs Wallace nodded and, picking up her sewing, began to stitch.

When they were out in the hall Sarah relaxed and said, "Say goodbye now, Rose, and I will come back in a few minutes to take you to your room."

Rose hugged her mother enthusiastically.

"I am so pleased, mother."

"So am I, Rose. I want you to remember that I shall always be thinking of you wherever I am. I will write to you as soon as I am settled and you must promise to write to me."

"Yes, I will and we can meet on my half day."

"We will have to hope that our half days coincide then won't we" her mother laughed.

She kissed Rose goodbye and walked to the door turned, smiled, and walked out shutting the door behind her.

Rose suddenly felt very much alone. Sarah coming down the hall and seeing her woebegone face said briskly, "Come on then, bring your bundle and I'll show you your room."

She led the way back to the kitchen. "This way," she said taking Rose through the door by the side of the kitchen dresser which led to a steep uncarpeted staircase. Rose followed Sarah up the stairs – they seemed to go on for ever. The staircase came out onto a small landing. At one end an uncurtained window let in enough light for her to see two plain white-painted doors either side of the top of the stairs.

Sarah walked to the left-hand door and opened it.

"In some houses the servants have to share a room. We are lucky, I suppose," she admitted grudgingly. "This will be yours. I am next door. I'll go and get you some bedlinen."

The room was small with a window high up in the wall. The roof sloped down nearly to the floor at one end of the room. A small brass bedstead took up all the room beneath the window. On the opposite wall a tiny black castiron grate containing a fan of paper. A small chest-of-drawers, a basin and ewer on a washstand completed the furniture.

It was much smaller than her room in College Road but much, much nicer than the one in Ratcliff Court.

Sarah returned with sheets, pillow cases and blankets. Rose hugged the blankets to her. They were thick and warm.

Sarah stood in the doorway with her arms folded and watched Rose make her bed, take her clothes out of her bundle and put them away neatly in the chest of drawers. Finally Rose threw the patchwork bedcover over the bed. Now she felt more at home.

Coming further into the room Sarah fingered the patchwork bedcover.

"Did you make this?"

"Yes, from scraps of material that we were given."

"You are a very good needlewoman, Rose. That could come in handy one of these days."

Sarah idly picked up one of the books which Rose had placed in a row on the mantelpiece over the grate.

"Books! What are you doing with books?"

"My father bought them for me." At the thought of her father Rose's eyes filled with tears.

"Oh, come on," said Sarah, "Let's go down to the kitchen and have a cup of tea."

Once in the kitchen Rose removed her shawl and Sarah noticed her brooch.

"We are not allowed to wear any jewellery. I should pin it on the inside of your dress. If madam can't see it you'll not get into trouble."

"Thank you," Rose was grateful. Sarah watched her as she carried out her instructions.

"I have an old print dress you can borrow. madam will give you a bolt of cloth to make up, I expect. You will need an apron and a cap. I might have something you can alter."

Rose thanked her. She was going to be busy with her needle this winter! Sarah got up and placed a large kettle on the range.

"Is there anything I can do?" Rose asked.

Sarah looked up from arranging the crockery on the table.

"You can make the tea – the caddy is on the mantelpiece – make it nice and strong. Madam gives me a weekly allowance of tea and sugar. She'll have to increase that now you're here." Sarah said with satisfaction.

As they sat drinking their tea Sarah instructed Rose in her duties as maid-of-all-work.

"You get up at 6.00, we are allowed an extra half-hour in bed in the winter. You stir up the kitchen range and set the table for our breakfast. At 6.30 *prompt* mind! you bring me a cup of tea. After we have had our breakfast you sweep and dust the dining room, that is *after* you have cleaned the grate and laid the fire. Then you sweep the hall and the front porch. All this *must* be done before the family come down to breakfast at 8 o'clock," she said severely. Then she paused, frowning as if trying to remember what else Rose had to do.

Rose wondered what Sarah would be doing all this time but had the sense not to ask.

"Then you help me get up the breakfast for the family. I will serve the breakfast in the dining room," she said grandly. "After the family have finished you will wash the dishes in the scullery," she waved her hand to indicate the scullery door. "I will tell you the rest of the morning's work later. Of course when Miss Mary and Miss Grace come home there will be more work for you to do."

Rose thought that what she had heard sounded quite enough! She had a thought and with Rose to think the thought was to ask the question.

"What does John do?"

"You must always call him 'Mr John,'" Sarah admonished. "I can see that I will have a lot to teach you about being in service! Mr John works with his father at the factory, so we don't see much of him. He sometimes works through the night if there is a lot of work. It's worse at Christmas time, of course."

"Why?"

"Mr Wallace owns Wallace & Son." Rose looked blank. Sarah explained, "They make children's toys. Mr Wallace designs them. At Christmas everyone is very busy. Mr Wallace and Mr John are hardly ever here, they spend most of their time at the factory. Mr Wallace often comes down into the kitchen and makes himself a sandwich. The family are not too much trouble although Miss Grace can be very difficult. She may be called Grace but that is as far as it goes. She seems to think that I have nothing better to do than fetch and carry for her all day long! I'm glad that you have come. Since Mrs Wallace has been ill I've had to let a lot of the work go."

Rose looked round the room.

"Yes, I can see that," she said tactlessly.

"I can't do everything, you know! Anyway, I hope to be leaving one of these days."

"Why?"

Sarah sat looking into the fire for some time, eventually she looked up and said, "I have been in service since I was twelve and I want a change. This household is different though."

"How?"

"Mrs Wallace is not as strict as most employers. Although she makes us go to Church twice on Sundays she doesn't interfere with the work. In a house this size we should have more servants. Mrs Wallace would like at least two more but Mr Wallace says he must put the money back into the business."

"How do you know that?"

"You hear a lot when you are a servant but you must *never* repeat anything – outside the house that is. I want to work in one of the big department stores and before you ask why – because I would meet more people and have more time off. And I want to get married and have a home of my own. I'm 24 – nearly too old. I never get a chance to meet anybody here. I only see the tradesmen and I don't want to marry a tradesman. When I have an afternoon off I have to go home and help my mother. She's a widow. But I can't leave Mrs Wallace now – not until she has had the baby. She has been ill for months. But I suppose" she looked speculatively at Rose "once the baby is born and I have you trained I could think about leaving."

"When is the baby due?" asked Rose.

"In about a month, I think."

"Then will you look for a job in a store?"

"Yes, I think I will – I don't like babies."

"But if you got married you would have babies of your own, wouldn't you?"

"Not necessarily."

"Why not?"

"That's not a subject for a young girl." Sarah was stern.

"Where are Miss Mary and Miss Grace?" Rose hastily asked.

"Since Madam has been so ill they have been staying with their Grandmother in Malvern. You do ask a lot of questions!"

Another bell jangled. This time it was the "Master Bedroom" bell.

Sarah slowly rose to her feet and left the room. Rose sat gazing into the fire. She could almost hear her mother's voice "Don't sit moping there, Rose, do some work – use your hands!"

She jumped up and began to stack the tea things preparatory to taking them into the scullery. She had just finished when Sarah came into the kitchen looking grave.

"I think madam is having the baby. I have to go and fetch the Doctor – you stay here in case she rings again," and snatching her shawl from a hook behind the kitchen door she was gone before Rose could ask her where Mrs Wallace's room was.

CHAPTER FOUR

Rose sat looking at the bell without taking her eyes from it until Sarah returned after what seemed a very long time.

"The Doctor is with her now." Sarah hung her shawl up. "We had best put some water on to boil."

A bell rang. They both looked at the bell board.

"That's the front door bell, go and open the door will you? It will be the nurse, she knows the way to Madam's room so you don't need to take her up. Come back here and help me. If the nurse stays we shall have even more work to do," Sarah grumbled.

There was a great deal of coming and going. The Doctor and nurse were in attendance all night. In the early morning hours the baby was born.

Rose sat at the kitchen table, her head on her arms, trying to sleep. Sarah sat dozing by the kitchen fire.

Doctor Thomas came into the kitchen and, walking over to Sarah, tapped her on the shoulder and ordered

"Go and fetch Rev. Oswin-Redway at once. Tell him the baby has to be christened straight away."

Rose raised her head.

"I thought anyone could christen a baby in an emergency." Rose spoke before she realized what she was doing. The Doctor swung round and, giving her a very straight look asked, "Who are you?"

"She's the new maid-of-all-work," Sarah was not pleased. It was not Rose's place to speak before she was spoken to and definitely not her place to question the Doctor!

Doctor Thomas turned back to Sarah,

"Your mistress is insisting that the baby be christened immediately."

"I will go at once, sir."

Sarah leapt to her feet. She knew her place even if Rose did not!

Once Sarah had left, Doctor Thomas sat down in the chair Sarah had vacated, stretched out his legs to the fire and sighed deeply. Then he said

"And where did you glean that piece of information?"

"It was in one of my books." Rose felt that she had broken some unspoken rule but did not know what it was.

"Do you have many books?" he yawned.

"Not many. I like reading." Rose told him.

"Good. You keep on reading. What is your name?"

"Rose – sir," she replied.

"Well, Rose sir, you don't seem the usual type of lowly servant. What made you take up this work?"

Rose had just launched into her history when the front door bell rang.

On opening it she found Sarah accompanied by a young man looking as if he had just got out of bed.

"This way, sir," Sarah pushed past Rose without looking at her "I'll take you to madam."

At that moment Dr Thomas came through the kitchen door into the hall and seeing Rev. Oswin-Redway and Sarah on their way upstairs he began to follow them. As he got to the small landing he turned and winked at Rose who was standing rather disconsolately at the bottom of the stairs. She smiled back at him and going back into the kitchen sat down at the table. She was tired, she had been running up and down stairs with hot water and towels all night. Sarah had decided that, since Rose was younger and therefore not so likely to get tired, she should be the one to carry up the hot cans of water, besides, as she told Rose, "You *are* the maid-of-all-work."

As she sat, half asleep, she remembered that during the night as she came downstairs after handing yet more hot water to the nurse a tall, grey-haired man had come running up the stairs.

"Who are you?" he had asked, startled.

"I'm Rose, sir."

"What are you doing here? Where is Sarah?"

"Mrs Wallace engaged me this morning and Sarah is in the kitchen boiling kettles, sir."

"I see. I'm Mr Wallace. I hope you will be happy here, Rose."

"Thank you, sir." Mr Wallace vanished up the stairs.

Now Rose was very tired. When Sarah returned she rather sharply informed her that there would be no time for sleep as the usual chores of the day had to be carried out whether they had any sleep or not.

During the morning the nurse came down into the kitchen with a list of instructions. She told them that she would be staying for several days at least. Sarah scowled – more work! Rose had only been in the house for twenty four hours but already knew that it was in her interest to keep Sarah in a good mood. Thinking to divert her

"What has the baby been called?" she asked.

"Amelia. She is still alive and every hour improves her chances. It is Mrs Wallace we are worried about now."

"Who does the baby look like?" enquired Sarah.

The nurse hesitated then said, "She looks like herself." She got to her feet. "I must get back to Mrs Wallace. I will be sleeping in the room adjoining hers. Perhaps one of you could make up a bed for me?"

"Rose will do that for you immediately," Sarah said grandly.

All the time Rose was making up the bed and lighting the fire she kept listening expecting to hear the baby cry but she heard nothing. Perhaps the poor thing had died after all.

Nurse came from Mrs Wallace's room to find Rose standing in a listening attitude.

"The baby is sound asleep and so is Mrs Wallace. You have done all you can. Thank you, Rose."

The household soon fell into a routine. Sarah doing the cooking and marketing, Rose doing the cleaning and any other jobs that Sarah gave her. The evenings she spent making her working dresses from a bolt of cloth she had purchased on Mrs Wallace's instructions relayed via Nurse Green.

Rose's day began before it was light but she did not mind. She would open the kitchen door and stand at the bottom of the steps that led up to the garden breathing in the frosty air, looking at the stars and thinking how nice it was to breathe clean air uncontaminated by the smell of wine, tobacco and spirits. Then, humming to herself, she would begin her work. Once the fire was going she would lay the table for breakfast and then take Sarah a cup of tea in bed.

One afternoon a few weeks after her arrival she had a letter by the second post. Sarah watched her as she put it carefully into her apron pocket to read later in her room.

"Letter from an admirer, Rose?" she asked

"Oh no, it's from my mother."

Sarah raised her eyebrows but Rose said no more.

She could not wait to get to her room that evening after her work was over. She lit her candle, undressed and getting into bed started to read. Her mother wrote that she had met an old neighbour of theirs from College Road days who was now a widow and worked as housekeeper to a very wealthy old lady. When she mentioned that she was looking for a position as a cook, Mrs Cove told her that the old lady's cook had just left under rather unfortunate circumstances and her advice was to write to Mrs Stritch enquiring if the post was vacant. She had written immediately and Mrs Stritch had replied by return of post asking her to go for an interview. She had been offered the post there and then and had started straight away.

She had told the housekeeper about Rose and she had suggested that, in time, they might be able to persuade Mrs Stritch to let Rose go and work there too but they would have to take things slowly as Mrs Stritch would not be pushed and could be quite cantankerous when the mood took her. The letter ended "I hope that you are being a good girl and working hard. Remember your promise to write."

Rose looked at the address which was in Belgravia. She read and re-read the letter. She would learn as much as she could from Sarah and then she would be ready to join her mother.

With this in mind she cajoled Sarah into giving her some cooking lessons. She even managed to persuade her to let her help wait at table from time to time. With all this work she was kept extremely busy but found time to write to her mother.

On her first afternoon off she took her letter to the post and then went for a walk in the park. It was very convenient that there was a park so close, it would be nice to get out for a walk on summer evenings. On a freezing cold February day that looked like snow it was not very pleasant, however, so she went back early and getting one of her books sat down to read by the kitchen fire.

"What are you reading?" Sarah had been hoping for a chat.

"Its a lovely book called 'The Coral Island,'" replied Rose.

"What's it about?"

"It's about three boys who are ship-wrecked on an island and of their adventures. You can borrow it if you like."

"I can't read. You read me some."

After that Rose spent the evenings, once dinner had been served and cleared away, sitting in the kitchen armchair reading aloud while Sarah either did some sewing or sat on the other side of the fire with her skirt above her knees enjoying the warmth. In this way they managed to get through 'The Coral Island', Sarah expressing a preference for Jack Martin: "A tall strapping broad-shouldered youth of eighteen with a handsome, good-humoured, firm face."

"Sounds just the boy for me," she said.

Two of their favourites were 'Arabian Nights' and 'The King of the Golden River'.

Rose enjoyed these readings. When they got to the end of her little library they started all over again.

They were engrossed in "Simple Susan" one evening when Mr Wallace came into the kitchen and stood watching them for some moments. Sarah, suddenly realizing he was there, hastily adjusted her skirts and leapt to her feet. Rose, absorbed in the story, carried on reading until, sensing that Sarah was no longer sitting opposite, she looked up to see Mr Wallace standing by the kitchen table listening.

"Oh sir, I am so sorry." She was red with embarrassment.

"Don't be sorry, Rose. You read very well."

"My father gave me all these books," she indicated her entire library which was stacked on the table.

"That's quite a good collection, Rose." He bent to look at the titles.

"You have some good books here. They look well read. You will have to get yourself some new ones."

"I will when I have the money, sir," Rose said eagerly. "I love reading."

"I came down to ask if you could make Mrs Wallace some weak tea. She seems to have a fancy for it. I didn't ring as I was passing the kitchen anyway and Nurse is busy with Amelia."

Rose could not think where he could be going that he would pass the kitchen on the way. Sarah had told her that he was "a bit different to other employers and he likes to walk round the house at odd hours." From her tone of voice she did not approve of such eccentric behaviour.

While he waited for Sarah to make the tea he picked up 'The Coral Island'.

"This looks a very good tale, Rose, may I borrow it?"

"Yes, of course, sir." Rose stammered. All those books in his study and he was asking to borrow hers!

CHAPTER FIVE

Rose eagerly awaited another letter from her mother which, when it came, was very cheerful. She was enjoying working for Mrs Stritch but she did not like Mr Stritch, the old lady's son, who came and visited his mother from time to time. She had found a nice Church to go to and hoped that Rose was attending Trinity on Sundays. Perhaps she would write and tell her her opinion of the sermons?

Rose had been attending the services with Sarah who grumbled the entire time that they could have been sitting in the kitchen reading. Sarah had asked Rose to teach her to read. She was a very quick learner and was beginning to want some books of her own, in the meantime she made do with Rose's little library.

Rose wrote to her mother telling her about their reading lessons and how she enjoyed reading to Sarah. She described her days and how Mr Wallace frequently came down into the kitchen, sometimes just for a chat. Mrs Wallace had still not recovered fully from the baby's birth. She had a reply almost by return of post expressing concern at the free and easy manner that Mr Wallace allowed in his home. Mrs Anderson realized that it was difficult for him as his wife was so ill but she did not approve of the master or mistress frequenting the kitchen. Rose thought her mother would get on very well with Sarah on this point – she didn't like Mr Wallace's sudden appearances either. She went back to the letter. Her mother was also insistent that they read only the Bible on Sundays and not story books. She had nothing new to report regarding employment but she was sure that one day they would be together again.

Rose hastened to reply and assure her mother that she would read the Bible on Sundays and that she was sure that once Mrs Wallace was up again things would get back to normal. As she sat biting the end of her pen and wondering how to continue she realized that she was not particularly disappointed that she could not join her mother. She wanted to see her again of course but she had grown used to the freedom that she had at No. 13. Re-reading her mother's letter her eye caught a passage asking about the baby.

She resumed writing.

"The baby has never been seen. Nurse Green looks after her and sleeps in a room adjoining Mrs Wallace's room. I go up and clean the room while Nurse takes the baby out in its perambulator when the weather is fine but the baby is so wrapped up in shawls that I have never seen her yet. Sometimes on my afternoon off I go as far as the park with Nurse. When Nurse takes the baby from the perambulator to take her upstairs the baby is always covered in shawls. She hardly ever seems to cry. Miss Mary and Miss Grace are still at their Grandma's in Malvern. Sarah says she thinks that they will not be allowed to come home until Mrs Wallace is better."

She was quite pleased with this missive especially as she had managed to circumvent the question of her leaving No.13. She knew that she didn't want to do so but how to tell her mother? She would be so disappointed. She waited with some anxiety in case her mother had read between the lines. Usually she had a reply within a few days but several weeks went by and there was nothing. She must have hurt her mother but it was not like her to sulk.

When another month had gone by Rose was really worried. Perhaps her mother had been taken ill and nobody knew where Rose lived! Finally she plucked up the courage to write to Mrs Cove asking her if she could tell her if her mother was ill. She had a reply within a few days. She was so anxious to read it that she did not put it in her pocket as she usually did but opened it immediately there in the kitchen. When she read the contents to Sarah's consternation she fainted. Mr Wallace, on one of his restless walks round the house, heard Sarah's panic-stricken cry and rushed into the kitchen.

"Go and get some smelling salts," he ordered.

By the time a breathless Sarah returned he had managed to get Rose into the armchair. Snatching the bottle from Sarah's hand he thrust it under Rose's nose. She coughed, moaned, opened her eyes, stared at him, then burst into tears.

"What happened?" Mr Wallace asked Sarah who knelt by the side of Rose patting her hand.

"I don't know, sir. She had a letter from her mother and when she read it she just fainted. It must be bad news."

"You are probably right." He picked up the letter from the floor.

"May I read it, Rose?" he asked gently.

Rose nodded and he swiftly read the short letter.

"No wonder you fainted."

Sarah so far forgot herself as to almost shout at him.

"What is it? What's the matter?"

"May I read it to Sarah?" He asked Rose who nodded wearily.

"I can read now, thank you, Mr Wallace." Sarah said proudly taking the letter from him.

It was brief and to the point. Sarah read silently mouthing the words as she did so.

"Dear Miss Anderson

I am sorry to have to tell you that Mrs Anderson no longer works in this establishment.

As she had informed me that she was a widow I was extremely distressed when a man insisting that he was her husband came to the house. He said that she frequently ran away from home. Unfortunately the Master was visiting his mother at the time and he immediately dismissed Mrs Anderson who had no choice but to go with her husband who was causing a scene.

She did manage to give me a message for you but since I had no idea where you were I could not deliver it until now. She asked me to tell you that she will be in touch with you and that you are not to worry.

I am sorry if this causes you distress.

Mrs S. Cove, Housekeeper."

Rose stood up, looking a little better.

"I am sorry, sir. It was silly of me to faint but it was such a shock."

"Of course it was, Rose. Sarah go and find Nurse Green and ask her to come here. I think we need an expert opinion."

"Oh, please don't get Nurse, sir, I'm sure I'll be fine now".

"I would be happier if Nurse had a look at you." William was firm.

Rose sank back down into the armchair.

When Sarah came back with the Nurse Mr Wallace took himself off to his study after telling Sarah to let him know Nurse's verdict.

Nurse Green asked Rose a few questions and took her pulse.

"Nothing to worry about. Would you like to go to bed for a while, Rose?"

"No thank you, I'm feeling much better now. I want to go and see Mr Wallace."

Nurse nodded and said, "Just as you like. There is nothing physically wrong. Just shock."

Knocking on the study door Rose waited for permission to enter. When he saw that it was Rose and not Sarah, William got up from his desk and led her to the leather armchair.

"Are you feeling better, Rose?"

"Much better, sir. Nurse says it was shock. I have come to ask for permission for time off to go and see if my mother is alright."

"Of course you can, Rose, and here," he fished in his pocket, "is enough money for your fare so that you can go on the omnibus."

"Thank you, sir. I will pay it back."

"Do you want to go now? As it is Sarah's afternoon off she can go with you for part of the way to make sure you are not on your own."

"Thank you, sir." Rose curtsied and left the room.

After she had gone William stared at the door for a while then nodded to himself as if he had made up his mind about something and went back to work.

As soon as they were safely outside the house Sarah told Rose she was going to go to every Department Store in the West End to see if she could get an interview. She was very excited.

"Don't say anything, will you? I don't want them to know," jerking her head backwards at the house.

Rose promised to keep it secret at the same time wondering what she would do if Sarah left.

Sarah chattered about her plans all the way to the omnibus stop. Sarah's omnibus came along first and she waved cheerfully to Rose as she jumped on.

After alighting from her omnibus Rose made her way to Ratcliff Court. They had never been accepted in the Court. The women seemed to take a malicious pleasure in taunting them, making loud remarks to each other every time Rose went to get water from the communal pump in the middle of the court. She learnt to ignore remarks such as "'ere comes 'er bleedin' Majesty – more water – must be cleanin' the palace again!" "There are some as think they're better than the likes of us." "Quick make yer curtsey Lena or yer'll get took to the Tower!" These sallies would evoke loud laughter from the women, all except one who seemed to keep herself to herself.

The other women treated her as if she did not exist. She did not even rate taunts. She would stand silently watching Rose as she queued for her turn at the pump, more often than not pushed roughly to the back of the queue. One day she came and stood by Rose's side. Rose was not pushed that day. Rose filled her bucket and turned to thank her but she had disappeared. Several times the woman came between Rose and her tormentors and once she rescued her from a group of men. She never spoke.

Now, as she walked further into the court, it appeared even worse than she remembered. Children, ragged and half-naked, still played on the filthy cobblestones watched by shabby, unkempt women who leaned in doorways with arms folded. Above their heads washing hung, limp, grey, dispirited, mirroring the women who had hung it there.

Rose no longer felt intimidated. She had grown-up in the last few months. She found she felt sorry for them. What had they to look forward to? A life spent in drudgery, frequently pregnant, more often than not nursing bruises inflicted by a drunken husband, alcohol their only escape from reality, an early death their only release.

She looked for her silent friend but she could not see her. Pulling her shawl close around her she made her way to her former home. The women stopped their gossiping and watched, silently.

Reaching the door she knocked, firmly.

No response.

She knocked again – louder this time. There was a snarl from the other side of the door and it was flung open and her step-father stood in the doorway. He peered through tiny, blood-shot eyes. He was filthy and looked as if he had been sleeping in his clothes for days. Below his rolled up sleeve his left forearm hung, limp and distorted. He frowned at her then, recognizing her, began to smile. It was an unpleasant smile which never reached his eyes. His expression became thoughtful as he looked her up and down.

"So you've come back, have you? I knew you would, one day. You've filled out. You could be useful to me – earn your keep."

She felt frightened but was determined not to show it.

"I've not come back. I came to see my mother. Where is she? Inside?"

He stared at her, then scowled, and said, "No, she isn't. She ran off again but I shall find her one of these days. I've a score to settle with her."

He touched his left arm with his right hand so that there was no doubt as to his meaning.

"You don't know where she is then?" Rose was dismayed.

"No I don't, more's the pity but you'll do. *You* can come and look after me."

Before she could step backwards he grasped the front of her dress. She struggled.

"No, I won't!" She was really frightened now.

His grasp tightened and he began to pull her, struggling, through the doorway. Her shawl slid from her shoulders. Anderson's right hand grasping her by the front of her dress fastened on her brooch and he began to pull it off tearing the dress.

"No! That was my mother's. You shan't have it."

Putting one hand over the brooch she pushed him violently with the other. Caught off balance, Anderson staggered and letting go of her grasped the door jamb with his good hand to steady himself. Rose took her chance and, picking up her shawl which had fallen to the ground, she ran from the court never looking back. She kept running until she got to the end of Ratcliff Highway where, wrapping her shawl round herself to hide her torn dress, she slowed down to walk to the omnibus stop. As she waited she tried to think where her mother might have gone. She would not have gone back to the house in Belgravia as she would not be welcome. Perhaps she would come to Rose. At the thought Rose began to convince herself that her mother was already at the house. There was only Nurse Green in! She was impatient to get back and when the omnibus eventually arrived hardly waited for it to stop before leaping on.

CHAPTER SIX

It was dark by the time she got back to No. 13 and let herself into the kitchen. Sarah was just setting out the tea things. Scarcely through the door Rose asked, "Has anyone come asking for me?"

"Not since I've been in. I haven't been in very long. What do you think? I have a new job in Harrington's in Oxford Street! It's just what I always wanted..."

Rose let Sarah's chatter flow over her. She pondered what to do next.

Seeing that she was not really listening Sarah asked, "Did you find your mother?"

"No, she was not there. He doesn't know where she is." As she spoke Rose removed her shawl. As she turned from hanging it up behind the kitchen door Sarah saw her torn dress.

"Did he do that?" she asked, shocked.

Rose held her dress together.

"Yes! He wanted my brooch but he didn't get it."

"Go and change your dress, then come and help me with the teas."

As she changed into her working dress Rose made up her mind that she would ask Mr Wallace if he could do anything to help her find out what had happened to her mother. She didn't know what he could do but he was a rich man with a factory of his own so he must be able to do SOMETHING. She didn't go straight back to the kitchen but up the stairs to the hall. Mr Wallace's study was situated next to the sitting room. Hoping he would be there she tapped on the door.

"Come in."

Mr Wallace looked up from a desk piled with papers.

"There you are, Rose. Did you see your mother?"

"No, sir – here is your change."

She handed him the coins and as he took them to her surprise and shame she began to sob. Mr Wallace got up from his chair and guided her to the large leather armchair. She sank down into it, still sobbing. William thrust a handkerchief into her hand then, with great patience, extracted her story from her.

How she had once lived in a nice house with her mother and father. They even had a servant. Her father worked in a bank in the City. She did not know which one. They were all very happy until the day the policeman came to tell them that her father had been killed by a horse which had slipped on the icy cobbles and crushed him.

How her mother had tried taking in lodgers and doing some sewing but it was no use, the money was not sufficient. Then Mr Anderson had come to lodge with them and had persuaded her mother to marry him. Once they were married he had changed completely and had ill treated them both.

When all the money had gone they ended up in Ratcliff Court – the last stop before the workhouse. Leaving nothing out she concluded by relating how her mother had brought her here and how kind Mrs Wallace had been.

"When I went today he said that she had gone and he didn't know where but he would find her. He wants revenge for his crippled arm."

"Would you like me to see what I can find out?" he asked

"Oh, would you, sir! I would be so grateful."

"Very well, I will try to find out all I can. Now you go and make yourself a nice cup of tea and then you will feel better."

She gave him back his handkerchief which he accepted with a smile and went back to a Sarah, agog with curiosity, who had to be content with the information that Mr Wallace had promised to see if he could discover where her mother was.

At the end of that week Sarah left. When it came to the point she was sad to go but at the same time pleased to get out of domestic service. She took a tearful farewell of Rose making her promise that she would go into the store on one of her afternoons off.

Nurse Green was still in the house and Rose was kept busy with the housework and the cooking. She was pleased to be so busy, it stopped her worrying. Mr Wallace had not said anything to her so she assumed there was nothing to report.

One sunny day in May Mrs Wallace was pronounced by Doctor Thomas to be fit enough to come downstairs for afternoon tea. Rose was delighted. She baked some very light cakes and made sure that the sitting room fire was burning brightly.

Coming down the stairs on her husband's arm Mrs Wallace looked thin and pale and her expression had a petulance which had not been there before.

Later that day, after Mrs Wallace had returned to her room, Rose and Nurse Green had their customary cup of afternoon tea in the kitchen.

"It was so nice to see madam up again," Rose said.

Nurse shook her head. "I am not happy about her."

"But surely Dr. Thomas said she was out of danger?"

"She's out of danger, yes, but she does not want anything to do with the baby. I am afraid that Mrs Wallace's illness has affected her very badly."

"Perhaps she will take to the baby when she is completely recovered," Rose said soothingly.

Nurse shook her head but said nothing.

Rose still hoped that Mrs Wallace would accept the baby but, although she appeared to make a good physical recovery, she was not the same. She spent her days lying on a sofa in the sitting room, either gazing listlessly into the fire or doing embroidery for a short time and then flinging it down with a sigh.

Mr Wallace was hardly ever at the office these days. He spent a great deal of his time with his wife, trying to get her interested in something, anything, but she was not interested in her music, she didn't want to go out to concerts which previously she had loved and she refused to entertain. She didn't want to do anything.

One morning Rose, who was behind with her work, was still laying the study fire when Mr John and Mr Wallace came into the room after breakfast. They were so deep in conversation that they did not see her where she crouched by the fireplace raking coals.

"It is no good, father." Mr John sounded angry. "They want *you* to go to Paris. After all, you are the designer – you are the best person to explain the designs. We also need some new designs for the Christmas trade if we are not to lose our oldest customers. I know you can design at home but we need you to go over the designs with the foreman. Mother will probably improve once you are not waiting on her all the time."

"I don't think you realize how ill your mother has been. This birth was not like the others. It's a pity that she can't take to the baby. The poor thing will have enough problems in life without being rejected by her mother. Dr. Thomas tells me that it is just a question of time so far as your mother is concerned, but how much time? He doesn't seem to know. But yes, you are right, John, I have been neglecting the business and you have been carrying the burden for far too long. I will come in for a few hours tomorrow."

He saw Rose where she was busying herself with the fire.

"Thank you, Rose, you can leave the fire now. You have looked after us very well but it is too much for one person, however willing." As she drew breath to protest he continued, "I have engaged a cook which should take some of the burden from your shoulders and no," as quite forgetting Sarah's oft repeated instruction not to speak unless spoken to, she again tried to interrupt, "I am not criticising your cooking! Mrs Coalport will begin tomorrow. She will arrive at 7.00 and depart after dinner has been served. I am sure you will work well together."

"Thank you, sir." Rose gathered her equipment together and left the room. On the way back to the kitchen she pondered on what she had heard wondering why Mrs Wallace did not like her own baby.

Mrs Coalport arrived prompt at 7.00 the next morning. A cheerful, motherly woman, wife of an ex-army sergeant, she soon became an integral part of the household, taking Rose under her wing and making sure she was well fed. She tut-tutted over Mrs. Wallace too and sent up delicacies to tempt her palate.

June being warm and sunny, Nurse and Mrs Coalport sometimes managed to persuade Rose to accompany Nurse Green and Amelia out to the park for some fresh air. Rose enjoyed these outings, it was hot in the kitchen even with the garden door open. Amelia was a good baby and hardly ever cried. Even Rose however could not pretend that she was a beautiful baby. Now that she was not smothered in shawls her lack of beauty was plain to see. Due to her difficult birth the left side of her face was slightly lower than the right. She was not ugly but she was not good looking either. Mrs Coalport always referred to her as "that poor little mite".

At five months Amelia was beginning to take notice of her surroundings. Sometimes other nurses would come and sit next to them on their favourite park bench. A conversation would begin between the two nurses. Inevitably the nurse would commiserate with Nurse Green on her charge's plain features. One afternoon as they sat on their bench a nurse walked down the path towards them pushing a perambulator with one hand and holding a small boy clutching a wooden horse on wheels with the other. As she began manoeuvring the perambulator into place by the bench the small boy walked over to Amelia in her perambulator. Amelia had her face turned away from him so, before Nurse Green, who was in conversation with Rose, could stop him, he grasped the perambulator handle and gave it a jerk. Amelia turned round. The child took one look at her lop-sided face and began to cry. Amelia smiled at him which seemed to upset him even more. His nurse immediately ran to him.

"Don't cry, Master Albert. You go and play with your horse over there on the grass where nurse can see you."

Once the child had gone, sniffing, she turned on Nurse Green.

"You should be ashamed bringing a child like that outside. It should be kept indoors. Master Albert will have nightmares and I shall be up all night!"

Before either of them could reply she got up, pulled her perambulator to the path, called the child to her and walked quickly away.

Rose was indignant.

"How dare she say that!"

Nurse sighed.

"I am afraid that Amelia will always be subject to such unkind remarks."

"Can't anything be done?"

"I'm afraid not."

"Are Amelia's looks why Madam does not like her?"

"She was very shocked when she first saw her. She may come round one day or she may not. In the meantime we must get Amelia home."

Rose was upset for several days by this incident but, as Mrs Coalport pointed out, "The poor little mite will have to get used to it, won't she. Let's hope she grows up with a nice nature, then she won't find it so hurtful. There is nothing you can do about it, Rose, and I do need those potatoes scraped for today's dinner. I have to get home prompt or Coalport will have something to say."

On her next free afternoon, Rose gave in to an irresistible urge to see her old home. She knew it was silly but she hoped to find her mother there.

Standing on the opposite side of the road she gazed across at the house, furnishing it in her mind's eye. It was newly painted. It had been brown now it was painted black. The wooden gate had been changed for an iron one. There was a plant in the downstairs window. As she watched, a woman and a young boy came out. As the woman closed the gate behind them she glanced casually at Rose then walked off down the road.

Rose knew that her mother would never come back here. Why should she? It was not her home now any more than it was Rose's. She turned away – she would never return.

One afternoon a few days later Mr Wallace summoned Rose to his study. As soon as she was inside the door he said, "Rose, I have found out as much as I can about your mother. A friend of mine, an Inspector in the police force, made some enquiries. Apparently your step-father dragged your mother back to Ratcliff Court 'by the hair of her head' according to one witness. Some of the residents said that they heard shouting and screaming. They did nothing about it of course – they didn't want to be involved. They saw Mrs Anderson coming and going for several weeks but then they didn't see her again. Nobody was inclined to ask Anderson where she was. The Police have arrested him for several burglaries and he will probably go to prison for some time. But where Mrs Anderson is nobody knows." He did not tell her that the Inspector was of the opinion that Anderson had "done away with her, like as not."

"Perhaps you will hear from her one day. She promised to get in touch with you, didn't she?"

Rose nodded but she was sure that if her mother had been able she would have contacted her somehow.

"I am sorry that I don't have anything more definite. Inspector Burridge has promised to carry on with his enquiries. Try not to worry."

"Thank you, sir. I am very grateful for all your trouble."

"One other thing, Rose. Mrs Wallace and I have decided that it is time to bring our daughters home. More work for you, I am afraid, but I know you don't mind hard work. That will be all."

Rose made her curtsey and left the room.

William had decided to bring the girls home in spite of his wife's protests in the hope that it would shake her out of her lethargy.

As she prepared the girls' rooms Rose wondered what they were like. Sarah had not liked Miss Grace but then Sarah did not like anyone who made extra work. She decided to wait and see for herself.

On the day of their arrival Mrs Coalport prepared a special tea. Rose laid the dining room table with the best china and arranged some roses in a low bowl as a centre piece.

William had taken the morning off to fetch the girls from the station. Posted by Sophia to keep watch for the cab from the morning room window, Rose announced, "They're here, madam!" as a hansom drew up at the gate.

Sophia became almost animated.

"I must meet them at the door – help me up!"

Nurse helped Sophia up from her sofa and out to the front hall. Rose, walking behind, watched through the open front door as William got out of the cab holding out his hand to help a graceful girl who managed her full skirts in an expert manner. As she stood, shaking out her skirts and adjusting her bonnet. William turned back to help his older daughter who, ignoring his hand, leaped to the ground showing off her cream satin boots and a length of red stocking.

Mary walked eagerly up the path to where her mother waited in the hall.

Shaking off the Nurse's arm Sophia walked to meet the girl and hugged her.

"Mary, my dear!"

As they embraced Rose saw Mary clearly and thought that she was one of the most beautiful girls she had ever seen. The hair showing under her bonnet was blonde and her eyes were bright blue.

"And my little Grace!" Sophia turned to her other daughter standing just behind her sister. Grace submitted to being kissed. Unlike her younger sister she made no attempt to hug her mother. Grace at thirteen was a miniature of Mrs Wallace with her dark brown hair and brown eyes.

"How are you, Mother?" Mary asked.

Before Sophia could reply, Grace turned to her father who was supervising the cabby carrying the trunks into the house.

"Papa, I am sure that man is damaging my trunk!"

As soon as the man had set down the trunk in the hall Grace opened it and began checking the contents.

After William had paid the cabby and shut the front door everyone made a move to the sitting room, Nurse helping Sophia who sank down on her sofa as if exhausted.

"Aren't you just longing to see our new sister?" Mary asked Grace, who, leaving her trunk with the contents scattered over the hall floor, had joined them.

"Oh, we can see her any time." Grace replied carelessly.

"Well, I can't wait. I'm going up to the nursery." Removing her bonnet and jacket and handing them to Rose with a smile and a soft "Thank you, Rose," Mary left the room.

"I have laid tea in the dining room, madam," Rose announced.

"Here, whatever your name is, take this." Grace thrust her bonnet at Rose. "Come along Mama, let's go and have some tea." Nurse Green, helping Sophia to her feet, caught Rose's eye and raised her eyebrows at Grace's retreating back. Perhaps Sarah was right after all, Rose mused as she served tea.

CHAPTER SEVEN

Rose was kept very busy and the days passed quickly. July was upon her before she realized it. Mary seemed very fond of her baby sister and would take her out in her perambulator accompanied by Nurse. Grace, however, made no secret of the fact that she did not like Amelia. Nurse told Rose and Mrs Coalport that when Mary saw Amelia for the first time she just gasped and then asked if she could hold her but Grace had said, "*That* is *my* sister? Take it away, do!"

Grace clung to her mother and Sophia seemed to be more animated when she was with her.

Sophia had had one of her good days. She and Grace had been looking at the Englishwoman's Domestic Magazine fashions. Grace was pleased to have her mother to herself and was extremely annoyed, therefore, when Nurse entered the room, carrying Amelia who was, for once, crying.

"Can't you take that nasty, ugly, noisy thing away?" she demanded. Nurse looked shocked.

"That's no way to speak about your sister," Sophia rebuked her daughter.

Stung, Grace lost her temper.

"She's the ugliest baby that has ever been born, Mama. Why can't we send her to an orphanage? I'm sick of her."

She ran over to the astonished Nurse and raised her hand to slap Amelia. Holding the baby to her protectively Nurse took a step back.

Sophia was instantly by Grace's side.

"How dare you call her ugly! She is my child and I will not have ANYONE call her ugly. Now go to your room this instant!" She then took Amelia from the nurse's arms and proceeded to soothe her. Fortunately Amelia chose that moment to stop crying and gazed with her beautiful brown eyes at her mother.

"It was a miracle," Nurse related the scene to an enthralled Rose and Mrs Coalport. "I am sure that I will soon be on my way!"

Rose was in Mr Wallace's study drawing the curtains one evening when William, looking up from his desk said, "I have something for you, Rose. If you look on the little table you will see a package addressed to you. Open it."

On opening the package Rose found it contained several books.

"They are for you. I hope you have not read them?"

"Oh no, sir, thank you so much!" Rose could hardly speak for pleasure. She wondered whether she should offer to buy them or were they a gift?

Seeing her frown and guessing the cause William said, "They are a present" as she opened her mouth to protest "When is your birthday?"

"February the first".

"As it is already July we can call it an early Christmas present."

"Thank you, sir." As Rose left the room, clutching her books, she thought how lucky she was to have such a good place.

The Summer faded into Autumn and still Rose had not heard from her mother. From time to time she asked Mr Wallace if he had any information from Inspector Burridge but he always shook his head and said he was sorry but there was nothing.

Anderson had been sent to prison for a considerable number of years. When the Police had raided the house in Ratcliff Court they had found nothing. William told Rose, with perfect truth, that her mother was not there. What Inspector Burridge had actually said was

"We have taken the place apart but have not found the body. We are now convinced that Anderson killed his wife but without a body there is no evidence. It will turn up eventually – they always do and then Anderson will hang."

William did not tell Rose Inspector Burridge's suspicions – time enough for that when, and if, the body was found. He also managed to convince Inspector Burridge that there was no necessity to bring Rose into the enquiry.

Christmas 1860 was a very busy time for both Rose and Mrs Coalport. Nurse Green departed. Sophia seemed much better and insisted that the festivities be observed. A large tree was set up in the hall and Sophia, Mary and Grace spent an afternoon decorating it.

Amelia on being brought down to see the tree lit laughed with pleasure. Sophia gave Rose a bolt of cloth for work dresses. Mrs Coalport was given an extra day's pay. Rose gave Mrs Coalport a blue glass necklace. She was delighted. "Coalport will be surprised," she said as she put it on. Mrs Coalport gave Rose a book of Mr Tennyson's Poems.

"I do hope you like it, I don't know anything about books." She watched anxiously as Rose untied the package breathing a sigh of relief upon Rose assuring her that she thought it was one of the best presents she had ever had.

Rose missed her mother very much but fortunately there was so much work to do that she never stopped all day long and sank into bed and sleep almost simultaneously every night.

January 1861 – a year since Rose had gone to work at No 13. She was no longer the skinny child she had been when she arrived. Good food and hard work had put flesh on her bones. At the end of February she was fifteen and the butcher's boy seemed to linger longer than usual – as Mrs Coalport remarked on more than one occasion.

After the excitement of Christmas, Rose noticed that Mrs Wallace seemed to sink back into a deeper depression. Mary patiently sat reading to her mother by the hour. Grace never offered to relieve her, instead she grumbled that they never entertained or went anywhere. She spent a large part of her day arranging her hair or turning out her wardrobe. She would pore for hours over the fashion plates in The Englishwoman's Domestic Magazine. Rose had to accompany her on her frequent trips to the dressmaker's no matter how busy she was. Mary did her best to keep Grace amused and, in the long winter afternoons when Sophia had gone to her room, she would play the piano in the drawing room so that Grace, dressed in all her finery, could practice her dancing.

On the few occasions when Sophia declared she felt well enough to entertain, William would come down to the kitchen and ask Mrs Coalport if she would mind extending her hours as a personal favour. Mrs Coalport always agreed and would take her menus to Mrs Wallace for her approval. Rose enjoyed these occasions and wished they occurred more often. She sometimes felt very lonely after Mrs Coalport had left for the night.

Amelia grew into a sturdy toddler. Rose had a soft spot for her and when she had a spare moment she would play with her. But Mary was the one that Amelia followed about and the two girls spent a great deal of their time together otherwise Amelia would have been neglected since her mother was more often than not confined to her room. Grace, whose personality did not improve with age, seemed to hate her small sister and Rose caught her in many spiteful acts towards Amelia.

One day, in the Spring of 1862, when Amelia was two and Grace fifteen neither of them could be found. After Sophia, Mary and Rose had conducted an extensive search of the house and garden without result and Sophia was on the point of sending Rose in a cab to fetch William and John the doorbell rang. On opening it Rose was confronted by a formidable female grasping Grace with one hand and Amelia with the other.

"I am Sister Aloysius. I wish to speak to your mistress immediately."

She strode into the house dragging Grace and Amelia with her. Sophia, coming through the sitting room door was overjoyed to see them both safe and sound.

"Grace, Amelia, wherever have you been?"

Sister Aloysius then informed her that she was in charge of a recently opened home for children in the Portobello Road. Apparently Grace had walked her two-year old sister the two miles to the home and once there tried to leave her outside. Sister Aloysius had detained her and demanded Grace's name and address.

"As it was perfectly obvious to me from the children's clothes and well-cared for appearance that they came from a good home, I thought it best to bring them back myself. I think a little discipline is needed," she added.

Sophia was inclined to faint but Sister Aloysius fixed her with such a firm gaze that she thought better of it. Instead she thanked

Sister for returning her daughters, gave her a substantial donation for her home, promised Grace would never do such a thing again, called Rose to show Sister out and retired to her room with a headache.

When William returned home that evening Rose informed him that Madam was in her room and wanted to see him immediately. William sighed and slowly climbed the stairs. Upon hearing the story from Sophia he first went to see Amelia who was sound asleep on Mary's bed. Mary assured him that she was unharmed. Then he ordered Grace to his study.

Nobody ever knew what he said to her but she was subdued for many days. From then on she hardly spoke to Amelia and when she did it was usually some spiteful remark. She could not wait to get away and on more than one occasion Rose overheard her telling Mary that she would get married to the first man who asked her. When Grace was in one of her more difficult moods Rose wished that the poor man would come along as soon as possible.

CHAPTER EIGHT

Amelia was seven when she first began to realize that she was not as other girls. There had been comments all her life but now she began to wonder what was so different about her that her mother's friends looked at her and then said things like: "Well, she has nice eyes" or "You must be thankful, Sophia, that she is so healthy – you can't have everything and there is always Mary." And then they would all nod very wisely and discuss her sister's beauty.

One day in Church Amelia looked at the stained glass window of Jesus surrounded by children. At the bottom was written "Suffer the little children to come unto me." She was little and she was a child. She prayed that Jesus would make her beautiful. She thought about this all day and every time she went past a mirror she looked in it to see if she had changed at all. But she had not.

That night she went into Grace's room and watched her as she put her hair into curl papers. At twenty Grace was well aware of her looks.

"Why do you do that?" Amelia asked. It looked very painful.

"To make myself look prettier." Grace replied

"I don't think I will do that when I grow up – it looks as if it hurts."

"You don't need to, do you?" Grace replied as she tugged at a particularly stubborn piece of hair.

"Why not?"

"Because, Amelia, you are not in the least pretty and you never will be so there is no need for you to bother. I intend to get married as soon as possible, in fact I think I will get married quite soon. Gerald is ready to propose and when he does, I will accept him."

Amelia privately thought that Gerald was silly the way he followed Grace around. He always seemed to be calling. At the moment she was more interested in her own problem.

"When we were in Church this morning I prayed to Jesus and asked him to make me beautiful like Mary but he hasn't done it yet."

Grace stopped, her hands in mid-air.

"You wicked, wicked girl! I shall tell Mama at once!" and she jumped up and ran to the door. Before Amelia knew where she was the room was full of females. Mary cuddling her, Grace informing everyone that Amelia was a "very wicked, vain girl" and Mama looking at her with a sad expression.

"She must be whipped!" Grace announced, self-righteously.

"Why?" Mary enquired hugging Amelia tighter.

"Because the devil must be driven from her soul," said Grace, quoting from one of the Vicar's sermons.

"She must be given a chance to repent," Mary replied. "Are you sorry for what you said, Amelia?"

Amelia thought about it.

"Jesus made the lame walk and the blind see so why can't he make me beautiful?" she asked.

"Are you sorry?" Mary asked again.

Amelia knew that it was a sin to tell lies because Papa had told her so.

"No," she said firmly.

Mary began to cry.

"You must whip her, Mama," Grace said, "for her own good," she added.

Sophia stood, trying to think what to do. Finally she said, "I will talk to your father about it."

Then, putting her hand to her head she turned and went to her room. Giving Amelia a vicious glare, Grace pushed Amelia and Mary out of her room slamming the door behind them. Without speaking Mary helped Amelia into bed kissed her good night and quietly left the room.

Amelia lay in bed and thought. She still could not see why she had been so wicked. She would ask Papa about it in the morning. Having resolved the problem she turned over and went to sleep.

Next morning Sophia did not come down to breakfast and Rose reported that "Madam is not feeling very well."

Grace, however, was determined that Amelia should get her just punishment. She waited until her father had nearly finished his breakfast and asked, with a vindictive, sideways glance at Amelia

"Papa, did Mama tell you about Amelia's wickedness?"

"If you mean Amelia's request in her prayers, yes, she did."

"Don't you think Amelia was wicked and should be whipped?"

William looked at his eldest daughter. He was worried about her. She had always been quick to seize any chance of getting Amelia into trouble. Looking at Grace's spiteful expression he knew that it was deeper than that. He suddenly felt very sorry for Gerald who had requested permission to ask Grace to marry him. William wondered if Gerald knew what he was letting himself in for.

"It is not my place to administer punishment to Amelia, that is her mother's job, however, I will speak to her. Amelia, come with me to my study."

John, who had been a silent witness to the scene said, "I don't think that Amelia meant any harm, father. She is only young after all."

Amelia smiled at her brother. Normally he hardly seemed to know that she was there but whenever she was in trouble he always came to her rescue.

"Come along, Amelia." Papa led the way to his study.

Amelia liked Papa's study. It smelt of Papa's cigars and she could lose herself in his big leather armchair. Now she was rather frightened. She had never been whipped in her life.

"Now, Amelia." Papa was very grave. "You must learn an important lesson from this. You must think carefully before you speak. Not everyone looks at things in the same way that you do. As for looks, it is true that you are not as pretty as either Grace or Mary, in fact you are not pretty at all and you must come to terms with the fact. You will have to reconcile yourself to staying with Mama and me always. I am sorry to be blunt, Amelia, but I am afraid that no man would look at you twice. I wish it were otherwise. You will always have a home with Mama and me."

"Thank you, Papa. I don't mind about getting married. I think it is stupid. Grace and Gerald look so silly just looking at each other all the time and Grace just wants to get married. I don't think she even likes Gerald, I think…"

"Amelia, what have I just told you! You must learn to control your tongue! We all have thoughts which other people would probably be shocked to hear but we keep them to ourselves."

Amelia was intrigued.

"Do you have thoughts too, Papa? What are they?"

Papa laughed and told her to run away as he had to get to the factory.

"Remember what I have said, Amelia. If Grace asks what happened tell her that I gave you a severe reprimand."

"Is that worse than a whipping, Papa?"

"Oh yes, much worse," he solemnly replied.

Later, when Amelia went down to the kitchen for her afternoon visit to Rose and Mrs Coalport she told them how Grace had tried to get her whipped. Mrs Coalport and Rose glanced at each other then Rose said, "Never mind, Miss Amelia. Good looks don't always mean a good person. Now drink up your milk so that Mrs Coalport can get on with dinner."

Amelia decided that Rose was the nicest person she knew next to Mary. She was always ready to answer any questions Amelia had about anything. She helped her with her reading when Mama had one of her headaches and took her to the park. Rose was always there. It therefore came as a surprise when, one Sunday morning a few months later during the coldest winter that even Papa could remember, Rose did not come to open her bedroom curtains or help her dress. Becoming impatient Amelia dressed herself and went downstairs to the dining room where she found the rest of the family just as puzzled as she was.

As she entered Mama was saying, "I have been to the kitchen and there is no fire and no Rose."

"Perhaps she is ill," Mary suggested

"Of course she is not ill. Servants don't get ill." Grace was scornful. "She is just being lazy. It's too bad! Rose knows it is the cook's day off. I want my breakfast!"

"We all want breakfast, Grace," said John. "Perhaps you could go and prepare it for us?" he suggested.

Grace did not bother to reply.

How silly everyone was, Amelia thought, all they had to do was to go to Rose's room. She ran quickly to the attics. As she got higher she could feel the cold. On the attic landing it was freezing and the window was coated with thick frost.

Not bothering to knock she entered Rose's bedroom. Rose was in bed and looked sound asleep. Amelia called her but got no response. Moving closer she called her again, louder. She reached out and touched Rose's face – it was icy cold, so cold that it made Amelia gasp. There must be something wrong with her. She ran down to the Dining Room.

"Come quickly, Papa."

"Where, Amelia?"

"To Rose's room."

"Papa cannot go up to a servants bedroom!" Grace was scandalised.

"But she won't wake up," Amelia told her.

"Of course she is awake, she just doesn't want to get up and do her work. She should be dismissed!"

"That is unfair!" Amelia said angrily.

Grace opened her mouth to reply.

"That will do," William said severely.

They subsided. Grace went and sat at her place at the table remarking to the table cloth.

"When I am married I will not let MY servants have a day off or stay in bed!"

William turned to Amelia

"Did you call Rose?"

"Yes, Papa. I called her and I touched her – she was so cold. I am sure she is ill."

Grace snorted in a very unladylike manner.

Ignoring her, William ordered.

"Sophia, you and Mary go up and see what is the matter."

Amelia followed them to the attic where Sophia began to shake Rose without result.

Sophia called Amelia to her from where she stood in the doorway.

"Do you know where Rose keeps her fire lighting materials?"

"Yes."

"Run down quickly and get them. Tell John to bring up a scuttle of coal." She turned to Mary. "Mary, fetch as many blankets and shawls as you can find. Take them from the beds. And hurry!"

Amelia departed on her errand and was soon back, closely followed by John carrying a scuttle full of coals. She watched while Sophia, removing the fan of paper from the grate, lit the fire. As the fire was beginning to catch Mary came in with a pile of blankets.

All this activity began to frighten Amelia.

"What is the matter with her, Mama? Why won't she wake up?"

"She is too cold, Amelia. I only hope we are in time. Mary go down and make some hot broth. Go with her, Amelia, and tell Papa that I will stay with Rose until she wakes up."

Amelia was inclined to argue but Sophia was firm.

By mid-day Rose was awake and wondering what had happened. When she saw the fire in the grate she was upset and told Sophia that Sarah had instructed her that it was forbidden for servants to have fires in their bedrooms.

Sophia thought for a moment and then said, "Yes, I did tell Sarah that she was not to light a fire but that was because she was very wasteful with the coal. I assumed that you had a fire in this bitter weather. You can light a fire when you think it necessary. I know you are a sensible girl and will not take advantage of this privilege."

Rose assured her that she would be very careful.

Once she was sure that she had recovered sufficiently to come downstairs Sophia left her to get dressed.

Grace was still sitting at the dining room table. John and William were in the study and Mary and Amelia were in the kitchen making soup.

"Rose is much better and will be coming down soon," she told Grace.

Grace did not respond. Sophia continued, "She would not have been the first servant to die from cold. I cannot believe that it nearly happened under our roof. Rose is a good servant. When you have an establishment of your own, Grace, I hope you find a servant as honest and hard working as Rose."

At that moment Mary and Amelia came in with the hot soup and Grace did not have to reply.

The cold weather continued and Rose was grateful for her fire. She did not mind the backbreaking task of carrying coal up to her attic.

The girls could not go out and occupied themselves in their own way. Mary read to Sophia, played with Amelia and practiced the piano. Grace complained a great deal and refurbished all her bonnets. Amelia read her books and tried to master the piano under Mary's patient tuition but even Mary had to admit that Amelia would never make a pianist and that she was incapable of singing in tune. When Mary was confined to bed with a bad head cold Grace refused to have anything to do with Amelia. Sophia was in despair and appealed to William. Giving Amelia some of his old designs he asked her to make copies for him. When he saw the completed work he was amazed.

"These are very good, Amelia. Did you enjoy doing them?"

"Oh yes. May I have some paper so that I can design too?"

Giving her a sketchpad he was relieved that he had found something to keep her occupied.

Soon after the snow and frost disappeared overnight,everyone became very cheerful and ordinary life was resumed with enthusiasm.

One afternoon William came home to find Amelia sitting on the stairs busily drawing. Handing his hat and stick to Rose he went over to see what she was doing.

"Can I see, Amelia?"

"Not yet Papa, this one is not finished but you can see this one."

She turned back several pages and handed him the pad. William studied the design then, turning to John who had followed him in, said, "Look at this, John. Amelia has designed a mechanical figure."

John took the pad. "It is quite good, Amelia."

"I think we have another designer in the family."

"Possibly father but I do need to talk to you urgently."

"Come into the study."

Forgetting Amelia they went into the study and shut the door. Amelia ran off to the kitchen and informed Rose and Mrs Coalport that she was going to be one of the best mechanical toy designers in England.

All that Spring and Summer she designed whenever she could. Sophia became worried. "You should not encourage her, William. She rushes through her lessons, she hardly goes to the park. It is not healthy. She should be learning the skills she will need as a wife and mother."

Looking up from his newspaper William spoke comfortably.

"She is very young, Sophia. She will probably grow out of it."

Sophia continued to lament.

"Why can't she be like other girls and do watercolours like Grace?"

Putting down his paper, William said gravely, "She will never be like other girls and to talk as if she is going to get married and have children one day is being unrealistic. If she has found something that she is good at then she should be encouraged."

Sophia continued as if he had not spoken.

"If she could only sing or play the piano or even sew. Her needlework is a disgrace, she has no patience for it and yet she can spend hours drawing designs."

William knew that Sophia was refusing to admit that Amelia was different and it worried him. Sooner or later Sophia would have to face the situation but not yet. She had been so much better lately and more like her old self that he did not want to say or do anything which would cause her to lapse back into apathy.

CHAPTER NINE

Simon Jarrett was perched on a high stool before his desk adding the long columns of figures in the large ledger placed on the desk before him, his pen moving rapidly down the columns before being dipped into the inkwell. The result of his calculations then being written neatly at the bottom of the page, the page blotted carefully, before turning to the next page of figures.

Had any of the other clerks employed by Wallace & Son looked at him they would have seen a man apparently engrossed in his work. Apparently, because one part of Simon's mind was on the figures and the other part was indulging in one of his daydreams. The one where he had his own factory and employed his own clerks. Simon was ambitious. He was determined to rise above his lowly status. He was far too superior for a mere clerical position.

This was the era of opportunity. He had decided that 1868 was the year he would begin his rise to the top. Anything was possible. He had severed all connection with his impoverished family years before and at twenty three he knew the time was right to take advantage of any opportunities which arose.

He knew that luck was on his side otherwise why had Mr Robson the Chief Clerk selected him to take a message to Mr Wallace's home? It was further proof of his inherent good fortune that the maid was out and Mary Wallace opened the door herself. He knew he was considered handsome, that women found him attractive and that nineteen year old Mary was attracted to him.

Being four years older he felt in complete control of the situation. He knew that he was destined for great things – all he needed was a chance. And he felt that the chance had arrived. All he had to do was to recognize the moment and the rest would follow. He looked up as Mr Robson called, "Jarrett!"

"Yes, Mr Robson?"

"Mr Wallace wants you to collect some papers from his home. You are to go immediately. I will give you some money from Petty Cash to pay for a cab as it is urgent."

Now the other clerks did look up. So Jarrett was being picked out again was he. They took in his dark wavy hair, his flourishing side whiskers and his immaculate clothes and thought they knew why.

★ ★ ★ ★ ★ ★ ★ ★ ★ ★ ★

Mary and Amelia were seated, one either side of the dining room table. Mary was hearing Amelia read. It was hot. She would much rather have been in the park but Mama had gone to rest complaining of the heat and Mary had been ordered to hear Amelia who could read very well and didn't need hearing.

Bored, Mary got up from the table and looked out of the window to the front garden which looked bowed down with the heat. Over the neat hedge which separated the garden from the pavement she could see the traffic passing on the road, not that there was very much.

Mary was just turning away from the window when she saw a cab stop outside the gate. When she saw who alighted from it she ran out of the room and looked at her reflection in the hallstand mirror. Her dark hair was matted to her forehead and her face was shiny. Quickly she took her handkerchief from her dress pocket, wiped her face and ran her fingers through her hair. When she looked in the mirror again she was almost pleased with the result. Her blue eyes gazed back at her and her cheeks were only slightly flushed. She stood by the inner door waiting for Simon's knock. When it came she waited a moment. The kitchen door opened and Rose appeared.

"I will open the door, Rose," Mary told her.

"I don't think your Mama would like that, Miss Mary. Why don't you go into the sitting room while I see who it is?"

The knock came again. Rose went towards the door and paused with her hand on the knob looking expectantly at Mary. With an impatient "Oh, very well." Mary flounced into the sitting room.

Shaking her head Rose opened the door. She thought she knew who it was – the clerk from Mr Wallace's office. She wished Mr

Wallace would send somebody else. The young man was far too good looking and knew it.

"Good afternoon." Simon was pleasant. He believed in keeping on the right side of servants, you never knew when they might be useful "I have been sent by Mr Wallace to pick up some urgent papers." He made it sound as if William had personally begged him to do this great favour. "They are on his desk in his study."

"Come in, please, sir," Rose held the door open. Simon came into the hall. As he did so the sitting room door opened and Mary came out giving an exaggerated start when she saw Simon which did not deceive either Simon or Rose.

"What is it, Rose?"

"This gentleman has been sent by the master for some papers, Miss Mary."

"Thank you, Rose – I will attend to Mr…?"

"Jarrett, Miss Wallace. Mr Wallace left the papers on his desk."

"Come with me." Mary led the way to the study and, once they had entered, shut the door firmly.

Shaking her head Rose went back to the kitchen where Mrs Coalport was putting the finishing touches to a cold dessert.

"Madam will be having trouble with Miss Mary before long," she told her.

In the dining room Amelia suddenly realized that Mary was no longer listening to her. She looked round but Mary was not in the room. Jumping from her chair she went to the window – there was a cab outside – perhaps Papa was home! She did hope so – she had an idea for a mechanical horse but she needed some guidance.

As she opened the dining room door she saw Mary open the study door opposite. She nearly called out but changed her mind. Mary seemed furtive. Amelia waited to see what she would do.

Mary beckoned to somebody and a man emerged. Mary then tiptoed down the hall, removed her straw hat from the hallstand, put it on, took up her parasol and they both left the house.

Amelia knew that this was wrong. Mama had told them never to go out without either herself or Rose in attendance and she would never countenance Mary going out with a strange man! She would follow them and see where they went. She had to hide behind the front door while the man paid off the cab.

Mary raised her parasol, took the man's profferred arm and walked away towards the park. It was quite easy to follow them without being seen since neither looked back once.

Once in the park they made their way to the bandstand in front of which were deckchairs where people sat listening to the band. The ladies in light frocks, each one with a parasol. Amelia preferred the uniforms of the bandsmen. She had decided that she would be a bandsman when she grew up. Some children with a little dog ran round between the deckchairs.

Mary and the man found two vacant deckchairs and sat down. Amelia gradually worked her way between the deckchairs until she was in the row behind Mary. The children playing with the dog had produced a ball which they were using to tease the animal. The ball rolled under two rows of deckchairs. The children stood irresolute, not knowing how to retrieve their ball without disturbing the grown-ups. They gathered in a group to discuss the problem.

In the meantime the ball had rolled to within inches of Amelia's feet where she stood at the end of the row of chairs behind Mary who sat at the end of the row in front. The chairs behind were empty almost to the far end. Amelia bent down as if to pick up the ball. If she tried hard enough she might be able to hear what was being said over the sound of the band. The cornet launched into a solo and Mary, who sounded annoyed, raised her voice at the same time. Amelia could hear every word.

"No, Simon, I will not do it. If you loved me you would not ask. I cannot steal from my own father!"

"It is not stealing, Mary. All I want is to look at one of his designs – just to give me an idea of the sort of thing he has in mind. I can then use it to develop my own ideas. That's all I want it for – as a help. If *you* loved *me* you would do it."

"Why can't you just ask Papa? I am sure he would assist you and if you told him we want to get married he would be only too pleased to help you."

"Dear Mary – you don't understand the business world, do you? Your father is never going to accept a mere clerk as a husband for his daughter. I have to prove myself and the only way to do that is to develop a design. A design so unusual that he will have to give me a chance as a designer."

"I still can't see why you don't just ask Papa. I think you only told me you loved me to make me steal the designs for you. All these months you have been leading up to this." Mary sounded tearful.

This was a little too near the truth and Simon hastened to reassure her.

"You are a lovely girl, Mary, and I want to marry you but I must get ahead first. I must be able to look after you. You must never regret marrying me."

Mary put her hand on his arm. She was beginning to calm down. He pressed home his advantage.

"Please say you will do this for me, Mary."

"I must think it over," she replied.

He became impatient and decided to take a gamble.

"I don't have time for you to 'think it over'. Either you do as I ask or you will never see me again!" Folding his arms dramatically he moved away from her.

"Very well. I love you very much, Simon, but what you ask is impossible. I have a loyalty to my father. I am sorry." She stood up.

"So am I." Feeling bitterly disappointed that he had misjudged her depth of feeling he rose and strode off, never looking back. By the time he reached the office he had persuaded himself that she would come round, he only had to be patient.

Amelia was certain she would be seen but Mary bowed her head and Amelia thought she heard a sob. Although she knew her sister would be angry Amelia could not bear to see her so unhappy. She went up to her and touched the arm holding the parasol that hid her face from passers-by.

"Don't cry, Mary. I am sure he didn't mean it."

Mary looked up, her blue eyes full of tears. She did not seem surprised to see Amelia there.

"I don't think so, Amelia." Then she began to talk to Amelia as if she were grown up and not just eight years old. She told her that she had met Simon when he brought a message from Papa. Normally she would have just taken the message and thought no more about it but he had been so charming that she had found herself agreeing to meet him in the Park.

They had been meeting regularly ever since. Lately he had begun to urge her to steal some of Papa's designs. Simon wanted to become a designer and said he needed the designs to give him a start in the right direction.

"Of course you cannot steal Papa's designs." Amelia was shocked at the very idea. "He will come back if he loves you," she said shrewdly.

Mary gave her a watery smile.

"Do you know, Amelia, sometimes I think you are a lot older than your years? We had better get back before Mama misses us."

But although they hurried through the hot streets as they entered the coolness of the hall Sophia was just coming down the stairs.

"Where have you been?" she asked, sharply.

"Amelia was so hot that I took her out for some air," Mary replied. "Isn't that right, Amelia?"

Amelia had never heard Mary tell a lie before.

"Yes, Mama." Amelia hung her head – she did not like lying to Mama.

Sophia, taking in her flushed face and quickened breathing, felt a stab of fear. Surely she was not going to lose another child? It had taken a long time for her to come to terms with Amelia's lack of beauty. She had wondered if it was something she had done or seen during her pregnancy. Dr Thomas had told her that that was a lot of superstitious nonsense but she was not so sure.

Surely Amelia would not be taken from her now that she had come to love her? Someday soon Mary would be leaving her to get married. She was nineteen and very pretty, it could not be long.

Grace was already engaged to Gerald. Sophia doubted whether Amelia would ever get married. She was far too plain, her one good feature her large brown eyes.

"You do not look at all well, Amelia. Go to your room and I will send Rose up with a cold cloth for your head."

Sophia was rather alarmed when, instead of arguing as she had expected, Amelia obediently let go of Mary's hand and started up the stairs.

For the next few days Sophia kept a careful eye on her youngest daughter but she seemed healthy enough, if rather quiet. After several days had passed without Amelia exhibiting any symptoms of illness Sophia breathed a sigh of relief and things seemed to go back to normal. Sophia was now completely absorbed in preparations for Grace's wedding which was due to take place at the end of July.

As the wedding day approached Sophia had no time to notice that Mary was getting paler and paler. As for Mary herself she was thankful that her time was fully occupied. She was to be a bridesmaid and her time was taken up more and more with dress fittings, and helping to write invitations. There were also endless discussions with Grace and Sophia on furnishing a home and engaging servants. No sooner had one problem been resolved than another took its place.

Amelia had no such worries. She was not a bridesmaid but she did not mind. One Sunday on the way back from Morning Prayer Papa started to tease her about having to stand still for dress fittings.

"You will never manage it, Amelia. You will walk down the aisle behind your sister in a dress half made!"

Amelia skipping along in her usual impatient way replied cheerfully, "I am not going to be a bridesmaid, Papa, so it will not matter." and she skipped off ahead of her family.

William became silent and thoughtful and when they reached home he caught hold of Sophia's sleeve as she was about to mount the stairs.

"Amelia is going to be a bridesmaid, isn't she?" he asked.

Sighing Sophia took her foot from the bottom stair and turned to face him.

"No, she is not. Grace did not want her as a bridesmaid."

"Why ever not – she is her sister!"

Sophia sighed, "I should have thought that was obvious, William."

"I know that Amelia is not quite as pretty as Grace or Mary, but even so…"

Sophia interrupted

"Gerald's sister is going to be the other bridesmaid. In any case it is too late to do anything about it now."

"I will speak to Grace – now," and William strode off purposefully to the dining room where Grace had begun unwrapping wedding presents. She looked up at his tempestuous entry.

"Look, Papa!" she said excitedly, holding up a crystal vase for his inspection.

William thrust it aside without even looking at it.

"Why is Amelia not a bridesmaid?" he asked bluntly.

Grace carefully placed the vase on the table before replying.

"Mama and I thought that it would be best if Amelia was not a bridesmaid."

"You are ashamed of her, aren't you?" he asked.

"Well, Papa, you must admit that she does get a great deal of attention because of her looks. Imagine what it would be like – she would be compared to the other bridesmaids and people would stare. I am only thinking of her." Grace added, putting on her best martyred expression.

"If," William said in the deceptively calm voice his family had come to know meant he was getting extremely angry, "you do not have your sister as a bridesmaid there will be no wedding because I shall refuse to pay for it and I shall make sure that everyone knows why. Amelia may not realize now why you refuse to let her follow you down the aisle but later on when she is older she will. And it will hurt.

I have never understood why you dislike your sister so much. Once you are married you can see her or not as you like, what you do will be the responsibility of your husband. You are not married yet, however, and still under my jurisdiction and will do as I say or, I repeat, there will be no wedding. Make up your mind which it is to be. I shall be in my study."

He then walked away.

As soon as he had gone Grace kicked an inoffensive footstool then flung a cushion across the room, all the time muttering through clenched teeth. "Amelia, always Amelia. I must get away from Amelia or I shall go mad!" She threw herself into a chair and closed her eyes which is how Gerald found her a few moments later.

"Are you ill?" he asked, anxiously.

Grace opened her eyes then, putting her hand to her forehead said in a faint voice

"Please go and ask Mama to bring some smelling salts."

As soon as he had left the room she restored the furniture to its accustomed place and was back in the chair with closed eyes when Gerald returned with Sophia.

"What is wrong, Grace?"

"It is the heat, Mama." Grace took the profferred smelling salts.

Sophia walked to the table and critically inspected the crystal vase.

"When you have recovered I think we should finish unwrapping these presents. I do hope that you are taking note of each one so that you can send a thank you note?"

"Yes, Mama, but I have to see Papa first. I want to ask him if he would mind if I changed my mind and had Amelia as a bridesmaid after all."

"But I thought you had quite made up your mind. I am pleased of course..."

"Help Mama, Gerald," Grace ordered as she got up and, wearing a grim expression, left the room.

Sophia looked after her and wondered what had made her change her mind.

Amelia was startled when, next morning at breakfast, Papa said, "Grace has something to ask you, Amelia, haven't you, Grace?"

Addressing the sideboard and speaking in a monotone Grace said

"I should like you to be one of my bridesmaids."

"Me?"

"Yes" Grace spoke through gritted teeth.

"Must I, Papa?" Amelia pleaded

"There – you see – she doesn't *want* to be a bridesmaid, Papa." Grace said hotly.

William rose to his feet.

"You will be your sister's bridesmaid, Amelia. Mama will be taking you to the dressmakers this morning so you had better eat up your breakfast."

He then strode from the room and the house.

After breakfast Amelia was reluctantly dragged off to the dressmakers where they met Gerald's sister Victoria. Amelia liked Victoria Mitchell who always treated her as if she were grown-up. Victoria showed no surprise at Grace's change of heart. Mrs Mitchell, Sophia and the dressmaker held a conference. The dressmaker assuring them that her girls would work day and night to ensure the dress was finished on time.

Amelia found it very irksome to stand still while the dressmaker fussed about taking her measurements but it was all over at last.

When she got home she immediately went down to the kitchen to tell Rose the news.

"My dress is blue and I am to wear a little blue hat tipped over my nose."

"What does the dress look like?" Rose asked.

"I will draw it for you." Amelia looked round for something on which to draw and saw the piece of white paper the meat had been wrapped in. Rose handed her a pencil stub. In a few moments Amelia had drawn the dress. A tight fitting jacket cut away to show an ankle length pleated skirt.

Mrs Coalport came and peered over Rose's shoulder.

"You are clever, Miss Amelia. Can you draw Miss Grace's dress?"

Amelia was happy to do so and as she worked she described the material and style.

"It is cream in a mixture of satin and tulle. You see this overskirt is tulle and here," she made a few more strokes, "it is looped up with a bouquet of flowers. The skirt is satin and there is more tulle pleating round the hem. The sleeves are full. It is very pretty."

"It looks lovely, Miss Amelia. What are the other bridesmaids wearing?"

"I don't know. I only saw the pattern for mine and then I watched while Grace tried her dress on."

"You will have to be careful not to tread on Miss Grace's skirt." Rose worried.

"Oh, I shall be *very* careful," Amelia said cheerfully. Suddenly she hugged Rose.

"I don't know what I would do without you. Don't you go and get married, will you?"

Rose did not answer and Mrs Coalport suddenly became very busy tidying the kitchen.

All the preparations were made. Sophia and Grace were convinced that the weather would be wet. William informed them that the weather would be fine and, sure enough, when they woke on the wedding morning the sun shone from a cloudless sky. A lovely July day. Everyone was up early.

Grace had lost her sulky look and seemed almost happy. Rose helped Amelia to dress and arranged her hat at the right angle. Amelia looked at herself in the glass. She had never really thought much about her looks. She knew that she was not as pretty as her sisters and that her mother was sad about this but it had never worried her.

Now she looked in the glass and saw an unbalanced face relieved by large, liquid brown eyes. Her hair, now arranged in ringlets, a chestnut brown.

"I am not very pretty am I, Rose?" she said.

Rose hesitated but realised that Amelia was beginning to grow up.

"As I have told you before Miss Amelia, it's not how you look but what sort of person you are. You go on being your own sweet self and nobody will notice your – slight problem. I can't stand gossiping here, I have to go and help Mrs Coalport. The poor thing is run off her feet with the extra staff getting in her way."

Amelia very carefully walked down the aisle behind her sister. She was so intent on making sure that she did not trip up or step on her sister's dress that she did not see the pitying looks from some members of the congregation.

At the end of the service when they all came out of Church they had to stand still for a very long time while some photographs were taken. Amelia was very interested in how the camera worked and she kept leaving her place in front of Grace and Gerald to go and ask the harassed photographer endless questions. Mary had to keep bringing her back. After Amelia had been returned to her place for the third time Grace bent down and hissed in her ear

"Stop making such a spectacle of yourself. Don't you DARE spoil my wedding day!"

Amelia stood stiffly to attention. The photographer heaved a sigh of relief and prayed she would keep still. Once the photograph was taken and she could move, she tapped her sister's arm. Grace bent down to her.

"I am glad you are married." Grace began to smile, a smile which froze as Amelia continued, "and going to live in Edinburgh. I won't have to see you then!" and she skipped away before an astonished Grace could give her the slap her hand was itching to deliver.

"Is anything the matter?" Gerald asked, concerned.

"No, nothing. Amelia was just saying how much she will miss me," Grace told him.

"She is quite a nice little thing, isn't she?"

Grace did not reply.

When Amelia returned with the other guests to the house for the reception the dining room had been transformed. The table decorated with swathes of flowers, candelabra and large silver bowls of fruit. Each place was laid with silver cutlery and intricately arranged table napkins.

There were strange servants and Amelia looked in vain for Rose. She wanted to tell her all about the service and what a splendid camera the man had had. As she was the only child present she was conscious of Mama's eye upon her and knew that she must wait until told that she could move. She had to wait a very long time.

Once the food had been eaten the cake was brought in, toasts were drunk and speeches were made. She began to feel sleepy. At last Mama, looking very elegant in a dress of deep magenta, her full skirt puffed up at the sides and back, took all the ladies up to the drawing room giving Amelia a chance to slip downstairs to the kitchen to Rose.

Rose and Mrs Coalport were sitting in the kitchen worn out with their efforts since before dawn. They welcomed Amelia as they always did and asked her to tell them all about the ceremony.

"Rose is particularly interested, aren't you Rose?" Mrs Coalport was arch.

"Why, Rose?" asked Amelia, uneasy for some reason which she could not explain.

Rose shot Mrs Coalport a look and shook her head slightly.

"Nothing, Miss Amelia. Tell us again about Miss Grace, I mean Madam cutting the cake."

Amelia was relating as much of Papa's speech as she could remember when Sophia came down to the kitchen to fetch Amelia and to tell Rose and Mrs Coalport they had permission to come up to the hall to see Mr and Mrs Mitchell off.

Grace came downstairs into the hall wearing a going away outfit of green silk. Her small hat, which Amelia thought looked rather like a plate, perched over her forehead. She wore her back hair loose. Amelia wondered what Mama would say as she knew that Mama disapproved regarding it as "a vulgar American fashion". Grace had shown Mama a picture of the style in a magazine and announced her intention of wearing her hair in this fashion in future, but Mama had forbidden it. Grace had sulked for days in consequence. Now, Mama did not say anything but Amelia saw her look of disapproval.

Grace smiled graciously at the two servants where they stood side by side.

"Thank you so much for all your efforts," she said, practising the voice she would use when addressing her own domestics.

"May we wish you every happiness, Madam."

Mrs Coalport replied on behalf of them both. It was the first time that Grace had been called Madam and she visibly preened herself, basking in her new status. She was debating whether to condescend to a few more remarks when Gerald and the rest of the family and guests entered the hall and a general move was made outside to where a cab waited.

Grace and Gerald stepped into the cab and drove away, the guests waving until the cab was out of sight. Once Grace and Gerald had gone Sophia began to wilt. The guests, taking the hint, began to disperse and Mrs Coalport and Rose went back to the kitchen to clear up while they discussed the day's events.

CHAPTER TEN

After the wedding came anti-climax. Sophia, missing Grace, seemed to be slipping back into her depression and, to make matters worse, the fine weather had broken the day after the wedding. It had been raining for several days and the girls were confined to the house. After two days of continuous rain Mary was feeling depressed. She tried to play the piano but it was very half-hearted and after a while she went to the window to see if it was still raining. It was.

She was just turning away wondering what to do next when she saw a figure walking up the path, the face obscured by an umbrella but she knew it was Simon. Running downstairs to the front door she opened it before he could knock and ran out into the rain. Giving him no time to speak she said, "I am so pleased to see you. I must talk to you." In her agitation Mary clutched his arm. "Mother is lying down and it is Rose's afternoon off. We can go into Papa's study. Nobody will think of disturbing us there."

Simon was delighted. She must have changed her mind. Soon all his plans would come to fruition. His mind racing through the possibilities he followed her to the study.

Amelia was at the table in the sitting room working on some designs for a new toy. She was completely absorbed. She was pleased with her new design. She was sure that Papa would like this one. He had been very interested in her horse and cart and she was hoping that he would let her produce this new design.

She was using a very fine nib to make the drawing. Suddenly it broke. She was vexed. How could she finish the design? She was sure that Papa would not mind her using one of his pens, she knew that he kept a supply on his desk in his study. She decided to get one. As she got to the study door she could hear the low murmur of voices. Good, Papa was back. She needed to ask him a question about some of the proportions.

"Papa..." she began as she entered the room. But it was not Papa it was Simon and he was cuddling Mary.

"Please, Mary – he will never know. He will just think he has mislaid them."

I can't," then they saw Amelia standing in the doorway a shocked expression on her face. They sprang apart. Amelia advanced into the room.

"Does Mama know you are here?"

"Please, Amelia – just go away and forget what you have seen," Mary pleaded.

"Yes – er, Amelia. Look, here is half a sovereign! Just go away there's a good little girl."

Amelia looked at the profferred coin then at Simon with scorn.

"I am going to fetch Mama," she said firmly and turned to walk to the door.

Mary ran after her, turned her round and kneeling at Amelia's level and with tears pouring down her face she sobbed, "If you tell Mama Simon will be dismissed. We are not doing anything wrong, we are going to be married, aren't we, Simon?" Mary kept her eyes on Amelia's face. Amelia looked up at Simon just in time to see him pick up some papers from Papa's desk and put them in his pocket.

Pulling away from Mary, Amelia took hold of his arm and tried to get the papers away from him.

"Give me those." Amelia tugged at his arm.

"Get away from me, you!" Mary got to her feet and turned in time to see Simon hitting Amelia round the head, his expression one of hatred. Amelia hung on tenaciously. Mary shrieked. She could not believe what was happening. Simon had changed in front of her eyes. None of them saw Sophia until she was actually in the room. Awakened by the noise she had come downstairs.

"What is going on here?" She demanded.

In the sudden silence Simon managed to shake off Amelia who staggered into Mary. Pushing past Sophia, Simon ran out of the house. Putting Amelia aside Mary called after him and went to follow him but Sophia stopped her in the doorway.

"Who was that man and what are you doing in Papa's study?" Sophia demanded.

"Mary has been meeting that nasty man, Mama, and he has..."

"Thank you, Amelia. Go to your room please while I talk to your sister."

Amelia went as far as the stairs and sat on the top stair listening to her mother and Mary shouting at each other. She had never known anything like it in all her eight years. She wished that Rose was here. When everything went quiet it was more frightening than all the shouting. Then the door burst open and Mary ran, sobbing, from the room and out of the house into the rain.

Sophia came out of the room and looked helplessly after Mary. She went to the door but Mary had gone. She sank down on the bottom step of the stair and leaned against the bannister. Amelia came down and sat beside her mother.

William came home to find them still sitting there in the dark with the storm going on all round them. Sophia was incapable of speech and all he could get out of Amelia was that Mary had been seeing a nasty man and that Mary and Sophia had had an enormous argument and Mary had run out of the house.

"How long ago?" he asked but Amelia did not know. At that moment Rose returned and he left her in charge while he went out to find Mary.

With Amelia's help Sophia got up to her room. Rose didn't have the heart to make Amelia go to bed so they sat in the kitchen to await William's return.

It was midnight before William came home with Mary who was soaking wet and already showing signs of a high fever. He had found her wandering up and down looking for Simon. She was completely delirious. While William went for Doctor Thomas, Rose and Amelia between them put Mary to bed.

Amelia knew that she had to tell Papa about the man taking the papers from his desk so she refused to go to bed. She kept trying to tell Rose who was not listening. At that moment William returned with the Doctor. After Doctor Thomas had made his examination he looked very grave and announced that Mary had pneumonia.

"I must be frank, William, and tell you that it is doubtful whether Mary will last the night. You must tell Sophia. Yes," as William shook his head, "If Mary dies and Sophia is not here with her child it could push her over the edge. I am sure Sophia is stronger than you think in a crisis."

William went and fetched Sophia who sat with Mary all night and, helped by Rose, placed cold cloths on the sick girl's forehead. But all to no avail, towards dawn Mary quietly died.

Sophia had lost yet another child. Her fourth out of seven children.

John, coming in early in the morning as was his habit of late, found Amelia sitting on the stairs.

"Whatever are you doing up?" he asked.

Amelia looked up. He was concerned at her white face.

"Oh, John, it has been awful. Mary is ill. Papa and Mama are with her. They won't let me in. I don't want to go to bed."

As John started up the stairs, Mary's door opened and William came out supporting Sophia who was sobbing. Rose came behind. After quietly shutting the door she put her apron over her head and sobbed.

"Is she?" John asked

"Yes," William replied, "she died fifteen minutes ago."

"Can I go and see her?" John asked

"Of course."

"I want to see her, too." Amelia had reached the top of the stairs.

Together John and Amelia went hand in hand to say goodbye to their sister.

There was much to do. Grace and Gerald had to be informed. All the arrangements had to be made for Mary to be laid to rest beside her brothers and sister. Sophia moved about like one of William's mechanical toys. As William spent all his time with Sophia Amelia did not get a chance to tell him about the papers.

Coming into the dining room one evening John found Amelia on her own staring at a bowl of soup which she had not touched. He sat beside her.

"You must eat something, Amelia." he said gently "Otherwise you will be ill and Mother and Father have enough to worry about."

"I can't eat, John. I keep trying to tell Papa but he won't listen."

"Tell Papa what?"

"That man took some papers from Papa's desk."

"Are you sure?"

"Yes. Then he pushed me, then Mary screamed, then Mama came."

Her lip began to tremble.

"Don't cry, Amelia. I will tell Papa. Now eat your soup."

Giving him a watery smile she obediently picked up her spoon.

Later in the evening, William called John into the study.

"I cannot leave your mother until after the funeral. Please inform Mr Robson that the factory will be closed on the day of the funeral. Also ask him the name of the clerk he sent for my designs last Monday."

Being reminded of Amelia's assertion that the man had taken some papers, John told William of her suspicions.

"Is there anything missing, Father?"

William quickly searched his desk.

"No, everything seems to be here. I think Amelia imagines things sometimes. It is a fact that one of the clerks came here and was alone with Mary, however. I want you to find out who it was and dismiss him at once. I want him off my premises immediately."

On arriving at the office the next day, John called in Mr Robson.

"It has been decided that the factory will close on the day of my sister's funeral. Please make all the arrangements. By the way did you send a clerk to fetch some papers from my home last Monday?"

"Yes, I did. Mr Wallace had left some designs on his desk."

"And the name of the person you sent?"

"Simon Jarrett."

"Oh yes, Jarrett – what do you think of him?"

"Well – he is efficient and quick with his work but there is something about him I don't like. I don't know what it is."

"Thank you, Mr Robson. Send Jarrett in will you?"

Greatly wondering, Mr Robson went into the main office and called Simon to him.

"I don't know what you have been up to my lad. Mr John wants to see you." He was gratified to see Simon go pale.

As Jarrett entered the room John observed him closely. The dark good looks, the carefully trimmed moustache, the clothes a little expensive for a humble clerk and the air of arrogance only lightly held in check. No wonder a vulnerable young girl like Mary was taken in. He did not invite Jarrett to sit down.

Simon had been mildly interested when Mr Robson had told them that the family had suffered a bereavement. One of the daughters had died. He assumed it was the ugly little girl Amy – no, Amelia.

John did not beat about the bush.

"I understand from Mr Robson that you were sent to get some papers for Mr Wallace."

"Yes, I was."

"Did you get the papers?"

"No, Mr John – there was nobody at home. I did tell Mr Robson when I got back."

John stood up, coming round the desk he confronted Simon who took a step back in surprise. John was white with fury.

"You are not telling the truth, are you, Jarrett? You entered the house and there was a scene."

"A misunderstanding, Mr John."

"Mary is dead and *you* are responsible. If she had not run out into the rain after you she would still be alive. You killed her."

"She's dead?"

How dare she die! All his plans gone for nothing! He unconsciously patted his pocket where the designs were hidden. He had looked at them last night. They were good, he could build on the idea. One corner was tucked over and he had smoothed it out. ASMW – what did that mean? He would wait until he had more time to puzzle over it. Now he was more concerned with the consequences to himself.

"How can I have killed her? *I* didn't ask her to run out after me. *I* am not responsible for the actions of a silly girl!"

Stepping away from Simon, John said coldly, "Take yourself off these premises immediately." he walked to the door, opened it and called "Mr Robson."

"Yes, Mr John?"

"Mr Jarrett is leaving us. Pay him what he is owed then make sure he leaves the premises."

Ignoring Simon, John walked back round his desk, sat down and, picking up a sheet of paper, began to read.

Simon came to life at last.

"You can't do this!"

Without looking up John replied

"I can and I have – now go before I have you taken in charge!"

"You will regret this. I will bring down Wallace & Son if it is the last thing I do!"

Mr Robson took Simon's arm in a firm grip.

"Come along, Jarrett – lets act like civilized human beings." Simon, still uttering threats of ruining the firm, was led away.

John looked up as the door closed and then resumed his reading.

After he had been escorted from Wallace & Son, Simon stood on the pavement wondering what to do. One thing he did know and that was that somehow, sometime, he was going to bring down Wallace & Son, then Mr John would be in his position.

Mr Robson watched him walk away then went back into the building to report to Mr John.

As Simon walked briskly away from Wallace & Son he began to plan. His main goal in life now was to ruin the firm. The best way to do that was to take away their trade.

He knew he could design mechanical toys but he also knew that he needed to know more and the best place to do that was Paris. From some of the correspondence he had seen when working at Wallace & Son, he knew that there were several firms in Paris producing mechanical toys. He would apprentice himself to one of these firms. He was confident that the designs he had taken from William's desk would open a few doors.

Having made up his mind he turned his steps towards the Shipping Agent's offices with a view to booking a passage on the first packet to leave England. He would not return until he was in a position to take his just revenge on Wallace & Son for their treatment of him.

CHAPTER ELEVEN

The days before the funeral were full of subdued busyness. Mourning clothes had to be made up for all the family including black work dresses for Rose and Mrs Coalport. The dressmaker seemed to be at the house day and night working in one of the attics which Sophia had turned into a sewing room.

Rose was kept busy answering the door to deliveries of flowers. Sophia ordered black-edged writing paper and envelopes then busied herself answering the many letters of condolence.

Amelia felt that she had no part in these proceedings and several times Rose found her sitting on her favourite stair silently crying.

William hardly spoke until he heard Sophia instruct Amelia on her conduct at the funeral.

"Amelia will not be going to the funeral," he told her. Sophia turned to her daughter.

"Run away and ask Rose to give you your tea."

Amelia could not find Rose in the kitchen. Mrs Coalport thought that she had gone up to prepare Mr and Mrs Mitchell's room. As Amelia went through the hall towards the stairs she heard, through the open morning room door, Sophia saying

"We MUST give Mary a proper funeral. It is expected. We have a certain standing in the community. Amelia must be there. She is one of the family."

"No matter how many horses with black plumes pull the hearse or how much money is spent on black edged writing paper, mourning dresses, professional mourners or any of the other trappings you think are necessary nothing will bring Mary back. However, I do understand that you need these things to help you grieve but I will not have Amelia walking behind the coffin.

I know it is what is expected but I don't want her to be upset more than she is already, and remember that comparisons may be made by otherwise well-meaning people. Grace and Gerald will be here. Let Amelia stay at home with Rose."

"Don't you want your daughter to be given a decent funeral?" Sophia sounded tearful.

"Of course I do, but I can't feel happy about all the frills that seem to be necessary. It's not a show, it's our daughter's funeral."

"I want Mary to have a proper funeral and I am sure that Grace would say the same." Sophia began to sound hysterical.

"Very well, but Amelia does not go."

Amelia thoughtfully climbed the stairs. She was relieved that she would not have to walk behind the coffin – everyone staring at her.

Grace and Gerald arrived later that day. Amelia had not seen her sister since the wedding. Now Grace was dressed in deep black with a black veil over her face which she threw back as she entered the house.

Ignoring Amelia who had followed Rose into the hall, Grace went up to the drawing room where she found Sophia. Mother and daughter embraced, then Sophia returned to her sofa, Grace and Gerald took chairs and Amelia sat on a chair between them. For some time everyone was silent. Grace sat fingering her black onyx brooch then she burst out, "Why, Mama?"

Sophia did not reply, just sighed and shook her head.

"She was so beautiful." Grace continued "Not like…" she stopped. Even Grace was not so insensitive as to say what hung in the air – "Why could it not have been Amelia?"

"Go and ask Rose to serve tea early." Sophia instructed Amelia, who slowly got off her chair and left the room. She vaguely wondered what Grace had been going to say but felt too miserable to care as she made her way down to the kitchen.

On the day of the funeral Mrs Coalport kept Amelia busy in the kitchen until Rose came in saying, "They have gone."

They both glanced at Amelia who kept her head bent over her work.

Mrs Coalport busied herself cutting up a seed cake then said, "First a wedding, now a funeral – that means the next will be a birth."

Neither Rose nor Amelia replied and they continued to work in silence.

When the funeral party returned Amelia was kept busy handing round plates. All she could see were black garments. Rose had opened the curtains which had been kept closed until after the funeral party had left and now the hot August sun poured into the room making it even hotter.

Amelia longed to be able to go to her room and take off her heavy clothes. She thought the day would never end but it was over at last and she was free to go to bed and cry herself to sleep.

The next day Grace and Gerald returned to Scotland. Just before they went Grace told her mother that in the New Year she hoped to make her a Grandmother.

Amelia spent a great deal of time down in the kitchen. Everyone in the house was subdued. She had even seen John wiping his eyes on his handkerchief. William shut himself in his study and usually stayed there most of the night.

John went out every evening after dinner telling nobody where he was going, coming home very late. Sophia retired to her room and had all her meals sent up. Amelia began having her tea in the kitchen rather than eat on her own in the dining room. Mrs Coalport was always making her little delicacies and calling her "poor little mite."

September came and Rose became quieter than ever. One day as she was giving Amelia her tea she said, "I have something to tell you, Amelia."

Amelia put down the piece of cake she was about to consume. Rose only called her Amelia when it was serious, usually she called her Miss Amelia.

"Yes, Rose." She said not quite sure if she wanted to hear.

"You know I think the world of you but I have a life to lead and one day you will be grown up and will probably forget all about me."

Amelia opened her mouth to protest.

"Oh yes, you will – it's only natural. Well, I have met somebody and I am going to get married. We would have been married before but Miss Mary dying like that made things difficult."

"You mean awkward." Said Mrs Coalport.

Rose blushed, "I will come and see you sometimes, Miss Amelia, and perhaps your Mama will let you come and see me."

Amelia remembered Grace's wedding and how Rose had said she would like her to be her bridesmaid.

"Can I be your bridesmaid, Rose? You did say that I could."

Rose looked surprised she had forgotten her light remarks.

"You can't, you're in mourning for your sister. I'll come and show you my dress after the ceremony and you can meet my George. How would that be?"

Amelia considered. Yes, she would look out of place going to a wedding in her black mourning dress and Mama had told her that she would have to wear black for a year. She had a happy thought, one which she was sure Rose had not considered.

"If you will wait until I am out of mourning, Rose, I could still be your bridesmaid."

Rose looked away.

"I'm afraid not, Miss Amelia – there are – reasons why I have to get married now."

"What reasons?"

"Grown up reasons, Miss inquisitive." said Mrs Coalport coming to Rose's rescue.

Amelia realized that she was not going to get any more out of either of them. She did think that grown ups were very peculiar at times. It was the first time that she had really considered Rose to be grown up. She looked at her as if at a grown up. Yes, she did look different – sort of fatter somehow. She didn't think she wanted to be grown up after all.

"You promise to show me your dress?"

"Yes, of course I will. Your Mama is interviewing girls to take my place this afternoon so you will have somebody here in the evenings to talk to."

"It won't be the same."

"I know, Amelia, but you'll get used to it."

Amelia finished her tea and went and sat on her favourite stair on the staircase to have a think. She could hear a murmur of voices from the morning room. The door opened and Sophia came out followed by a thin girl with severe features.

The girl said, "Thank you, Madam. I shall be here as arranged Monday week."

Sophia called for Rose and when she appeared said, "This is Agnes. She will be taking your place. Show her the kitchen. Tell her everything she needs to know."

Once Rose had taken Agnes away to the kitchen Sophia sighed, put her hand to her head and began to climb the stairs. When she came to where Amelia was sitting she stopped and looked down at her.

"You will be sorry to lose Rose I expect, Amelia. You have never known any other servant. You must remember that servants come and go. We were lucky to have Rose for so long but then there were special circumstances." It was almost as if Mama was talking to herself. "But they all leave in the end.

I would have been forced to give her notice in a few weeks anyway. At least she is getting married. Now Mary has gone there is only John and you left. I expect John will be off soon." Then, as if she realized she was speaking her thoughts aloud, "You will always stay with me, won't you, Amelia?"

"Oh yes, Mama, always."

Rose was very sad leaving Amelia but she was also excited. She would soon have a home of her own and she was looking forward to it. George had a very good job working for the Electric Telegraph Company so she was sure of a good weekly wage.

There would be no return to the conditions of Ratcliff Court for her! At this particular time she missed her mother more than ever. She had come to terms with the fact that her mother was, in all probability, dead. Only death would have prevented her from getting in touch with her daughter. Rose was sure that her stepfather had something to do with it.

She had told George all about it. He had agreed that her mother probably was dead and added that, as they could not prove it was Anderson, there was no point in worrying about it. George was a very practical man and Rose loved him dearly. She would never have left Amelia for any other man.

They had rented a little house only a half mile from No 13. Rose spent most of her spare time getting the house ready. They had few possessions but she didn't mind. So long as they had a roof over their heads she was happy.

The night before her wedding Rose slept at No 13 for the last time. Mr Wallace had told her that, had they not been in mourning, they would have been pleased for Rose to be married from the house. He would have been honoured to give her away. Rose shed fresh tears at this unexpected statement.

As she had no family of her own George's Mother, Mrs Brett, had taken over and arranged everything. Mr Brett was to give her away and George's three sisters were to be bridesmaids.

Rose found George's mother, Mrs Brett, rather a formidable lady who questioned her closely on her background. She was very impressed that Rose could read, write and reckon. Rose told her that she had been an orphan for many years. Mrs Brett took it into her head that Rose's parents had been killed together somehow. Rose did not disabuse her of this.

Neither did she mention Ratcliff Court and definitely not her stepfather. That was all in the past. It was no longer part of her life. She was going to begin a new life now.

On her last morning at No 13 everyone came to the kitchen to say goodbye. Mrs Coalport shed tears. William and Sophia gave her a handsome sterling silver cake basket. William thought that this was rather unsuitable but Sophia insisted.

He was pleased that Sophia had roused herself so much so he let it go. Mrs Coalport produced a butter pot. Even John managed to take time off from his work to present her with a tea service plus tray with roses all over it.

"I thought it would remind you of all the times you have prepared tea here," he said.

Rose was overwhelmed with all the presents.

"How am I to get these to Mrs Brett's?" she worried.

"That's all been arranged," and William led the way out of the kitchen. He opened the front door for her and outside the gate was a cab all ready to take her to her future mother-in-law's where she was to dress.

"It's all paid for, all you have to do is get in and off you go. We all wish you the very best of luck."

Rose was quickly installed and, surrounded by her possessions, she left No 13.

Amelia ran out after the cab. "Don't forget to show me your dress, Rose," she called as the cab gathered speed. Rose leaned out and waved her handkerchief. Then she sat back in the cab and had a good cry.

"What was that about a dress?" William asked as they all trooped back indoors.

"Rose promised me that she would come and show me her dress. It's because I can't be a bridesmaid because I am in mourning." she told him.

William smiled at her but his mind had already turned to a new design.

Amelia waited impatiently. She didn't know how long a wedding would take. She remembered that Grace's wedding had seemed a long time but when they had arrived back from church she had looked at the brass clock on the dining room mantelpiece and found it was quite early. She decided that she could expect Rose at 4 o'clock. That was when Mama had tea in the drawing room when she was well enough to be up.

Four o'clock came and went. Mrs Coalport served tea. Sophia called for Amelia to come and bring her lessons with her so that she could see what she had been doing. Amelia liked these sessions with Mama. For one thing it usually meant that Mama was feeling better and might even play a game of cards with her. Today, however, after looking at Amelia's copybook Sophia declared that she had a headache and would lie down until dinner time.

Amelia was at a loose end with no Rose to talk to. Normally she would seize this occasion to go down to the kitchen and chat to her as she went about her work. She wandered down to the kitchen where Mrs Coalport was just starting the dinner.

"I have no time to talk to you today, Miss Amelia, I am afraid. With no Rose I have to do everything myself. Goodness knows when I shall be home tonight. Coalport is not happy but, as I said, its only for a few days. Madam did ask me to live in until the new girl comes on Monday but I can't leave Coalport – he would never manage on his own!"

"When do you think Rose will come, Mrs Coalport?"

"Rose has gone Miss, you know that. She's got her own home to run now."

"But she promised to show me her dress because I couldn't be a bridesmaid because I'm still in mourning."

"Are you sure that's not one of your little daydreams, Miss? You know what a one you are for daydreaming. I sometimes wonder if you know when you are awake! Now out of my way there's a good girl. Go and play with one of the toys your father gave you. There aren't many little girls who have so many new toys to try out. I am sure there is one that your Papa wants an opinion on."

Amelia went and sat on her favourite stair. The hall clock chimed five, still no Rose. What could have happened to her? Perhaps she could not get married because she had no bridesmaid! Amelia went into a daydream in which she got to the Church and Rose was crying and everyone was crying until they saw Amelia who was instantly transformed into the most beautiful bridesmaid that ever was.

Without remembering quite how she managed it she found herself outside the front gate and walking along the road. She knew that Rose was getting married in Church. She didn't think it was the same church that Grace got married in because she had asked Rose and she had said a different saint but which one? Amelia went through all the saints she had heard about in her Sunday School lessons. None of them sounded like the right one.

What else had Rose said? She wracked her brains. Then she remembered hearing Rose talking to Mrs Coalport about a place called Ratcliff Court – that must be where Rose had gone. Amelia had no idea where Ratcliff Court was. It must be at least as far as the corner because Rose had taken a cab. She decided to keep walking and read the street signs until she came to one that said Ratcliff Court.

She became interested in the activity in the street. There were so many people. Where did they all come from? She saw a pastry shop and realized she was hungry but she had no money. She walked a bit further – now the roads were narrower and the people looked more ragged. She came to a street market.

Small boys with ragged trousers and shirts, filthy legs and unshod feet encrusted with dirt fought each other for rotten fruit. She was beginning to feel uncomfortable and encountered several sideways looks from some of the more disreputable.

She was almost sorry that she had come. Perhaps she had been foolish. She would have to go back. She walked down an alleyway hoping to find a road but it only led to another court. A man leaning in a doorway called out "Come here, little girl." She backed away and then began to run.

She ran down the alleyway. When she got to the narrow street she did not know which way to turn, to left or right. She was beginning to feel frightened. Although it was late afternoon on a bright August day and the sun shone on the upper stories of the houses it did not penetrate the narrow gorge-like street. Left or right?

She began to sob then told herself not to be a cry-baby. If Grace could see her now she would laugh at her being so silly. She closed her eyes and prayed hard. When she opened them she knew her prayers had been answered. She saw the familiar sight of a policeman slowly walking towards her. He saw her at the same time and quietly approaching her asked her where she was going.

"To see Rose," she replied.

"Where would this Rose be?" he asked.

"I think she is in Ratcliff Court. Do you know where that is?"

The policeman peered more closely.

"And what would your name be, Miss?"

"Amelia Sophia Margaret Wallace. My papa owns Wallace & Son."

"Does he now. And does he know that you are out by yourself?"

"Not exactly. I think I should like to go home now, please."

"Well you come with me, Miss, and we will get you home to your Mama."

When Amelia arrived on the doorstep accompanied by a policeman Sophia thought that she would die from humiliation.

"I found this young lady wandering along Ratcliff Highway. She said she was looking for a Rose who lives in Ratcliff Court. I didn't think it was right for a child to be wandering around in that neighbourhood so I brought her home, madam."

"Thank you so much, constable."

"Is the master in, madam?"

"I will take you to his study. Amelia go to your room!"

"But Rose said she would show me her dress because I can't..."

"GO TO YOUR ROOM AMELIA! Rose has left us. Servants come and go. They are not family, they are a different class. Rose probably only said that to you to keep you quiet!" Sophia snapped.

Amelia could see that Mama was upset. She went slowly up the stairs. She heard Papa's study door open and close and then nothing. In her room she sat on the bed and thought about Rose. What did

Mama mean, Rose was only a servant? And what was a different class? She had always considered Rose to be, not her sister exactly but definitely a friend. She would ask Papa about it in the morning.

She didn't have to wait until the morning. Soon after she had gone to bed Papa came to see her.

"Are you awake, Amelia?" he asked.

"Yes, Papa. I have a question I want to ask you."

"Only one! That's unusual for you! What is it?"

"Mama said that Rose is a different class. What does she mean?"

"Well, Amelia, that is something that people have been trying to define for years. What I think Mama means is that Rose does not come from the same background as ourselves. You can't make friends with a servant, Amelia, they are not like us, they have their own ways of doing things.

I consider that I am a good employer but I don't make friends with my workforce and they would not like it if I tried. That way everyone knows their place in society and that is what it is all about. Do you see?"

Amelia was not quite sure that she did but nodded anyway.

"Now I want you to promise me that you will NEVER, NEVER do anything like this again. Your Mama was frantic and you know how delicate she is. There are some places in London that are not safe for a young girl. Do you understand me, Amelia?"

"Yes, Papa."

"Now promise me you will never do anything like this again."

"I promise, Papa. I am sorry that Mama was worried. I didn't mean to do it. It just happened."

"Well, make sure that it doesn't 'just happen' again. I don't enjoy being lectured by a policeman in my own study. Now go to sleep and we will start afresh tomorrow."

"Goodnight, Papa. And thank you for explaining about class and servants and things."

"Goodnight, Amelia."

William realized that Amelia needed more stimulation. Under normal circumstances he would expect Sophia to be responsible for her education as she had been for her other daughters but Sophia could not be relied upon, she changed from day to day.

He did not entirely agree with the education of women beyond a certain point. They needed to know how to read and write in order to be able to run a household. A rudimentary knowledge of arithmetic sufficient to deal with the household accounts was all that was necessary. He considered any further education to be a waste of money and he therefore set out to find a school whose curriculum accorded with these ideals.

He was very fortunate in finding an establishment close to Brondesbury Villas run by twin sisters, the Misses Black, two spinster ladies of impeccable respectability and uncertain age.

There were only fifteen young ladies in the school ranging in age from 10 to 16. William had to keep his irritation in check as the Misses Black, as like as two peas, frowned and bit their lips in unison. Amelia was younger than their usual pupils. She was also – unusual. Special provision might have to be made, etc., etc.

William had almost decided to go elsewhere when they made up their collective minds to take Amelia on a trial basis as a day pupil. The fees would, of course, have to reflect the special circumstances . . . William left, thanking God that women would never be in charge of the education of boys.

CHAPTER TWELVE

The days quickly fell into a pattern. Whilst Amelia did not forget Rose she got more involved in school and William had begun to take an interest in her designs. They spent many happy hours in his study discussing each others' designs and the latest ideas from France.

Christmas was strained. Mary's place was vacant and it was strange to have Agnes instead of Rose serving at table. William was disturbed that they had heard nothing from Rose. When he mentioned his disquiet to Sophia she was dismissive. "What can you expect from a servant?"

Sophia found Christmas very hard to bear, she did not even have Grace to comfort her. Grace, at five months pregnant, could not manage the journey from Edinburgh in the depths of winter. Sophia was reminded all the time of the previous Christmas when they had all been together.

Strangely, the person Sophia seemed to turn to most was Agnes. Agnes could get Sophia up when she had said she would stay in bed. Sometimes she had even managed to persuade Sophia to go out for short walks in the park.

One afternoon in January Agnes went into the sitting room to draw the curtains and found Sophia studying a miniature of Mary which she kept on the table with the others.

"Is that the daughter that recently died, madam?" she asked.

Normally Sophia would have dealt swiftly with such impertinence from a servant but she had been feeling very depressed for some time. William was out all day and when he was home spent most of his time in his study and Amelia was usually with him. John did not always come home for dinner and when he did he went out immediately afterwards not returning until the small hours. Her friends had drifted away since she seldom entertained. To talk to anyone, even a servant, was a relief.

"This is a better likeness." Taking off her gold locket and chain she opened it holding it out for Agnes to see Mary's picture inside. Agnes gazed at it intently.

"She was very beautiful, madam."

"Never to see her again, that is what I cannot bear," said Sophia. "I know that the Church says we shall meet one day but that seems such a long time to wait. I want to know that she is happy now, Agnes."

Shutting the locket with a sigh she replaced the chain round her neck.

Agnes looked at Sophia's sad face then going to the open door she shut it and went back to stand in front of her chair. Bending down she spoke softly.

"Well, madam, there might be a way."

"Whatever do you mean, Agnes? Mary is dead – I shall never see her this side of the grave."

"There are ways, madam, of course it costs money." Sophia looked at her, startled.

"How?" she breathed.

Agnes bent closer.

"I have heard of a lady who is a medium, madam. She can get in touch with those who have 'passed over'. I understand that she is very good. A friend of mine got in touch with her husband who had recently died."

"The Church teaches that such dabbling is wicked. I don't want to hear any more about it, Agnes."

Straightening up, Agnes replied, poker faced.

"Very well, madam. There is probably nothing in it," and quietly left the room.

Sophia brooded for several days. She tried to speak to William on the subject but he was always too busy to listen. She considered consulting Rev. Oswin-Redway but decided against it. In the end she convinced herself that there was probably nothing in it but if there were she was missing an opportunity to get in touch with Mary. Finally she spoke to Agnes who was setting out the tea-things.

"I don't really think there is anything in this idea, Agnes, but I am quite willing to meet this medium and make up my mind then."

"Very well, madam, I will try and get in touch with her – I think she will agree to a meeting, although she does not work with unbelievers." Agnes spoke matter-of-factly.

"I am not an unbeliever, Agnes, I just have not made up made my mind."

"Very well, madam."

Agnes did not let her smile show until she was outside the drawing room door.

★★★★★

Amelia was on her way home from school. Since Rose had left she had been allowed to come home alone. She enjoyed these walks to and from school. She felt free. Although people still stared at her she had grown used to it. She walked part of the way with her friend Geraldine.

Geraldine at ten was the nearest in age to Amelia at the school. She was also rather young for her age and sometimes Amelia felt the elder of the two. Geraldine didn't seem to care what Amelia looked like and would happily chatter away about school, her family and home.

Amelia liked to listen to her talking about her family. As her friend was one of nine children there was plenty to talk about. Amelia had told Geraldine all about Mary dying and Rose never coming to show her her dress. Geraldine was of the opinion that it was not worth worrying about.

As time went by without any news of Rose Amelia began to believe that Rose had forgotten all about her. She had been very hurt for some time but Geraldine had convinced her that servants were servants.

This coloured Amelia's attitude towards Agnes. Amelia didn't like Agnes very much. She did not know why. Agnes was always polite but Amelia felt she was playing a part. She also smelt faintly of mustiness which Amelia found unpleasant. She had mentioned this to Mama who had told her not to be so silly and anyway Agnes did her work very efficiently and that was all that was required. She was not required to be a friend.

Amelia was sure that Mrs Coalport didn't like Agnes either. Although Mrs Coalport had never said anything to confirm this sometimes, when Amelia went down into the kitchen, the atmosphere was charged, almost as if there had been what Mrs Coalport called 'words'. Mrs Coalport would be quite flushed and Agnes would be sitting in her usual place by the table looking faintly contemptuous.

Walking home one day, after she had waved goodbye to Geraldine, Amelia turned all these things over in her mind. Looking across the road she was surprised to see Agnes talking to an older woman. As this was not Agnes's afternoon off she assumed Mama had sent her to escort her home. Amelia felt resentful – she was not a baby!

She was glad that she had already said goodbye to Geraldine, she would not want Geraldine to see her being met by a servant. As Amelia carefully crossed the road she watched Agnes show the woman something which she held in her hand. As Amelia approached she heard Agnes say

"Give me several more days to work on her, Auntie, and I will be sure of her. She is desperate to..."

Seeing Amelia she pushed her hand inside her shawl but not before Amelia had seen that it held a miniature like the ones in the sitting room at home.

"What are you doing here?" Agnes asked, sharply.

Amelia looked at her in surprise.

"I'm going home – I thought Mama had sent you to meet me."

Recovering herself, Agnes patted the other woman on the arm who, nodding slightly, walked away down the street. Agnes turned to Amelia.

"I had to run an errand for madam. I did not realize it was so late. Come along then, Miss Amelia."

"Who were you speaking to?"

"It was a lady who was asking me the way to the Doctor," Agnes replied smoothly.

Although Amelia did not believe her she said nothing and as soon as they got home she went into the sitting room to see Mama. Sophia looked up as she entered and seemed disappointed when she saw it was Amelia.

"Agnes is just bringing the tea, Mama," Amelia announced. She decided to tell Mama what she had seen "I saw..."

"Agnes is back?" Sophia interrupted, jumping to her feet.

"Yes, she is in the kitchen," Amelia was astonished when her mother ran from the room and down to the kitchen.

Sophia rushed into the kitchen where Agnes was laying a tray for tea and Mrs Coalport was at the range, basting a joint. Agnes looked up and Mrs Coalport turned round in surprise. Seeing their amazed faces Sophia smoothed down her dress and forced herself to speak calmly.

"Please come into the hall, Agnes, I wish to speak to you. Carry on with your work, Mrs Coalport."

As Mrs Coalport put the roast back in the oven and closed the door she wondered what it was that needed to be said in private. She hoped Agnes was getting her notice.

As soon as they were in the hall Sophia turned to Agnes.

"Did you see her?" Sophia asked eagerly.

"No, madam, there was no sign of her. I don't really know where to start looking." Agnes replied calmly.

Sophia slumped down onto one of the hall chairs. Amelia, who had come out into the hall in search of her mother saw Agnes give Sophia a speculative look.

"Come back to the drawing room, Mama, and Agnes will bring the tea," Amelia coaxed. Sophia let her lead her back to the drawing room where she collapsed onto the sofa.

As Amelia drank her tea she turned these puzzling events over in her mind. She felt that she wanted to confide in someone and in the end decided her brother John would be the best person.

John was very seldom at home these days but today he surprised them all by appearing just before dinner.

"You're going to sit down to dinner with us then, John?" asked his father.

"Yes, father, but then I must go out."

"Again?" William raised his eyebrows.

"I have an appointment," John said, making for the stairs. "I will just change and then I will be down."

Amelia, sitting on her usual stair, stood up as John ascended.

"I have something to ask you, John," she said.

"What is it, Amelia? I have to change before dinner."

"Can we go to your room, please, I don't want anyone to hear."

John led the way to his room. Once the door was shut he sat down on the bed and patted the coverlet beside him.

"Come on then, Amelia, what is the problem? Are you in trouble with one of the Misses Black again? Do you want me to speak to Papa on your behalf?"

"Not this time thank you, John. Its about Agnes."

"Agnes? Ah, the maid. What has she been up to? Stealing the silver?"

"No, John, please listen. I don't like Agnes very much – do you?"

"I have never given it much thought. She is not as nice as Rose, certainly. Is that what you want to talk to me about – whether or not I like Agnes?"

"I think she is telling lies but I don't know why."

"What makes you think that?"

She told him about Agnes and the part-conversation she had overheard and how Agnes had told her that the woman was asking directions and she had never seen her before.

"But she must have seen her before if she was her aunt, mustn't she, John?"

John sat still for a moment.

"Yes, on the face of it it does sound rather strange. Probably nothing in it."

"Should I tell Papa?" asked Amelia anxiously.

"No, don't worry him at the moment. We have some problems at the factory and we have no proof that Agnes is up to anything. It's probably your imagination, Amelia. You spend too much time alone."

"I don't mind being alone, I am used to it. I shall keep watch on Agnes and see what I can find out and when I have found something I can go to Papa."

"Yes, that's the best thing to do. Now off you go, Amelia, I have to get dressed for dinner."

Amelia left the room and then remembered that she had not told John about the miniature. She turned and went back into the room. John looked up with an impatient expression,

"I don't want to hear any more about this, Amelia. I am late and I want to get dressed. If there is anything else you want to say you must tell me tomorrow."

He took her arm and pushed her through the door which he shut and she heard the key turn in the lock. Sighing she went downstairs and into the sitting room where she counted the miniatures on the small table. They were all there. Perhaps she had been mistaken.

It was difficult to keep an eye on Agnes and go to school. She considered confiding in Geraldine but decided it would be better if nobody except herself and John knew about it until she could find proof.

For several days nothing unusual happened. Amelia was beginning to wonder if anything would happen. She was feeling bored. For the first time she could remember there was no snow for her to play in. January and no snow, just rain all the time. Mrs Coalport considered it "unnatural – we will suffer later!"

Upon returning from school one wet afternoon Amelia found Sophia in a state of excitement. As soon as she walked into the sitting-room her mother grasped her arm.

"Thank goodness you are back, Amelia, I thought you were never coming. Help me to re-arrange the furniture," and she began bustling about – setting the table in the middle of the room, and putting four chairs round it. She then drew the curtains although it was still daylight outside. Amelia was puzzled.

"I am expecting a visitor. It is important that you do everything she tells you, Amelia."

The doorbell rang. Amelia heard Agnes' voice in the hall then she appeared in the doorway followed by a woman who, although now dressed in a shapeless, voluminous garment of a sickly green and wearing a gaudy scarf, Amelia recognized as the woman Agnes had called Aunt. Her small eyes, one with a slight squint, darted here and there lingering on the miniatures on the table by the window. Realizing that Agnes was watching her closely, Amelia kept her face as blank as possible. It seemed important not to let Agnes know that she had recognized the woman.

Sophia gushed "How do you do, Madam Freda. I have arranged everything as instructed."

Madam Freda walked round the table as if inspecting the layout of the table and chairs. She peered at Amelia who was standing watching her.

"Who is this, then?" her voice sounded hoarse.

"My daughter Amelia. I hope you have no objection to her being present – I understand that you need more than one person?"

"Yes, that's right – four is the minimum. Perhaps your maid could also stay."

Amelia noted that she did not say "my niece."

"I am not sure that I should, madam," said Agnes sounding scandalized.

"Well, in that case..." and the woman began to move towards the door.

"Yes, she can stay if you are sure that it is absolutely necessary," Sophia hastened to reassure her.

"We would be more likely to get a result. Let's begin. If you sit here next to me, Mrs Wallace, and Agnes," she seemed to realize her mistake and paused but Sophia didn't notice, "your maid can sit on my left and the little girl can sit on her right and opposite me. That's it. Now, I must have complete silence. The spirits can be very shy. They may not come at all. Now we must all join hands."

"What spirits?" Amelia was getting frightened. "I don't want to do this, Mama," and she got up from her chair.

"Do be quiet, Amelia – if you don't sit down and do as you are told I will never speak to you again!"

Startled, Amelia re-seated herself.

They all sat in silence for some time. When Madam Freda gave a sharp cry, Amelia jumped. "Sit still, Amelia," her mother hissed. The medium now began to breath slowly and regularly. After she had been doing this for sometime she sighed and let go of Sophia's and Agnes' hands.

"I am sorry, the spirits are not happy. There is something wrong here. Perhaps you do not believe that it is possible to communicate with those who have passed on, Mrs Wallace?"

"Oh yes I do, indeed I do." Sophia made haste to reassure her.

"Then perhaps it is the little girl that is blocking the flow. She is not – normal, is she? The spirits are very sensitive to these things. It would be better perhaps if next time it was just the three of us."

"Will it work with only three?" asked Sophia.

"Yes, the spirits are quite happy with only a few people. Sometimes they appear when we have only one person present."

"But you said..." Amelia began. Agnes sitting on her right gave Amelia a sharp kick on the ankle.

"I'm sorry, miss," she said, "I think I am nervous, I have never sat in on a seance before."

Amelia decided to keep quiet. Madam Freda stood up.

"When will you come again?" Sophia asked eagerly.

"Oh, that depends. I have a great many people who rely on me to keep them in regular touch with their loved ones."

"Can you come tomorrow?"

"Tomorrow – no, I think not. I have promised to see another client tomorrow. I can only manage one seance per day – it's so tiring."

"Could you not put this client off?" pleaded Sophia.

Madam Freda looked shocked.

"The lady has begged me to help her. She is most anxious to contact her nephew. Money is involved – something to do with a will, I believe, and of course she is willing to pay for my services quite handsomely. I am only a poor woman, Mrs Wallace and cannot turn down money. I should like to give my services for nothing but I have to live."

"Yes, yes, of course. If I pay you double do you think you could see your way?"

"Well, I am not sure, the lady is desperate. She may go to somebody else and I have then lost a regular sitter," she said, reasonably, spreading her hands and shrugging, indicating an impasse. Her sharp little eyes watching Sophia closely.

"If I promise that you will be required to come regularly – say, once a week for the forseeable future, would that make a difference?"

"I can see that you are anxious for my help, Mrs Wallace, and I have always been too good hearted for my own good – yes, I will come again at the same time tomorrow but the young lady must not enter the room."

"Thank you so much. I am very grateful." She turned to Amelia. "You won't mind will you, Amelia? You must be quite bored I should think."

Amelia smiled but did not reply.

"I will show you out, madam," said Agnes.

Once they had left the room Amelia asked, "What was she trying to do, Mama?"

"Trying to contact your sister Mary. I must know that she is happy where she is. You have no idea how much I miss her."

"I know you do, Mama, so do I but are you sure that Papa would approve? That woman frightens me."

"Don't be so silly, Amelia, there is nothing to be afraid of. And there is no need to concern Papa with this. I will tell him when we have contacted Mary but until I have something to tell him there is no point, is there?"

Amelia shook her head to appease Mama but she had made up her mind that she would tell Papa as soon as possible. She was sure that Madam Freda and Agnes were being deceitful otherwise why would Agnes call her own Aunt 'Madam'?

She sat up on her stair waiting for Papa to come home until she got so sleepy she had to go bed. She would tell him in the morning.

CHAPTER THIRTEEN

Papa was not at breakfast. Neither was John. Agnes said that they had had a very early breakfast and gone off to the factory. Amelia didn't know what to do. She knew that Madam Freda was going to come back again that afternoon and she wanted Papa to know about it before she came.

Amelia was late home from school as she was kept behind due to inattention in class and had to write: "I must not be so rude in class" on the blackboard fifty times. When she got to the front door Agnes was just letting Madam Freda out. Amelia saw a conspiratorial look pass between them.

She found her mother in the drawing room setting the room to rights.

"Has Madam Freda been here again, Mama?" Amelia asked.

"Yes, she thinks that we are nearly there. Mary didn't come though today but another spirit did who knew her and said that she would pass on a message. I am so excited Amelia. Madam Freda has agreed to come again tomorrow although she does not usually like to conduct seances so close together but I could not wait. Tomorrow I will know how Mary is. I may even speak to her!"

"You will tell Papa today then, Mama, in case he wants to speak to Mary too," Amelia stated.

"I don't think Papa would understand, Amelia. He might not like it."

"Then why are you doing this, Mama, if Papa would be cross?"

"One day when you are grown-up you will understand. Now go and ask Agnes to give you your tea. I must go and lie down. I feel very tired." Sophia walked slowly to the stairs and started up them. Amelia watched her. As her mother got to the top of the stairs Agnes came from the dining room.

"Your tea is ready, Miss Amelia."

"I don't think I want any tea thank you, Agnes."

Agnes looked at her closely.

"Why not? Has it anything to do with your Mama seeing Madam Freda?"

"No, Agnes. I think perhaps I am not very well."

"Very well, miss."

Amelia knew that Agnes was watching her as she went up the stairs. She tried to walk like somebody who was sickening for something. By the time she got to her room she was feeling quite ill. She thought it was because she was hungry but she could not now change her mind, it would make Agnes suspicious. If only Papa would come in. To pass the time she began work on a design for a toy horse which could move its head from side to side.

She was absorbed in her design when a tap came at the door. Forgetting that she was supposed to be ill she cheerfully called, "come in!" and was overjoyed when Papa walked into the room.

"You don't sound ill, Amelia. Agnes seemed to think that you were at death's door," he said.

"Have you spoken to Mama?"

"No, she's gone to bed with a headache."

"Papa there is something I must tell you. John said that I must get more evidence and I have so now I can tell you."

"Tell me what, Amelia?"

She told him of her suspicions of Agnes, the conversation she had overheard, the seances and her suspicions regarding the miniature. Looking anxiously into his face she asked, "Have I done wrong, Papa? Mama told me not to tell you because you would not understand but I don't think Agnes and Madam Freda are very nice. I am sure they are taking money from Mama."

"I am certain they are. You haven't done anything wrong, Amelia. Are you afraid of all this talk of spirits and the afterlife?"

"A little, Papa."

"There is nothing to be afraid of, Amelia. Unfortunately there are some people who prey on others' unhappiness and I am sure that

that is what Agnes and Madam Freda are doing. There are some mediums who appear to be able to get in touch with people who have died but I don't know whether they really do or not. I am sure however, that Madam Freda is not one of them. I have heard talk in the city about a spate of such people. I will take over now, Amelia. You go to sleep – its getting late."

"Will you tell me what happens, Papa? And it was not Mama's fault. She misses Mary very much. I wish..."

"What do you wish, Amelia?"

"I know it is wicked, Papa, but sometimes I wish I had died instead of Mary. Everyone loved her so and she was so beautiful." she said wistfully.

"Never think that nobody loves you, Amelia. Yes, we did all love Mary. She was a beautiful girl but God saw fit to take her away from us. He also saw fit to make you as you are and you must be content with that."

He kissed her goodnight and left the room.

Amelia sat up in bed again. She had just thought of a way she could make the horse's tail swish from side to side. She picked up her design pad and pencil and was soon once more absorbed.

The next day Amelia made sure that she was attentive at school. She didn't want to run the risk of being late home. To make doubly sure she told Miss Black that she felt unwell. It was only a small lie and, as it was in a good cause, it didn't count as a lie.

Miss Black was not to know that her pale face and the dark rings under her eyes were the result of a late night working on a design. Thinking that Amelia might be incubating an infection which could run through the school with subsequent loss of income, Miss Black was only too pleased to suggest that Amelia go home early.

Once out of sight of the school windows Amelia ran all the way home arriving breathless at the garden door. When she went into the kitchen she saw Mrs Coalport peering through the door to the hall with her head on one side, listening. Seeing Amelia she waved her over.

"Come here, Miss Amelia." she whispered, "That Agnes is getting her come-uppance at last. I never did trust her. Nasty sly one.

Always listening at doors," said Mrs Coalport listening harder than ever. She turned to Amelia.

"The master came in about fifteen minutes ago. Into this very kitchen. 'Where's Agnes?' he says looking fierce. "In the sitting room with madam and that Madam Freda." I says. Then he goes marching up the hall and straight into the sitting room. You should have heard them scream! Then he came out with your Mama and "Take her to her room, Mrs Coalport," he says to me. Madam was sobbing fit to bust. I took her upstairs and put her to bed. I've only just come down. It's been quiet in there ever since."

Amelia and Mrs Coalport stood side by side at the kitchen door. Suddenly the sitting room door opened and Agnes and Madam Freda came out followed by William. Agnes was crying. Madam Freda looked annoyed.

William was clearly extremely angry. He addressed the sobbing Agnes.

"You are dismissed without a reference. You have five minutes to pack your bags and take yourself out of my house."

Agnes ran, still sobbing, up the stairs.

"And as for you," turning to Madam Freda, "if you come anywhere near my family again I will get you taken into custody. Mrs Coalport," he called. Mrs Coalport ran out into the hall. "see that these women leave the house."

Mrs Coalport smiled. "It will be a pleasure, sir." she said.

Amelia came into the hall to watch. Catching sight of her Madam Freda pointed at her shouting.

"It's all that one's fault – nasty ugly child!"

Before William could say anything, Mrs Coalport confronted Madam Freda and, raising her arm shouted, "You mind your tongue!"

Madam Freda drew herself up as if to defend herself.

Amelia's eyes were round. It looked as if there might be a fight there in the hall. William moved forward intending to calm the two women when they were all distracted by Agnes coming down the stairs carrying a bundle. Mrs Coalport turned from Madam Freda. Lowering her arm she asked with relish.

"Shall I search her, sir?"

"No, let them go, Mrs Coalport. Let's get them out of the house." William sounded weary. "I am going up to see my wife." He started up the stairs.

Mrs Coalport escorted Agnes and Madam Freda to the door which Amelia opened. Mrs Coalport gave them each a push through. Shutting the door with a bang, she caught hold of Amelia and they did a dance of triumph down the hall.

Amelia and Mrs Coalport went back into the kitchen where Amelia sat by the fire having her tea while she told Mrs Coalport how she had become suspicious of Agnes and how she had told Papa.

"Well I never, Miss Amelia, you are a clever girl. That horrible woman's remarks didn't upset you did they?"

"Not really, Mrs Coalport, I am used to it. Rose used to say 'handsome is as handsome does'. I wonder where she is?"

"So do I. Do you know, I have been round to her house at least four times and there has never been anyone there. I don't think she lives there any more. Perhaps it was something to do with the baby."

"What baby?" Amelia asked surprised.

"Rose's baby. She was expecting, Miss Amelia. That is why she had to get married but perhaps your Mama hasn't told you about these things yet."

"Oh yes, she has," lied Amelia who didn't have any idea what Mrs Coalport was talking about, but she wanted to know.

"Well, Rose got pregnant and had to get married. That's all there is to it. She must have had it by now. We could do with her now and no mistake. The mistress is going to take this very hard."

Amelia thoughtfully finished her tea, wished Mrs Coalport goodnight and went to bed.

Amelia was very puzzled about the baby. She had seen Geraldine's mother before she had her baby. She had looked quite fat. She did not know why that was. On the way home from school the next day she asked Geraldine about it.

"Well," said Geraldine, importantly, "Mama tells us that she is going to have another baby. Then nothing happens while she arranges it. Then a Doctor comes and a nurse. Then I get sent away to my Aunt Louise's and when I come back Mama has got the baby."

"But *where* does it come from?" Amelia asked.

"It is something to do with the Nurse. You cannot have a baby without a Nurse. I think she brings it and if the mother likes the look of it she keeps it but if the mother does not like the look of the baby she sends it back with the Nurse. My Mama often says that she wishes she could send the boys back but I suppose it is too late now."

Amelia thought this over and when she got home surprised Sophia by asking her why she had not sent her back when she saw how ugly she was. Sophia was shocked and could not think what to say for a while, then, "I would not have sent you back, Amelia. You are the one who will stay with me when I am old. You must look after me."

Amelia then knew that she had been kept so that she could look after Mama for always. She was quite pleased to do this but was still not certain she had got all the facts.

As Mrs Coalport had predicted, Sophia was very upset at William breaking up the seance. Sophia tried to reason with him but he was adamant.

For several days afterwards whenever William tried to speak to her she would leave the room or pick up a book and pretend to read. When she did speak to him again it was to inform him that since he had dismissed the servant he could go about engaging a new one. In the meantime Mrs Coalport found she was suddenly promoted to housemaid and parlour maid.

William was extremely busy at the factory and had no time to engage domestics. He considered that to be woman's work and told Sophia she was neglecting her duties and he ordered her to engage a servant immediately. Sophia called him cruel and unfeeling and flew into a fit of hysterics; it took William and Mrs Coalport half an hour to calm her down and get her to her room.

William then called in Dr. Thomas who, cheerful as usual, told William that he was of the opinion that a change of scene might do her good. On being informed of this Sophia decided to take Amelia and go and stay with her parents in Malvern for a few weeks.

William was quite happy with this arrangement. It was going to be difficult replacing Agnes at short notice and it would give him some time. Mrs Coalport was quite willing but had her own house to run. From what he could gather Mr Coalport was still "not happy about me being away so much, sir".

CHAPTER FOURTEEN

The evening of the day that Sophia and Amelia had been put on the train to Malvern William took a long walk. He wanted to think and he thought best when he was walking. He had had a disturbing conversation with Arthur Douglass. He liked Arthur, they had been friends and rivals for years. In the old days, before Sophia had been ill Arthur, Sophia and Arthur's wife Patience had frequently dined together at each others houses.

For some years Arthur had been trying to persuade William to sell his smaller factory and go into partnership with him taking his automata expertise with him. William knew that Arthur had no son to inherit the business and that he could make a condition of the partnership a seat on the board for John but he preferred to be independent. Arthur usually made this offer each time they met but today he had told William.

"I have found a designer of automata who is nearly as good as you, William. We will give you a run for your money this Christmas!"

William could not persuade him to say more than that. When William asked the name of this designer Arthur just grinned and shook his head. Arthur's firm could easily swallow up William's smaller one if it came to a fight between them for customers. Arthur was a friend but he was also a businessman. William decided to wait until he saw the quality of the automata before he worried. Arthur could be bluffing – trying to push him into agreeing to the merger. Then there was Sophia...

Deep in thought his brain took no notice of where his feet were taking him until the noise of men shouting made him take note of his surroundings. The noise was coming from a group of men fighting outside a public house which, according to a badly cracked wooden notice on its wall, was improbably called Paddy's Goose. He stepped across to the other side of the narrow alley to avoid the fists which were hitting anything within reach.

He looked round and found that he was a long way from home. Realizing that his business clothes could attract unwelcome attention, he was preparing to leave the alley as quickly and unobtrusively as possible when he felt a light touch on his arm.

He shook off the girl only to have another tap his shoulder. He turned impatiently. The girl gasped and covered her face with her shawl but not before he had recognized her.

"That is you, isn't it, Rose?" he caught her arm and guided her beneath a gas lamp.

"Yes, sir. I am sorry I didn't realize who you were." She pulled her arm out of his grasp and turned away.

William walked after her and grabbed her arm in a tight grip. Several of the girls were looking on with interest.

"Don't go, Rose. What has happened to you?"

Rose shook her head.

"Let me go, sir, I must earn some money."

"No, Rose, not like this," and William held on to her tighter than ever. "You are coming home with me." Taking her arm firmly he led her back down the alley to a brighter lit thoroughfare where he hailed a cab.

Neither of them spoke until they got to No 13. They went in by the garden entrance. Mrs Coalport had damped the range down and had left him some sandwiches on the table.

"Make us some tea, Rose," said William, sitting down at the table and picking up a sandwich.

Rose looked round the familiar kitchen as if she could not believe that she was there. Slowly she filled the kettle and put it on the range to boil. Once the kettle was boiling she made the tea. William indicated a chair. They sat at the table. And still neither of them spoke. Rose began to relax and William asked what had happened. In fits and starts she told him her story.

"Everything was going well at first, sir. I was so happy. We had a fine baby boy. He was beautiful. Then George became ill. He coughed a lot. He could not get to his work and he was sacked. Then the baby got sick. We did the best we could but with no money coming in it was hard.

I had to try and get some money somehow – George never knew where the money came from. I said that a kind lady had given it to me. It did no good – they both died one after the other. I had to let the house go. The landlord said I was not a respectable tenant. I ended up where I was before I came here – Ratcliff Court."

"With your step-father?"

"No, he was long gone. I think he is in prison."

"Couldn't George's mother help you out?"

Rose shook her head

"Mrs Brett helped out when George got sick but after he died I had to ask her to look after the baby while I went out. I told her I had a job in a match factory but somehow she found out what I was doing. She told one of her sons to follow me. When I got back she confronted me and said how could she be sure the baby was George's and that I had only married him to give the baby a name, then the baby died. After that I didn't care."

"Why didn't you come to me, Rose?" William reproached her.

"I was too ashamed, sir. I didn't think you would want anything to do with me."

"I could have helped you, Rose. No one need have known."

Rose reluctantly got to her feet.

"Thank you for the tea, sir, I must be going. The mistress won't like me being here."

"We have been having our own troubles, Rose. Mrs Wallace and Amelia are away in Malvern. Mrs Wallace has been quite ill. Agnes has gone."

He told her how Agnes had deceived them and tried to take advantage of Sophia's grief.

"We are now without a servant, Rose. I don't suppose you would consider coming back?"

Rose's face lit up, then it dropped.

"The mistress would never take me on now. It would be a disgrace." she began to pull her shawl round her shoulders.

"The mistress doesn't need to know does she, Rose? She only needs to know that your husband and baby died. I am sure she would be pleased to have you back again. I think that it would be better for her to have someone that she knows here. She is going to need some careful looking after when she comes home. Amelia has been missing you, I know. It is not us who will be doing *you* the favour, you will be doing *us* a favour. Please consider it. At least stay the night. You can stay here in the kitchen if you like. I am going to work in my study for an hour or two, perhaps you could bring me some hot milk later?"

Rose smiled.

"I should very much like to come back sir. I promise I will never let you or Mrs Wallace down."

"That's a good girl." William patted her on the head and left the kitchen.

Rose leant back in the old kitchen chair with a sigh. She had found peace for the second time at No 13.

In the morning an astonished Mrs Coalport found Rose fast asleep in front of a dead fire. She gently woke her and asked what she was doing there. Rose told her that her husband and baby had died; that she had met Mr Wallace by accident and he had offered her her old job back. Mrs Coalport took in Rose's shabby clothes and thin form and came to her own conclusions which she conveyed to Mr Coalport that evening. She began to feed Rose up and Rose began to put on weight. She had her old room back and began to feel as if all the rest had been a dream. She missed her family but that was now a chapter in her life which was closed.

By the time Amelia and Sophia came back from Malvern Rose was almost her old self. William had written to tell Sophia about the new arrangement. Sophia was glad to have a servant that she could trust. While she had been at Malvern she had had several long talks with her mother who, although shocked, had very sensibly not condemned Sophia for using a medium but let her talk it through and Sophia had finally been able to express her grief at Mary's loss.

She had been wrong to try and get in touch with Mary. She would always remember her of course, but she had to let her go. In his letter William had written that Rose had lost her husband and baby in one of the frequent Cholera epidemics which periodically swept the poorer parts of London. He did not mention how he had come to find Rose. Sophia assumed she had come to the house on the off-chance of a job of some kind. Sophia felt some sympathy with Rose. They had both recently lost a child.

When informed of the contents of William's letter Amelia was delighted. She could not wait to get back to No. 13. The first thing she would ask Rose was why she had never come back. She pestered Sophia to take her home. Sophia was feeling better than she had in a long time. She did not know how long it would last but hoped that now she had finally come to terms with Mary's death she might even begin to entertain once more.

Rose had been eagerly awaiting their return having been informed by William that they could be expected in a few days. She had given the whole house a thorough clean – Agnes had not been much of a housemaid she discovered and neither had Mrs Coalport. Once William had taken a cab to the station to fetch them she could hardly wait. As soon as she heard the cab at the gate she opened the front door.

Amelia ran to her and hugged her hard.

"I am so glad to see you, Rose. I am sorry about your baby. What did it die of?" she asked curiously.

Sophia quickly intervened.

"Now don't stand here on the doorstep, Amelia. And don't ask so many questions."

Giving her a grateful look Rose stood aside for them to enter. The house shone from top to bottom and Mrs Coalport had cooked a special dinner.

Amelia spent that evening with Papa in his study looking at designs. By the time he finally realized what the time was and sent her to bed she knew Mama had long ago gone to her room. She did not immediately go upstairs but went instead through the hall door and along to the kitchen, where she found Rose just finishing scrubbing the wooden kitchen table. Rose looked up in surprise,

"Why aren't you in bed, Miss Amelia?"

Walking to the wooden armchair Amelia sat down in front of the range and gazed at the flames through the fire bars. After glancing at her face Rose continued with her work. When she had finished she sat on the opposite side of the range and waited for Amelia to speak. After a time Amelia blurted out, "Why didn't you come and show me your dress as you promised? I went to look for you and got lost in a horrible place. A policeman brought me home. Papa was cross."

Rose sat very still for a minute.

"I am sorry, Amelia. I did not forget about you it was just well... difficult."

"How – difficult?" Amelia was relentless.

"Mrs Brett, my mother-in-law, is used to her own way. She has always been in charge and her husband and sons always do as she tells them. When I said that I wanted to come back and show you my dress because I had promised she was very angry and George backed her up."

"Why was she angry?"

"She had been in service herself. She knew that this was my first place and said she had more experience. She said that I did not understand that servants were servants and employers and their families were in a different class. They were not friends, they were just employers and she was certain that you would have forgotten all about me as soon as I had left and that I would be making a fool of myself if I came back. I should have known you would be upset. I am sorry."

"Mama said the same thing about you, Rose. About servants being a different class. Why can't we be friends? I don't understand."

"It's the way the world has always been. I think we could be friends if we keep it secret. Perhaps one day things will change. Now I think you had better get to bed."

"Yes, Rose. Thank you. We will be friends. I won't tell anyone. Not even Geraldine. Good night."

After Amelia had gone to bed to dream of all the exciting things she and Rose would do together one day, Rose sat for a long time gazing into the fire.

Soon the days slipped into a rhythm. One morning Rose realized that she had not cried herself to sleep for several nights. She still went to the cemetery on her afternoons off but the pain was beginning to fade.

Amelia finished her horse design and was very pleased with it. She managed to catch William one Sunday afternoon as he was about to go into his study and told him about it. William was inattentive. He had still not discovered any more about John's activities nor the identity of Arthur's new designer.

"Not now, Amelia," he said and went into his study and shut the door.

Rose found Amelia sitting on the stairs gazing at the study door with a mutinous expression on her face.

"What is the matter, Miss Amelia?"

"I wanted Papa to look at my design but he won't listen. It's a good design, Rose, one of the best that I have ever done," and she thumped the stair in frustration.

"I expect your Papa is very busy just now. Perhaps he will look at it later. Why don't you come into the kitchen and explain it to Mrs Coalport and me? And you haven't told us about what you did when you were in Malvern."

Amelia jumped up from the stair and went into the kitchen where she gave Rose and Mrs Coalport a lecture on how her design could be made up. Rose nodded and smiled and Mrs Coalport kept saying "Well, I never!" and "That's clever," which made Amelia feel much better.

Later that evening when Rose took in William's hot milk as usual, she found him sitting by his study fire gazing into the flames. She had had a long conversation with herself and resolved that she would speak to him about Amelia's design.

"Excuse me, sir."

"Yes, Rose? Nothing wrong is there?"

"No, sir, everything is fine. It's about Miss Amelia."

"What has she been up to now?" William sighed. He was rapidly coming to the conclusion that Amelia was worse than two boys put together.

"Nothing, sir, that is to say nothing bad. She has been showing me some of her designs. I don't know anything about these things of course..." she hesitated.

"Yes, Rose, carry on."

"Well, she was upset when you didn't look at them, sir." She said in a rush.

William frowned,

"Is that what she was talking to me about. I was too deep in my own thoughts to take in what she was saying. It's a design, you say?"

"Yes, sir."

"Thank you for telling me, Rose. I'll make sure I ask her about it tomorrow. Who knows she may come up with something which will make all our fortunes!"

Rose smiled and left him to go back to his thoughts.

That Christmas Arthur Douglass brought out his first mechanical toys. William and John sent one of the clerks to purchase a selection. They studied them together in William's office.

"This looks familiar, John. I'm sure I did a similar design years ago. I didn't continue with it because it did not came up to our standard. It could almost be mine," he said, thoughtfully.

"I agree that the style is similar to yours, father but I don't suppose it is unusual for designers to work along similar lines without even knowing the other one exists."

"Yes, I expect you are right." All the same, for some reason which he could not explain William felt uneasy.

CHAPTER FIFTEEN

William and Amelia sat one either side of the big desk in William's study each working on a different design. It was late and these days Rose took in two glasses of milk. She was not sure that it was right to keep a fourteen-year old up so late at night but Sophia didn't seem to mind. Sophia didn't seem to mind anything.

Rose was not the only person who was worried about Sophia. William had been concerned for a long time. He had thought that she was better when she came back from Malvern after Rose's return but she gradually sank back into depression. He wished that Grace lived nearer. Sophia seemed to wake up a bit when Grace was there but Grace had her own problems. She now had three children all boys and a handful.

When William went to Edinburgh on business he always stayed with Grace and Gerald. Lately he had the strong impression that all was not well with their marriage.There were nasty little remarks and undercurrents. He knew that Grace was a selfish and self-centred woman and he was sorry for Gerald but wished he would stand up for himself more. There was, however, nothing he could do, it was their business. He could only watch from the sidelines.

Sophia, on the other hand, was his business and he wished that he could do something to help her. He had consulted numerous Doctors who had all told him the same thing – give it time – but how much time? Sophia had not been herself since Amelia's birth fourteen years before.

He looked at Amelia; her face full of concentration as she worked on her design. From time to time she bit the end of her pencil and frowned, then her face would clear and she would smile and bend her head and begin drawing once more. He supposed that she was happy, it was difficult to tell. She must be quite lonely. He had asked her about friends at school but she only said that, since her friend Geraldine had left, she did not have any friends then added, "But I really do not mind, Papa."

He turned an idea over in his mind then said, "Amelia, I have been very impressed with your designs. Do you think you could do, say, half a dozen for the Christmas trade?"

"Oh yes, Papa," she eagerly replied.

William considered. "You will soon be leaving school. Once you leave and if Mama can spare you, I could perhaps make you an official designer for the firm. Of course I will have to consult John now he is a partner. I don't know how he feels about women in offices. I will see what I can do."

The last five years had been very good for William. He had enlarged the factory and business was booming. Every one seemed to want mechanical toys. The order book was full. He had been in negotiation with a firm in Edinburgh and hoped this would be a breakthrough into the Scottish market.

William and John argued over the advisability of purchasing a factory in Scotland. William was adamant – it was just what he needed – a new factory to fuss over. He swept all John's objections aside.

"We must expand, John. If we don't go forward we will not keep up with the market, especially the market abroad. You saw the last exhibition in Paris. We must keep ahead or die and that brings me to another point. You seem to be spending rather a lot of time away from the office. You are hardly ever at home. You have seemed rather pre-occupied of late. Is it a woman?"

"No, father." He hesitated and William waited.

"As a matter of fact I have been rather foolish."

"Show me a young man who has not and I will show you a dull fellow! We have all been silly at some time. Let me guess – I should say – gambling?"

John looked relieved.

"Yes, father. I win and then I lose it all but I am sure I will recoup, then I win some back and then the cycle starts again until now I find that I owe considerable sums all over London."

"This has been going on for some years I take it?"

"It began soon after Mary died. I was bored, father. After I had finished for the day in the office there was nothing to do. I ran into some fellows I had known at school and we began to go out to the clubs. I knew I should stop but I couldn't. Then I was in too deep. For the last two years I have been trying to win back enough to pay my debts."

"How much do you owe, John?"

John looked at his feet.

"I'll make it easier for you," William pushed a paper, pen and inkwell to the edge of the desk "write it down."

Taking up the pen John dipped it in the ink and wrote. William picked up the paper. John, watching him closely for any reaction, only saw his jaw clench.

"This is quite a considerable sum. I will pay the debts. I am not going to give you the lecture you deserve on the sins of gambling but it must stop – now. You will come into the office at 8.30 like everyone else and you will spend more time at home.

There is another point to consider. You need to make some provision for the future. I am not getting any younger and we need an heir. I hope to be with you for some time to come but I must give up sooner or later and I should like to know that the firm is in good hands and likely to continue for many years to come. You will, therefore, need to look round for a wife. Do you have anyone in mind?"

"No, father, I have never given it much consideration. Time has just drifted on."

"We will discuss it again when I come back from Scotland."

"You are determined to investigate the possibility of a factory there then?"

"Yes, I think it is in our interests. There are one or two enquiries I wish to make.

John tried to dissuade his father.

"Must you go up to Scotland now? It is not a good time. You promised us some new designs."

"You will get your new designs when I come back. I will not be away long. I think I have a new toy which will put us back on top." He unlocked a drawer in the desk and took out some sheets of paper. John got up and came round to his side of the desk. After looking at the designs for some minutes he said.

"This is good – very good, it should sell well. Did you draw these up? It does not look like your work."

"No, I think I have discovered a new talent."

"Who is it? We must engage him immediately before he goes elsewhere or is it somebody we already employ?"

"I don't think this designer will desert us. I am not prepared to say who it is at the moment. I think it best if I keep it between the designer and myself."

"Surely you can tell me!" John was indignant.

"Let's just say that you would find it hard to believe!" William smiled to himself. He could quite imagine John's reaction to being told that the designs were by his fourteen year old sister!

CHAPTER SIXTEEN

Anderson was feeling pleased with himself. He felt in control of his life again. Prison had reinforced his philosophy of life – make sure you do unto others before they do unto you.

He had scarcely been out of prison an hour when he had a bit of luck. Having nowhere to live and very few possessions to pawn he had decided to look for a house with lax security and steal something worth selling. He was walking down one of the suburban streets – always a good place for easy pickings – when he saw a housemaid cleaning the upstairs windows of one of the houses.

He just gave her a glance and then looked again. His luck was definitely in – it was Rose! He had found her. He would make her come with him. She looked even more attractive than she had the last time he had seen her fifteen years before. She could keep him. He need never worry about money again.

How to persuade her? If she was as stubborn as her mother had been it could take some time to break her but break her he would. He felt that he was being watched. He looked up at Rose – she was not looking at him. He looked across the road to see a man watching him. He didn't like being watched. Swiftly crossing the road he confronted him.

"What's your game?"

Simon had been watching the house for several days. He had come back from Paris full of ideas and thirsting for revenge. Who was this large, smelly individual? Why was he so interested in the house?

"More to the point – what are *you* up to? No good I suspect."

Anderson took in Simon's good clothes. His air of well-fed opulence – might be good for a touch.

"I'm down on my luck, mister. I have just lost my job. Can you spare a shilling?" he whined.

Simon studied him. The man had the prison pallor so was probably a rogue and he could be useful.

"Let's go somewhere and talk. I might be able to put some work your way."

"Nowhere round here – we could take a cab."

Simon knew he was taking a chance being alone in a cab with this hulking brute. It was broad daylight however...

"Come along then."

Refusing to go any further the cabby deposited them at Rosemary Lane just off Ratcliff Highway. Simon hung back uneasily when he saw the narrow street. He knew he was too well-dressed to be able to walk safely here. Seeing him hesitate Anderson reassured him.

"Nobody will dare to touch you once they know you are with me." He boasted.

Simon reluctantly paid off the cabby who murmured with one eye on Anderson, "Are you sure you don't want to come back with me, sir?"

Simon shook his head and followed his guide into the Highway. Fortunately they did not have far to go. Anderson turned into the Kettle Drum.

Pushing his way through the men and women crowded inside he waved to the barman.

"You're out, are you?" the barman said. He saw Simon.

"Good morning, sir – what can I get you?"

Before Simon could answer Anderson replied, "You can get *us* a nice quiet corner and two pints of beer."

Coming from behind the bar the man walked over to an alcove where two old ladies, heads together and little fingers delicately extended sipped their gin.

"Here you two, move!"

One looked round ready to argue but seeing Anderson glowering at her nudged her friend who slowly rose to her feet clutching her glass.

"Here," Simon gave one of them a shilling, "thank you for moving."

The grimy face broke into a gap-toothed smile.

"Thank you, sir – you're a gent! Anything else I can do for you, dear?" she leered.

"Move!" Anderson gave the slower of the old ladies a none too gentle shove.

Once they were seated in the alcove and Anderson had taken a long pull on his pint he asked.

"What is this job you want me to do? I might be able to fit you in." he said grandly.

"Since you have only just got out of prison I think it very unlikely that you are overworked. Why were you keeping watch on that house? Thinking of a little burglary were you?"

Anderson was not sure what to reply. This cove was not as stupid as he had thought. He would have to tread carefully.

"I might have been."

"I hope you were because that is the job I have for you. I want you to break into that house and take what I tell you and only what I tell you."

"What's in it for me?"

"Ten sovereigns."

"Twenty."

"Very well, twenty."

Anderson was delighted – this job must be very important. There might be further pickings here if he played his cards right. It might also be an opportunity to get at Rose.

"What is it you want taken and when?"

Taking out his design notebook Simon swiftly drew a plan of the ground floor of No 13, marking the study with an X.

"This is the room. It is a study. On the desk or possibly in one of the drawers there will be drawings."

"What sort of drawings?"

"Drawings of mechanical toys."

"Mechanical toys – what use are they?"

"None to you but a great deal to me."

"When do I get paid?"

"Half now, half when I have the drawings."

"Why do you want these drawings?" Anderson asked.

"That's nothing to do with you! Let's just say I have a score to settle." Simon counted out ten sovereigns. "There is your first payment. When do you think you will have them?"

"Meet me here a week from today – same time."

After he had escorted Simon away from the Highway and seen him into a cab, Anderson returned to The Kettle Drum, ordered another drink and sat in thought.

He had a perfect opportunity to earn some money and lay his hands on Rose. If he could make it look as if she had helped him steal the drawings she would be dismissed immediately and he thought he knew how to do it.

Some days later Rose was kneeling by the kitchen fire trying to get it to burn up. Mrs Coalport had just gone home declaring that the fire was always awkward when the wind was blowing from the West.

Rose had just attacked the fire with a poker when Mr Wallace appeared. For once she was not pleased to see him. Putting the poker down she got to her feet.

"Sorry to trouble you, Rose. Have you been clearing out my study?"

"I have swept and dusted, Mr Wallace, but that is all."

"And you didn't open any of the drawers?"

Rose was indignant – first the fire defied her and now Mr Wallace was accusing her – of what?

"Of course not! Is anything missing, sir?"

"Yes, some designs I was working on. I was sure that I put them into the drawer but there is no sign of them. What I did find was this." He showed her what he had in his hand – a hair comb. Instinctively Rose put her hand to her hair. William, misinterpreting the gesture said "You *do* have a comb missing then, Rose. Do you know where I found this? In the drawer in my desk!"

Rose flushed red, not with guilt but temper.

"That is not my comb and I have *never* opened any of the drawers in your desk."

William looked at her for a long time then he made up his mind.

"No, of course you didn't, Rose. I'm sorry. It was a shock when I found it. I couldn't think of anyone else who goes into the study except Amelia and she doesn't put her hair up yet. My wife never sets foot in there and John does not wear combs."

This last was rewarded by a reluctant smile.

"Where do you think it came from?"

"I have no idea, sir. The person who took the designs left it there, I suppose."

"I wonder how they got in?"

Rose shook her head.

Sitting down in the armchair by the fire and idly picking up the poker William began absentmindedly poking the fire. Rose was vexed to see the fire blaze up.

William talked to himself, "Why would anyone want to take the designs and leave a comb? The comb was obviously left to implicate you, Rose. Who? Do you have any enemies?" he looked over at her where she stood by the table.

"No, sir. My step-father was the only person who disliked me that much but he is in prison."

"Time has passed, Rose. It could be that he has completed his sentence. I will ask Inspector Burridge, he might know. Why take the designs? Probably to make it look as if you were selling them to a rival firm? To get you dismissed? I don't like it, Rose. I think I will go round and see Inspector Burridge now."

Once Mr Wallace had left the house Rose went back to the fire which was now burning fiercely, sat in the kitchen chair and tried to work out why her step-father, if it had been he, would want to have her dismissed. Not for any good reason she was sure. In spite of the blazing fire she shivered.

When she opened the front door to Mr Wallace some time later he just thanked her as usual and asked where Mr John was. On being informed that he was in the sitting room he handed her his hat and coat and went into the room.

William was glad that John was home for once. He found him talking to Sophia. William was pleased to see her animated face. He was sorry to take John away but what he had to say could not be said in front of her.

"I have to speak to you immediately, John, come to the study."

"Must you take John away, William?"

"Yes, I am sorry Sophia, it is urgent."

Sophia sighed and picked up her book.

As soon as the door was shut John asked anxiously, "Is it the works, father? Has something happened?"

"So far as I know everything is fine at the works." He told John about his conversation with Rose and continued, "I have just been to see Inspector Burridge who made some enquiries. Anderson, Rose's stepfather, has recently been released from prison. I think he may be trying to get Rose dismissed so that he can live off her earnings. He has tried this once before. That is why her mother brought her here all those years ago.

Rose does not know this of course. I am ashamed to say that I almost believed that she had betrayed our trust but of course she has not. She has no family of her own now. We are all she has. We must always look after Rose, John, no matter what happens."

"I agree, father. How did Anderson get in?"

"Inspector Burridge thinks through the window and he left the same way closing it behind him, apparently that was his usual method of working which is why the Inspector is pretty certain the intruder was Anderson."

William and John then spent several hours making plans.

William worked far into the night as was his habit. At twelve he roused John then, after they had quietly let several men into the house through the garden door, he went back to his study, put the designs he had been working on into the desk drawer, turned out the light and left the room. All was silent.

One o'clock came and went. Two o'clock sounded from the clock on the mantelpiece. At two-thirty there was the sound of a window being raised and a man climbed over the window-sill into the room. He only needed the glow from the dying fire to see his way as he walked straight to the desk and to the drawer where the designs had been placed by William only hours earlier. Opening the drawer, he took out the designs, stuffed them into his pocket and moved towards the window only to be seized and held. William and Inspector Burridge accompanied by John came into the room. John turned up the gas lamps.

The burly constable holding the burglar dragged him over to the gas light. The man did not struggle.

"Anderson! I thought it would be you!" the Inspector said with satisfaction. More policemen crowded into the room guarding the door and window.

The Inspector took the papers from Anderson's pocket and gave them to William who questioned Anderson.

"Who were you taking the designs for? They are no good to you."

Anderson smiled "That's my secret – what's it worth?"

"That's enough of that, answer the gentleman." The constable held Anderson in an even tighter grip.

"Someone who hates you and your family as much as I hate that Rose. Tell her that I shall be back one day. As for who paid me – you will never find that out from me."

"Don't you be so sure, my lad!" Inspector Burridge said grimly. "Take him away." He watched as Anderson was removed none too gently. Then turning to William, "Who is Rose, sir?"

"She's my servant. A very loyal servant and before you ask, no, she is not involved in this. What will happen to him?"

"He was caught red-handed and has a long criminal record so there is no doubt at all that he will go to prison for quite some time I should think. It would be a good idea, sir, if you got a safe to keep your designs in." The Inspector sounded reproachful.

"Yes, I know." William smiled, "I have a man coming from Chubb's tomorrow or rather today."

Inspector Burridge nodded.

"Well, there is nothing more to do here. We will be going, sir – and don't forget about that safe!"

After the Inspector and his men had left William gathered up the designs and put them into the desk drawer.

The activity had woken Sophia and Rose who reported that Amelia was sound asleep. Sophia was inclined to be nervous until reassured by John that the intruder had been taken into custody. While John was reassuring his mother William took the opportunity to tell Rose

"There is no need to worry about Anderson any more. He is going to prison for a long time."

He did not tell her about Anderson's threat. It was probably just talk. The relief on Rose's face was proof of how worried she had been.

As William was helping Sophia to her room he told her that he had to go to Scotland the next day. He would be away for several days. She begged him not to go.

"I must, Sophia – believe me if I could get out of it I would." he told her.

Sophia disengaged herself from his arm.

"Thank you. I can manage now."

As she got to the door of her room she turned.

"After what has happened here this evening the least you could do would be to stay with me."

"The man has been locked up, Sophia. The danger, if there was any, has gone. John will be here."

Sophia did not reply, turning, she went into her room and closed the door.

William sighed. He despaired of Sophia ever becoming normal again. He went down to the kitchen where he found that Rose had made some hot milk.

"Thank you, Rose. You are happy here, aren't you?"

"Oh yes, sir! This is my home. I shall never leave. This may sound presumptuous, sir, but I think of you all as my family. It is the only one I have."

William smiled remembering his conversation with John.

"I am happy you feel like that. We are all very fond of you. I have to go away to Scotland for a few days. I leave them all in your capable hands, Rose. Look after them for me until I come back."

"Of course, sir."

He was glad they had Rose. She had repaid their giving her a home many times over. He sometimes wondered if she thought of her husband and child. He supposed she must. Early the next morning he left for Edinburgh.

★★★★★

Rose was feeling happy. It was a crisp January day, the sun shone, Anderson was out of her life at last and she could go out without looking over her shoulder in case he was there and in four days it would be her 27th birthday. She sang to herself as she dusted Amelia's bedroom.

She heard the sound of a cab. It stopped outside the gate. Glancing out of the window she saw Mr John alight from it. What was he doing home at this time of day? She hurried to open the door for him.

"Rose, get the mistress and Miss Amelia into the sitting room immediately, will you, and you had better stay within call, I may need you." He looked grave and older than he had when he had left for the office that morning.

Rose had a nasty feeling in the pit of her stomach. It took her back to the day many years before when the policeman had come to tell them about her father's death. She had a sudden premonition.

"Is it the master, sir?" she asked fearfully.

"Just do as I say, Rose, will you." He sounded curt.

Rose ran to the mistress's bedroom. Sophia was just finishing dressing. She seemed better today and questioned Rose closely as to what John wanted. Rose left Sophia making her way downstairs and ran Amelia to earth in the study poring over one of William's sketch books. She was not happy to be disturbed but Rose's agitated manner made her throw the book down on to the desk and follow Rose to the sitting room where her mother was saying to John.

"What is it, John? What has happened?"

Rose just had time to hear him say

"Please sit down both of you. I have some very bad news," before she shut the door.

Remembering Mr John's instructions she waited in the hall.

She heard Amelia cry out and half started towards the door. Then there was silence. After a time Mr John opened the door and beckoned Rose to go in. Sophia was sitting on the sofa looking stunned, she had her arm round Amelia who was sobbing. Sophia was completely dry-eyed.

"What is it, sir? Please tell me," Rose pleaded.

"It is the master, Rose. He has been killed in a train crash. Apparently the express ran into a goods train at Manuel Station. I have to go to Edinburgh to identify the body but there is no doubt that it is father. They found his card case with the firm's name and contacted the local police station by telegraph. They came to me at the office. Take Amelia to her room. I will look after the mistress."

CHAPTER SEVENTEEN

Simon was anxious to get to The Kettle Drum for his weekly meeting with Anderson. The designs Anderson had supplied were very sketchy and Simon wanted something better this evening. He hoped that William was beginning to feel uneasy about the missing designs. Simon would leave it for a few weeks and then start again when William thought it had ceased.

Since his first meeting with Anderson he had been back to The Kettle Drum several times, taking the precaution of wearing old clothes. Sometimes he took a walk down The Highway. The colourful life amused him and he enjoyed the touch of danger.

Tonight, however, he was anxious to get away. He had other ways of passing the time in mind – he knew of a cock-fight out on the marshes.

He watched the comings and goings. He could have ended up like that man over there. Perpetually drunk. Nothing to look forward to. Any ambition he might have had long gone. But *he* had not allowed himself to sink to the bottom.

He had shaken off his drunken father and slatternly mother as soon as he was old enough. He had no idea what had happened to them or his brothers and sisters. For all he cared they could be dead. In fact he hoped they were. He did not want them arriving on his respectable doorstep one of these fine days. He congratulated himself on his cleverness.

On his arrival in Paris, thanks to the designs he had taken from William's desk, he had been able to apprentice himself to one of the best mechanical toy makers in France. When he had eventually returned to England he had gone straight to Arthur Douglass who had been very impressed with his experience and letters of recommendation. Arthur's designer was getting old and Arthur wanted new ideas and Simon had them. Two years after joining the firm Simon was the sole designer for the company.

Then late one dark November afternoon Arthur, on his way home, had walked past Simon's office and seeing him still working walked in.

"Not finished yet, Simon? It's getting late you know."

"Yes, I know, Mr Douglass. I want to finish these designs ready for the meeting tomorrow. My lodgings are not very comfortable and I prefer to work here."

"You aren't married are you, Simon? No, I thought not." As Simon shook his head. "Come home with me for dinner. I am sure Patience won't mind. It will do you good. I have a daughter, Eleanor, she doesn't see much young company. Come on now leave that, you can finish it in the morning." Arthur would not take no for an answer and waited while Simon put his things away.

When they got to the house he found that Mrs Douglass was a tiny woman. Eleanor on the other hand was more like her father. She had his large features and loud voice. Her high complexion was not improved by the puce gown she was wearing.

"I have brought a young man home to meet you, Eleanor." Arthur pushed an unwilling Simon forward. "Perhaps you could play to us after dinner, my dear."

"Really, father, you should not bring people home without notice. Cook gets so upset."

Eleanor ignored Simon completely. He began to feel angry. He was not just anybody! He was her father's chief designer not some common workman! Out of sheer pique he decided to make himself as pleasant as possible to Miss Eleanor. So pleasant did he make himself that three years later, how he was not quite sure, he found himself walking down the aisle with a simpering Eleanor on his arm.

Arthur Douglass' wedding present to Simon was a seat on the Board of Directors. It was all that Simon wanted but he was of the opinion that the price was too high. Eleanor was barren. He would not have the sons he had envisaged. Possibly due to her childlessness Eleanor was even more waspish than she had been before their marriage. She was also vicious. By their first anniversary he very rarely saw her as he dined out most evenings.

Coming out of his reverie he looked round for Anderson. The bartender came over.

"No good waiting for Anderson, sir – he's been arrested!"

"Arrested! What for?"

"Breaking into some toff's house. It will be a long stretch this time." The barman sounded pleased.

Simon rose and thrust his way to the door. Anyone in his way was ruthlessly pushed aside. He began to walk home careless of the rain. Supposing Anderson talked? But who would believe him? Perhaps he should visit Anderson in jail and tell him what would happen to him if he did talk! No, that would only call attention to himself. The best thing to do would be to act normally. He would find out soon enough if Anderson talked. Anyway it was the word of a twice convicted villain against his, a respectable businessman. Simon cheered up and hailed a cab to take him to the cockfight.

*****

The morning after the cockfight Simon did not feel like work. He had got home in the early hours to find Eleanor waiting for him. She had begun by asking where he had been. He did not think it was any of her business and told her so. She had then flown into hysterics whereupon he had left the room. She came after him and, grabbing his arm, began shouting in his face.

Naturally he had hit her. She should know her place after all these years. She then had the temerity to lash out at him so he hit her again. This time she fell, sobbing, to the floor. Leaving her there he went upstairs to his room and to bed. He had not seen her this morning.

Breakfast was more badly cooked than usual, the domestic having been given her notice the previous day for some minor misdemeanor. The domestics never stayed long enough for him to remember their names. Eleanor seemed incapable of keeping a servant. He would have to do something about Eleanor soon, she was becoming a nuisance.

Once in his office he picked up the newspaper which had, as usual, been left on his desk. A headline caught his eye "Railcrash! Five Dead!" he began to read. When he got to the list of fatalities he stopped and re-read the item. So, William was dead was he. Simon began to think quickly. If William was dead that meant the firm was without a designer.

William Wallace & Son was the only firm which was a serious rival to Douglass & Co. He knew that John was no designer. He wondered what they would do. Perhaps if he spoke to Arthur he could get him to agree to buy the firm. If they stepped in quickly they might make a killing. He knew that, although Arthur and William had been good friends as well as rivals, Arthur was not over-sentimental when it came to business matters.

He also knew that Arthur and William used to meet for lunch and that the two families dined regularly with each other until Sophia's illness when the custom gradually lapsed. He did not know how long it was since William and Arthur had last met. Getting up from his chair and, taking the newspaper with him, he went down the corridor to Arthur's room.

Arthur was not pleased to see him. He had been well aware for some time that Eleanor was not very happy in her marriage. So far he had not mentioned it to Patience as he did not want to worry her but he thought he would soon have to ask her advice.

He could see that Simon was quite excited about something. His rather handsome face, which was beginning to show signs of the late hours he kept, was alight with glee.

"Have you seen this?" Simon thrust the newspaper under Arthur's nose. Arthur read it through. He was shocked by the news.

"This is very sad. Poor Sophia, she's not in the best of health. This will be too much for her, I am afraid."

"Don't you understand! William was the designer. Without William they have no designs."

"They will get somebody else. I told William it was a mistake not to have another designer but he kept saying that he had one who would astonish us all one day but I never met him."

"We must make an offer for the factory before they have time to recover from this blow! It is our chance! We can put Wallace & Son out of business for good!" Simon said, impatiently.

Arthur glanced up sharply. He sometimes wondered if he knew his son-in-law as well as he thought he did.

"We don't need to take over Wallace & Son. There is enough trade for both firms. *I* have no plans to expand." He emphasized the "I". He went on, "Do you have some personal reason for taking over the firm?"

Simon knew that he would have to be careful.

"What could there be? I only thought that it would be an ideal opportunity to get rid of a rival, that's all."

Arthur noted that Simon could not look him in the face, so there was some secret which it might be wise to uncover if only for his poor Eleanor's sake.

"Never mind." Simon stamped back to his own room where he sat and brooded for some time.

*****

At No. 13 each member of the household reacted to William's death in their own way.

Mrs Coalport cried a great deal and sat by the fire in the kitchen saying over and over again, "He was such a lovely man!"

She had to be roused to cook such meals as they ate.

Rose cleaned the house from top to bottom and when she had finished she began all over again. It felt like losing her father once more.

John was kept busy with all the arrangements. He had to find time to collect Grace and Gerald from the station. They would stay until after the funeral which could not take place until after the inquest. Sophia was annoyed when she realized that they had not brought the children with them. She had wanted them walking behind the hearse but both Grace and Gerald had decided that they were too young so they were left at home in charge of Gerald's parents. John and Gerald attended the inquest which was a formality only.

Once Grace and Gerald were staying in the house Rose had more work to do but she was glad of it. She worked without cessation all day so that when she went to bed at night she was so exhausted she fell asleep immediately.

Amelia spent two days in her room on her own. When she came out she looked very pale but composed.

Sophia was the one that astonished everybody. Once the initial shock had passed she seemed to throw off her accustomed lethargy and became as she had been before Amelia's birth. It was as if the shock of William's death had jolted her back into reality.

She plunged into arrangements for the funeral. John as the nearest male relative was in charge of this but Sophia insisted on being consulted on every point down to the finest detail. She was determined to have what she called a "funeral in keeping with your father's standing in the community." Which meant black horses wearing tall black plumes to draw the hearse.

She also decided that William would be buried with his children. John pointed out that it was the depths of winter, the journey would be long and slow. Everyone would be frozen. Sophia and John argued long into the night until Sophia suddenly gave in saying

"I suppose I must remember that you are the head of the family now, John. Do whatever you think best. I will, however, make all arrangements regarding mourning clothes. We must all be properly dressed."

The Englishwoman's Magazine was consulted and as a result Amelia, Grace and Sophia received the attentions of a dressmaker who specialized in mourning clothes and within twenty-four hours of William's death all three were in deep black. The dressmaker's task was made even more difficult as Sophia stood over her to make sure her dress had the correct number of tucks.

Sophia called a meeting of all the females in the household and issued her instructions. Grace and Amelia were informed that they could not wear any jewellery unless it was black and preferably none at all. They were also informed that they would be in full mourning for nine months and three months of half mourning. Rose was put into a black dress and Mrs Coalport was also requested to wear black.

"Although who will see me in the kitchen, I don't know." she grumbled to Rose afterwards.

When Amelia first saw her mother in her widow's cap she thought how old it made her look, the white of the cap and the deep black of the dress giving her face a pale, washed-out look.

Sophia also ordered black-edged writing paper and envelopes with black seals. Artificial black silk flowers were ordered for the vases in the rooms. William's portrait which hung in the sitting room was draped in black crape. Everything was black everywhere Amelia looked. Even the sky was black. She went about the tasks Sophia gave her in a daze. She became thin and pale. When Rose tried to get her interested in her designs again she rounded on her.

"What do you know, Rose! I shall *never* be happy again! I shall *never* design again! You don't *understand* how I feel!"

"Yes, I do, Amelia. My father was also killed. He went out in the morning to his work and never came back – alive that is. I know what it is like to have a policeman call and tell your mother that she is a widow. I know what it is like to wake up in the morning expecting to hear his voice calling goodbye before he goes out to his work. I know all this, Amelia, so don't tell me that I don't understand!"

Amelia was shaken – Rose had never spoken to her like that before.

"I am sorry, Rose, I didn't know. You have never spoken of your parents. Is your mother still alive?"

"No, Miss Amelia, she has been dead these many years."

"Then you are an orphan, Rose."

"Yes, Miss, I suppose I am. Now you bestir yourself and get downstairs and help your Mama with her letter writing. There have been so many letters from people who knew and liked your Papa that your Mama will need both you and Mrs Mitchell to help with the replies."

Amelia pondered Rose's revelations as she addressed envelopes. She realised that she knew very little about Rose's life before she came to them and not very much since she had lived under the same roof. She had never considered that Rose had parents. She, of course, knew that she had a husband and family once but she had never asked her about them. They seemed nothing to do with HER Rose. Rose had always been there and Amelia had expected Rose to go on being there for as long as she, Amelia, required her to be.

On the day of William's funeral the snow lay deep. One of the horses pulling the hearse slipped on the icy cobbles and looked as if it might fall to its knees but the driver held it up. By the time they arrived at the church they were all frozen. Amelia remembered very little of the service. She felt as if she was not really there. It was all happening to some other person.

Rose would have liked to go to the funeral but she was busy getting ready for the return of the funeral party. Mrs Coalport had recovered herself sufficiently to do a mound of cooking. Once she was working with her hands she felt better.

John watched his father's coffin being lowered into the grave and thought of all the times he had wished he ran the Company so that he could carry out his plans without any opposition – well now he did run the Company. He hoped that he could command as much respect as William had.

There were many little tributes from individual workers as well as a large wreath from the entire workforce. The foremen of the various departments were present behind the family, the factory having been closed for the day and representatives of the various firms they had dealings with. He noticed that Arthur Douglass was there and remembered what William had said about the new designer. They were going to need him. For the first time he realized that they now had no designer.

His eyes roamed further – anything rather than look at the coffin being lowered into the grave. He noticed a heavily veiled woman on the outskirts of the crowd of mourners. He wondered who she was. There were no other funerals taking place so she could not be a mourner from another funeral. All the family women were here with him. Sophia behind her veil; Amelia trying hard not to cry; Grace leaning on Gerald's arm. Who could the woman be? He resolved to speak to her at the end of the interment.

Just then Sophia swayed and seemed about to faint. Once the commotion was over he looked round for the mysterious veiled lady but she had gone. A suspicion began to take form in his mind. Should he do anything about it? If his suspicions were correct it would not do to upset his mother.

Now he turned his attention to getting everyone back to the house where they found that Rose had made up a blazing fire in the dining-room and Mrs Coalport had laid the funeral feast out.

Later the family Solicitor, Mr Triston, gathered the family together for the reading of William's will.

They all sat round the dining-room table. Mr Triston had requested that both Rose and Mrs Coalport should be present. As was expected the business was left to John, together with the house, Sophia to retain residential rights during her life-time plus a large sum of money. Both Amelia and Grace had substantial sums. Amelia's in a trust fund not to be touched until she had reached thirty. Rose was surprised to find that William had left her £300 and Mrs Coalport began to sob into her apron when informed that she had been left £50.

"There is one other bequest but that is all that concerns us here." Mr Triston said smoothly.

Sophia offered Mr Triston some sherry which he accepted. John was determined to get him on his own and ask about the other bequest. If it was to the benefit of the person he thought it was his suspicions were confirmed.

Mr Triston was reluctant to discuss the matter at first as he "thought it proper that it should be confidential". After much urging on John's part and after a solemn undertaking from John that he was not interested in contesting the will, Mr Triston conceded that yes it was to a lady, he would not divulge that lady's identity under any circumstance but he would only say that there were no children to complicate matters.

He thanked Mr Triston and assured him that the information he had given him would never go any further.

"It was a long standing relationship – some ten years, I believe." Mr Triston volunteered.

As Mr Triston finished speaking John glanced at his mother. Just as he did so he saw Rose attract her attention and speak to her. Sophia looked distinctly vexed. Surely the woman had not come here? He made his way swiftly to his mother's side.

"What is the matter?" he asked apprehensively and was relieved when she replied.

"That girl Sarah has come to the door asking for her old job back. It seems that working in a Store was not all that she thought it was going to be. I must deal with it. Will you make sure that everything goes well here. Tell Grace she must stop clinging to Gerald and take my place as hostess."

John was sorry for Sarah as Sophia strode from the room but pleased to see his mother back in charge as she used to be.

CHAPTER EIGHTEEN

Mr Robson was very upset by William's sudden death. He wondered what Mr John would do. They would have to get a new designer but good English designers of mechanical toys were few and far between. So far as he knew Arthur Douglass & Co were the only other firm of any significant size in England, the main manufacturers being in France and Germany. They could try to get someone from the continent – perhaps Mr John had someone in mind. Then he remembered something Mr Wallace had said. He must tell Mr John. Leaving his office he passed Mr John's old office knocked on Mr Wallace's door and upon being invited to enter found Mr John sitting behind his desk staring into space. He looked worried.

Before Mr Robson could speak John asked, "Mr Robson, you have been with the firm for a long time, haven't you?"

"Oh yes, Mr John. I was with your father when he first began to design. We used to work in the cellar of the old London house. We had some very hard times but we ended up with this factory. I shall miss him very much."

"Did he tell you the name of the new designer that he found just before he went on his last trip? As you will appreciate we badly need a good designer."

"That is what I have come to talk to you about. He did mention something. I do not have a name but Mr Wallace seemed to be quite amused by it, I have no idea why. He said to me 'when the identity of this designer is known it will cause a stir'. He also mentioned something about putting the designer on a more official footing when he came back from Edinburgh. But of course he never came back. I have been through all the papers and there is nothing at all that gives us a clue as to who it could be. What will you do?"

"I am not quite sure. My father was the man with the ideas. We might be able to get somebody from one of the French or German factories but they will take a great deal of persuading. If only father had not been so secretive. He had other secrets too, I believe?"

"I believe so, Mr Wallace."

"Do you know anything about the lady who appeared at the funeral?" John decided to be blunt.

"I have seen the lady on several occasions but concluded it was none of my business. Now it does not matter, does it?"

As Mr Robson fixed Johnwith his steady gaze he was transported back many years to his school holidays when the Chief Clerk used to show him round the factory and tell him not to touch anything fixing him with that same look.

"No, it doesn't matter now."

John sighed.

"Thank you, Mr Robson. I am sure we can find a designer. There must be some around only too anxious to design for a prestigious firm such as ours."

Mr Robson nodded and left him to continue staring into space.

*****

Amelia felt numb for several days after the funeral. She went about in a daze and at the end of the day she had no idea what she had been doing. She got up in the morning and lay down at night. Sometimes she slept and sometimes she did not. She had a suspicion that Rose put something into her milk before she brought it up at night but she did not question her about it.

When she could not sleep she used to go down to Papa's study and sit in the old armchair. She felt near to him there.

One night she felt she could not stay in bed any longer. She crept downstairs to the study. Rose had banked up the fire as she used to do for Papa. Amelia supposed that she had done it out of habit or perhaps she expected John to come home late and work in the study as Papa had done.

John would not be designing. Papa had been the only one who designed – apart from herself of course. She sat down in the old armchair and thought of Papa and how they had sat one either side of the desk far into the night sketching out their designs – asking each other's opinion. For the first time since William's death she felt the stirrings of an idea. She left the chair and rummaged round in a drawer for her sketch book and began work. Soon she was experiencing the absorption she always found when into a design. She forgot about everything except the work.

★★★★★

John was very dispirited. He had tried not to let Mr Robson know how he felt but did not think that he had succeeded. He worked late at the factory. They had enough orders for existing lines to keep them going for some time but at Christmas time there would be no new toys. Their customers would be disappointed unless he found a designer soon. Although it was only the end of February it took at least nine months to design, test and set up the production of new toys. He *had* to find a designer by the end of March at the latest.

It was late when he got home but he thought he would have one more look in William's desk to see if he could find something he had overlooked. It was a very forlorn hope as he had searched the desk several times already. As he opened the study door he felt the warmth of the fire and saw Amelia at the desk, her head down, busily drawing something in her sketch book. He was annoyed with her. She should be in bed. He knew that she was missing father. He remembered coming in on several occasions and finding her sitting opposite William at his desk happily drawing away at something or the other.

"Amelia," sounding more abrupt than he intended.

She jumped and looked up.

"John! I thought you were at the factory!"

"I was but it is very late. You should be in bed."

"I couldn't sleep so I came down here to sit in Papa's old armchair. I feel close to him here."

"Yes, I do understand, Amelia, but you must begin to pick up your life again. Mama needs you."

"Not very much. She is too busy ordering Grace and Gerald about."

John grinned. His mother regaining her vitality had been a mixed blessing especially as far as Grace was concerned. Gerald's father had sent him to London to oversee their London branch and Sophia had begun house-hunting with enthusiasm. She was rarely at home. He supposed that Amelia was lonelier than ever. Perhaps he should look at her drawings. It was probably something she had to do for school.

"What have you there, Amelia? May I see it?"

"Oh no, it is nothing." She shut the pad, jumped up and hastily made for the door. A page detached itself and fell onto the floor. John quickly bent to retrieve it glancing at it as he went to hand it back. He paused, looking at the design. He had seen something like this before – it was similar to the design he had seen on William's desk!

"Amelia, where did you find this? Was it in the desk? You must tell me, it is very important." He was shaking with excitement.

Amelia knew that the time had come to tell her secret. She was sure that Papa would not mind.

"They are mine, John," she replied.

"Yours! Don't play games with me, Amelia. I must know where you got these designs. The whole future of the factory is at stake. I have to find this designer, he is one of the best I have seen. We must have him designing for the factory. Now, where did you get the designs? If you have been up to one of your pranks I will make sure that you don't get into trouble with Mama but *I must know* – where did they come from?"

In his anxiety to make her divulge the information he took her by the shoulders as if to shake it out of her.

"They *are* mine, John – I designed them. I have been practising designing for a long time. Papa said you would not understand!" she added irritably.

John could not believe it. Then he remembered half seen things. Amelia and William poring over books. Amelia for ever sketching. William's words came back to him, "let us just say that you would find it hard to believe". Indeed he did!

"May I see what you are working on now?" he asked, still not sure but when she showed him her rough designs there was no doubt in his mind that here was the mysterious designer – under his nose the whole time – his fourteen year old sister!"

"Why didn't you tell me you were doing these?" he asked.

"Papa told me it was best we kept it to ourselves until he could take me into the firm as a designer. He said it would be difficult as I am a girl."

"It would indeed." John was thoughtful. "These are very good designs, Amelia, and I need good designs just now. However, you are a girl and a young girl at that. Girls are not supposed to do this sort of thing. Girls are expected to draw dainty watercolours of ruined churches and paint flowers, not design toys!"

"I think it is unfair that I can't do what I want to do. You said yourself the designs are good. Why can't I come to the factory with you and see my designs made up?"

"There is nothing to stop you coming to visit the factory, but it would not be acceptable for you to work in the office and design. The only women in the firm are factory women, not properly brought up young ladies. I think the best thing would be for you to continue with your designs here at home. I will take them to the factory, get them made up, then bring them home for you to test. You need never come to the factory and no one will ever know."

"Papa said that when he came back from Edinburgh he would see about me having an official position as designer." Amelia stated.

"I do not think that Papa really meant to do that, Amelia." As she began to protest. "He would have said something to me about it but he did not" he thought it best to forget his last conversation with his father. He had more than once deplored William's apparent disregard for convention. Having his sister or any other properly brought up young girl for that matter working in the office was unthinkable – it would never happen – it was against nature.

"In that case," Amelia was angry, "you can't have my designs," and plucking the sheet from John's hand left the room shutting the door with a bang.

John thought that she would soon get over her sulks but several days went by and although Amelia spoke to him and acted as usual she never mentioned the designs. It was now John's turn to be angry. She was only a child after all. What she could do, surely he could? He had never done any designing because William had always done it. He had just never tried, that was all.

He spent much time, effort and paper trying to design something unusual and marketable but in the end he had to admit that he did not have the necessary flair. It was grossly unfair but it would appear that Amelia had inherited William's inventiveness and then, just when he was in despair, Amelia walked into the study, placed the designs on his desk, and left, without a word. He was sure that Rose had something to do with her change of heart but he did not care what had caused it – he had the designs!

*****

A positive result of William's death and Sophia's recovery was the resumption of visits between the Douglasses and the Wallaces. On one of these visits by Arthur and Patience John called Arthur into the study and showed him several of Amelia's designs without saying whose they were. Arthur was enthusiastic.

"These are very good, John – you need to hang on to this young fellow. He could not have appeared at a better time. Your father did tell me about a new talent he had discovered but would not say who the fellow was. He seemed quite amused in fact and said it would cause the biggest stir this century!"

"It might well do that," John replied.

He debated whether or not to tell Arthur the full story. He plunged in before he could think twice.

Arthur was astounded.

"Your sister designed these? That's unbelievable. Of course – excuse me saying so – she is different. Perhaps this gift was given to her as some sort of compensation for being ug— er, not quite like other girls."

"What do you advise me to do?" John asked.

"You are the oldest living male relative, you therefore have full charge of all the females in your immediate family. Grace is of course subject to her husband but your mother and Amelia are considered in law to be your responsibility. The best thing you can do is to order Amelia to give you all her designs for you to do with as you like. You can market them as your own since she has no property in her own right."

"Isn't that a bit harsh?" John was uneasy.

"It may seem harsh to you, John, but the law was made for the female's own good. They are incapable of looking after themselves. Why, it has been scientifically proved that their brains are smaller so it is our *duty* to look after them and make sure they don't do anything silly, such as marrying an unsuitable person as they are apt to do if left to their own devices. It is a great responsibility for us but it is one that we must shoulder gladly. Saint Paul knew the problems that we have to face. Consult your Bible, my boy" patting him on the shoulder.

John was thoughtful as he saw Arthur and Patience out of the house later that night.

★★★★★

When Arthur went into the office the next day he had barely sat down when Simon came in

"Well?" Simon was abrupt.

"Well what?" Arthur was puzzled.

"Have you made an offer for the firm and what did John say? I know you were there last night."

Arthur had forgotten about Simon's suggestion of taking over John's firm. He had never given it any serious thought.

"I went as a friend. I have no intention of making an offer for the firm. In any case they have a designer and a very good one too. I have seen some of the work."

"They have a designer? Who?" Simon almost grasped Arthur in his desire to know.

"I think that is John's business. If you want to know any more I suggest that you ask him. Now I do have a very great deal of work to catch up on, Simon. By the way I believe that you and Eleanor are coming for dinner tomorrow? Patience won't take any more excuses so please make sure that you both appear this time."

Arthur watched Simon as he went back into his own office. He had made up his mind that he would talk to Eleanor tomorrow in private. He knew that she was quite a difficult person but she was his daughter and if she was unhappy he had to do something about it. He had already consulted Mr Hisk, his lawyer, regarding a possible divorce. Mr Hisk had looked grave.

"It is difficult for a woman to obtain a divorce. The only grounds are rape, sodomy, bestiality or adultery linked with incest, bigamy, cruelty or desertion, which have, of course, to be proved. Your daughter has no proof I take it?"

Arthur was shaken.

"I have not yet spoken to my daughter on the subject."

"Cruelty might be the best option but I am not very optimistic." Mr Hisk shook his head.

Saying that he would consult Mr Hisk when he had more information Arthur went back to his office.

This conversation went through his mind as he heard Simon shouting at one of the clerks. He was afraid that Simon was becoming obsessed with the idea of ruining Wallace & Son and he would very much like to know why. No good reason he was sure. It was his intention to retire at the end of the year. So far he had not even informed Patience. He had intended to leave Simon in charge of the firm but now he was not so sure. Simon seemed to be becoming unstable. He knew that Simon was expecting to step into his shoes but now he made up his mind to sell the firm. Perhaps John would purchase it! With a grim smile he began to tackle the pile of papers awaiting his attention.

CHAPTER NINETEEN

For a day John turned Arthur's advice over in his mind. He was sure Arthur was right. He felt the full burden of the responsibility for Sophia and Amelia. He knew that he would have to marry soon and that would be yet another responsibility. He asked himself for the hundredth time why did William have to be on that particular train at that particular time? When he got home that evening he sent for Amelia. On entering the study she found him standing in front of the newly lit fire warming himself.

"Ah, Amelia." He rather pompously began. "I have been thinking about our last conversation. Since I am your sole male protector," he liked the sound of that so he said it again "your sole male protector, I have decided that you will stay at home and help your mother. You will also carry on with your designing but only until I can find a male designer." He thought he had said that rather well. He found that he enjoyed being in a position of power. He rocked himself backwards and forwards on his heels.

Amelia did not like this new John. She knew that she was in a very vulnerable position.

Without replying she went to the kitchen where she found Rose rolling out dough.

"What is the matter, Miss Amelia?" Rose could see that she was upset.

"John has just told me that I have to stay with Mama for ever and that I have to give him my designs but only until he can get a male designer. Its not fair!" She almost stamped her foot.

"Mr John is the head of the household now and he can do as he likes," Rose said, comfortably.

"But why, Rose?"

"Because, Miss Amelia," Rose said patiently, "he is your brother. He is male and you are only a female, that is the way things are. If you had been born a boy it would be different but you weren't so you must be content with the situation in which God has placed you."

Amelia threw herself into the kitchen chair.

"You don't have to be male or female to design, Rose. I can design just as well as any man. Father said so. I will refuse to do any designing for John, then the factory will have to close and it will be John's fault!" and she crossed her arms in triumph.

"Have you thought about all the people who work in the factory, miss? What about them? You are only thinking of yourself. The men will lose their jobs and their families will starve. Women and little children that have never done you any harm – what about that?" Rose stopped her rolling and placed her floury hands on her hips and waited for Amelia's answer.

Amelia had not thought about this. She supposed that people DID rely on their wages from the factory to live. Life was very difficult!

"I still don't see how it is that John can tell me what to do," she stated sulkily.

Rose resumed her rolling

"Because that is the law, miss. He is your guardian."

"Well, it's a stupid law!"

"I wish I had a guardian to look after me."

"But I want my *freedom*, Rose." Amelia banged her fist on the table making the loose flour jump.

"I don't know what you mean by freedom, Miss Amelia. It seems to me that you have had more than enough freedom in your life. You are beginning to sound like one of these silly National Union of Women's Sufferage people and please don't bang the table, you'll ruin my pastry!"

Sighing, Amelia got up and left the kitchen. She would never make Rose understand. She only knew that she resented anyone having power over her life, even John. Remembering Rose's words she wondered who these Sufferage people were and how she could contact them.

★★★★★

John felt he had dealt very well with the situation and was happier now that he had a designer especially as Amelia would not need to be paid!

His relaxed state of mind was short-lived however. One afternoon Mr Robson came in to say that Mrs Mitchell was in the outer office in a distressed state. John told him to bring her in and fetch some tea.

Once he had Grace sitting down by the desk with a cup of tea in her hand he asked her what was the matter.

"It's Gerald," Grace burst out, nearly spilling her tea in her agitation.

"Is he ill?" John enquired.

"No, not ill, John, I don't know which way to turn," and she burst into tears.

This was so unlike his selfish and overbearing sister that John was stunned. He did not think that he had ever seen her cry before.

"Please try and tell me what is the matter, Grace."

"Gerald has begun to neglect the business. I have had all sorts of strange people calling at the house saying that Gerald owes them money. They were most unpleasant. When I spoke to Gerald about it he shouted at me and told me I was one of the most selfish people he had ever met! Me! Of all people! Do you think I am selfish, John?"

When John did not reply she continued. "He even said that the boys were ill-behaved and needed a good beating."

Privately John agreed with Gerald. So, the worm had turned at last, had he! Now he said, "Can you account for this change in Gerald, Grace?"

"I think that he is drinking more than usual – he does not come in until late and will not tell me where he has been."

"I will speak to him – go home, Grace, and lie down."

He helped her to her feet, called Mr Robson and told him to put Mrs Mitchell into a cab. Then went back to his desk. No sooner had one problem been solved than another took its place.

Later as John left the office he saw Gerald getting out of a cab. Gerald looked relieved to see him.

"Can we go somewhere and talk?" he asked.

John had not seen Gerald for some months and was shocked by his appearance. Gerald had always had a round, well-fed face which made him look quite child-like but now his face was thin and he had deep frown lines.

"We can go into my office – we can talk freely there." John led the way into the building.

Gerald sat in his chair but did not say anything. John waited for a time then said, "How bad is it?"

"Pretty bad. My father does not know yet but he will have to be told."

"What happened?"

Gerald hesitated for a long time studying his clasped hands then braced himself, sat up straight and began.

"Your mother happened. Now she has begun to take an interest in things again she and Grace are never apart. That is not so bad but they encourage each other. The house has had to be re-furbished from top to bottom. Another servant was absolutely necessary. The boys must go to the very best school. Grace must have her own carriage. We must entertain. I must escort them everywhere.

It is too high a life-style John. I had to borrow money from the firm to keep us going. I am never in the office and things have got slack. I don't know what to do. I came here to ask your advice." He looked at John expectantly.

John thought for a moment then said, "First you must tell your father. Then you must tell Grace what you have told me. I know that she is selfish and inclined to be domineering." Gerald looked startled. "She is my sister and I know her as well as you do. We both know that what I have said is true. She will never change but she will listen to reason if you are firm enough.

You have to be master in your own house, Gerald. Women expect to be led and Grace is no exception in spite of what she says. Tell her that this extravagance must stop. Give her an allowance and make sure she keeps proper accounts. Insist on knowing where every penny goes. If she overspends on her allowance take it off the next. She will soon learn." Gerald looked doubtful. "It's the only way."

"I suppose you are right. I will go up and see my father. I am not looking forward to it. Thank you, John." He got up to leave but when he reached the door he turned and looked over at John sitting at his desk.

"Mrs Wallace will miss Grace."

"I am sure she will find something to fill the gap." John assured him.

John was not surprised therefore when a few weeks later Sophia indignantly informed him that Gerald's father had decided that he needed him back in Edinburgh.

When John next saw Gerald and Grace it was at a farewell dinner party given by Sophia. Gerald was very attentive to Grace who seemed less overbearing than she had been and more relaxed. He did not see either of them alone but when Grace kissed him goodbye at the end of the evening she whispered "Thank you" in his ear. As he watched Gerald hand her into a cab he hoped they would be able to start again in Edinburgh.

CHAPTER TWENTY

It was some days after Amelia's sixteenth birthday. She was sitting in front of her mirror while Rose put up her hair. Amelia studied her reflection. She was still not used to seeing such a grown-up person staring back at her. She was just beginning to realize that being a young lady was just as restricting, if not more so, than being a schoolgirl. She sighed. Rose, misinterpreting her sigh, said, "Don't worry, Miss Amelia, I am sure she will like you."

Amelia could not think what she meant for a moment but then remembered that this was the day when John was bringing Miss Trevise and her mother to tea.

"I had forgotten about Miss Trevise, Rose. I don't think it matters very much whether she likes me or not, it's John she is marrying."

"It's all been very sudden, Miss Amelia. I had given up hope that Mr John would ever get married."

"Oh he must, Rose, because he needs an heir to carry on the business." Amelia was practical.

"Putting up your hair has not made you more careful in what you say, has it, Miss? If Mr John marries Miss Trevise what will you and your Mama do?"

"What will we do? Why nothing, Rose. Everything will go on as usual."

"But it can't, Miss." Rose was horrified that Amelia had not realized the situation. She stopped putting in hairpins and stared at Amelia in the mirror.

"Miss Trevise will be the new mistress here and she may not want you and your Mama living with her."

Amelia had never considered this possibility. She shrugged.

"I expect John has thought of that. After all," she added, "he is my guardian and my only living male relative as you have pointed out more than once!"

She yelped as Rose thrust in a hairpin with unnecessary force. "There you are, now you can face anybody."

Feeling rather worried as to whether her hair would stay in one place, Amelia made her way downstairs. She could not help thinking about her father. She still missed him very much but no longer felt that her entire world had collapsed. During the last two years she had furnished John with over two dozen designs. Although he had come to rely on her and had given up any attempt to find a new designer he refused to acknowledge her officially. She was not happy with this arrangement but she could not think what else she could do so she let things drift for the moment.

As she reached the bottom of the stairs she heard the front door bell and Rose, who had just made her way down the back staircase, hurried along to answer it. Amelia paused on the stairs, she wanted to see Miss Trevise before she saw her.

Amelia watched as John entered the hallway and turned to usher in a young lady and an older woman. Amelia craned her neck to see round Rose who had come forward to take their cloaks and bonnets.

Glancing up, John saw Amelia standing on the stairs.

"Amelia! You do look grown-up." He turned to the older woman "Mrs Trevise, this is my sister Amelia."

Mrs Trevise smiled and said, "So pleased to meet you, Miss Wallace. Your brother has told us all about you."

Before Amelia could reply John continued, "And this is Miss Trevise, Amelia."

Miss Trevise, who had been supervising the handing over of the cloaks turned. She was a small girl. Very blonde, very pretty. She smiled at Amelia. At the same time her eyes took in everything about Amelia who was sure that all her hairpins were falling out.

"How do you do? You are just as your brother described."

Amelia was not quite sure what to make of this but at that moment Sophia, having heard their voices, came down the stairs to meet them.

"Do come to the fire, Mrs Trevise, you must be frozen." She led the way up to the drawing room where a bright fire blazed and tea was laid out.

Amelia was the last to enter the drawing room where Rose was waiting to dispense the tea.

Rose, standing waiting for the guests to seat themselves, thought how pleased William would have been that John had, at last, brought home a prospective bride. She watched as they all seated themselves. Mrs Trevise in a brown walking dress, Miss Trevise in blue which contrasted with Sophia's mourning black. Sophia had declared her intention of emulating Queen Victoria by wearing mourning only from now on. She looked at Miss Trevise as she sat close to Amelia. Miss Trevise was extremely pretty with long blonde ringlets, a beautiful complexion and china blue eyes. She looked rather like one of Amelia's dolls but she was a little plump – she would go to fat in a few years if she was not careful, Rose thought with satisfaction, but even Rose had to admit that Amelia did not come up very well in contrast. She suddenly realized that Sophia was signing to her to hand round the cakes. As she did so she listened to the conversation.

"It is so nice to meet you at last, Mrs Wallace," said Mrs Trevise.

Sophia smiled at the same time thinking back to a morning a few days earlier. They had been seated at breakfast. John, looking up from his newspaper, had said, "By the way, Mother, I have asked a Mrs and Miss Trevise to tea on Thursday. I hope you will make them welcome."

Sophia was astounded.

"You have never mentioned these people before. Who are they?"

"I hope you will like Miss Trevise – Selina, that is, I think I am going to marry her."

Everything seemed to stop. Rose, who had just entered the room with a fresh pot of coffee, nearly dropped it. Amelia paused, her fork in mid-air. Sophia carefully and deliberately laid down her knife.

"I wish your father were here, John. He would be pleased that you are thinking of settling down at last. Can you give us some more details – where did you meet? How long have you known her? What is she like?"

"Mrs Trevise is a widow like yourself and Selina is the most beautiful girl you have ever seen. I met them several months ago in the park. I didn't say anything because I was not sure myself until recently but I do want to marry Selina. As there does not seem to be a male relative I have approached Mrs Trevise who seems to be quite in favour of the match provided Selina agrees. I do not think there will be any problem there, after all I am quite a catch!"

Amelia thought that John sounded very conceited. Expecting the poor girl to fall into his arms! John continued, "She will be like another daughter to you, Mother, and a sister to Amelia, I am sure."

"How old is Miss Trevise?" Amelia asked

"Just twenty, that makes an age gap of sixteen years. Not too much, I think." John replied complacently.

Sophia, coming back to the present, was not so sure. She smiled and turned to Miss Trevise.

"Tell me, Miss Trevise…"

"Do call me Selina," Miss Trevise simpered.

"Very well – Selina. I understand you met my son in the Park?"

"Yes, Mama was taken ill and he came to our rescue. Just like a knight in shining armour!" she turned and looked up at John with what Amelia considered to be a stupid expression on her face. John seemed to enjoy it though.

"Not really a knight, Selina – not yet, anyway."

"Do you think you might have a title one day, John? How divine!" Selina was clearly taken with this idea.

Mrs Trevise turned to Amelia.

"And how do you occupy yourself? Do you play the piano or sing?"

Before Amelia could answer Sophia said, dismissively, "Oh no, I am afraid that Amelia has no accomplishments." she turned back to Selina. "Do you play, Selina?"

"Oh yes, I play very well – do you not think so, John?"

"Yes, you must play for us one day Selina."

He turned to Amelia.

"Miss Trevise also sings and can sketch in water colours. She could teach you a lot Amelia."

"I don't particularly want to play the piano or sing or sketch in watercolours, thank you, John." Amelia was polite.

Selina raised her eyebrows, clearly vexed at Amelia's dismissal of the opportunity to learn at the feet of an expert.

"Perhaps Amelia sews and embroiders," Mrs Trevise hastily intervened.

"No, I am afraid not," Amelia replied cheerfully.

"How very strange," Selina was a little shrill. "I should have thought you would be only too eager to acquire such accomplishments. I should have thought," she was clearly getting into her stride, "you would need such skills if you are going to be a governess."

"I am not going to be a governess, Miss Trevise. I am going to stay at home and look after Mama."

"To stay with your Mama until you get married is exactly what a young girl should do." Mrs Trevise smiled at Amelia.

"Don't be silly, Mama. She will never get married – who would have her looking like that?"

There was a shocked silence. Sophia drew in her breath sharply. John blinked. Selina bit her lip and, catching her mother's eye, flushed. Rose was indignant and seriously considered pouring the contents of the tea she had just poured for Mrs Trevise over the girl regardless of the consequences, as it was her hand trembled and some tea slopped into the saucer.

"Do be more careful, Rose." Sophia was sharp, sharper than she intended.

"Do not trouble yourself, Mrs Wallace," Mrs Trevise said comfortably. Turning to Amelia who was sitting very still and silent she said "I don't think that Selina meant to be unkind, Amelia – I may call you Amelia, may I not? – she sometimes speaks without thinking. A fault for which I am constantly rebuking her. Am I not, Selina?"

"Yes, Mama. I am sorry, Amelia, I did not mean to offend you." Selina looked enchantingly contrite. John was clearly entranced.

Amelia remained silent looking down at her hands crumbling the cake on her plate into little pieces.

John wishing to smooth over the awkwardness said, "I am sure Amelia did not take offence, did you, Amelia?"

Amelia opened her mouth preparatory to making a blistering retort, guests or no guests, when she caught Mrs Trevise's eye on her. Mrs Trevise smiled and shook her head slightly so instead of the rude reply Amelia had been contemplating she found herself saying

"Of course I am not offended, Miss Trevise."

Everyone breathed a sigh of relief. Rose, who had watched the scene with interest, thought Mrs Trevise seemed a very nice understanding woman. She could not think how she had allowed Selina to become the vain, empty-headed creature she clearly was.

John looked on with satisfaction. He was sure that Selina had not meant to be rude. He wished, however, that she had not mentioned Amelia becoming a governess. It was an idea that had come to him when Selina had asked him if his mother and sister needed to live with them. He had said that he was sure his mother would be happy to live with his sister Grace and that he supposed Amelia could become a governess. He still thought that it would be an excellent solution. After all, if he told Amelia that was what she was going to do she would have to do it.

He had every intention of marrying Selina Trevise. He was the head of the house after all. Then he remembered that Amelia was still doing the designs – perhaps she could combine governessing and designing. He would have to give the problem some thought. There was plenty of time between now and the wedding. He frowned slightly, he wished he could get a good designer then he could dispense with Amelia's services altogether.

Selina, seeing him frown and misunderstanding the reason, said "We must not tire Mrs Wallace, Mama. I think it is time we went."

"Yes, indeed," agreed Mrs Trevise. There was a general putting down of tea plates and getting up and shaking out of skirts.

In the hall Rose stood holding the cloaks and bonnets. Under cover of the fuss John made helping Selina with her cloak and Sophia making polite remarks, Mrs Trevise said to Amelia who had trailed downstairs into the hall, "I am very pleased to have met you, my dear. I hope that you will come and visit me sometime soon."

That was all she had time to say but Amelia immediately felt drawn to the older woman. She promised that she would visit her and the guests departed with John who was intent on getting a cab and seeing them safely back home.

Once the door had closed Sophia led the way back up to the drawing room. While Rose collected the used crockery Sophia sat looking into the fire. Amelia came and stood by her chair. Sophia glanced up and sighed.

"John had to get married one day and I am pleased, of course, but it will mean changes for us, Amelia." She turned in her chair and looked at Rose. "You will have a new mistress, Rose – I will no longer be mistress here. Will you stay?"

Rose stood holding the tray of crockery. She had already considered her answer to this question.

"I stay where Miss Amelia is, madam. Mr Wallace was very good to me and helped me when I needed it. I shall never desert Miss Amelia."

"Thank you, Rose, you have been a very good servant. I bless the day that your mother brought you to us all those years ago."

Rose was quite moved and hardly knew what to say.

"Thank you, madam," she murmured and fled to the kitchen.

Once back in the kitchen she sank down into the old kitchen chair. Mrs Coalport looked at her with concern.

"Are you alright, Rose?"

"Yes, thank you. Its just that Mr John is talking of getting married."

"Is that a fact! Well not before time. I have often said to Coalport 'if that young man does not rouse himself soon it will be too late'. When is it to be? There will be a lot for us to do. There's the wedding cake for a start. That should be begun as soon as possible then there's ..."

"I expect Mrs Wallace will issue her orders when she is ready." Rose sounded weary.

"What does the new mistress look like?" Mrs Coalport was curious as ever.

"She is very pretty but I don't think she is very sensitive to other people's feelings," and she described what had been said.

"Well I never! Poor Miss Amelia! She can't help how she looks! If only people knew her as we do, Rose. She has always been misunderstood in this house. I remember many a time she has come down into this very kitchen..."

As Mrs Coalport launched into one of her reminiscences Rose let her mind wander. She had been surprised that Mrs Wallace had remembered the circumstances of her arrival. She found that she was wishing that things could stay the same. There had been too many changes these last few years.

First Mr Wallace dying and now Mr John getting married. Everything seemed to be changing. She always read the newspapers from cover to cover before using them to light the fire. There seemed to be all sorts of new jobs – girls called Type Writers worked in offices. She had read a report of a machine which would enable people to talk to each other over long distances. Only yesterday when out marketing she had seen her first horse-drawn tram. The world was changing and she was not sure whether she approved or not.

John duly proposed to Selina who, after a show of astonishment, accepted. John was pleased but not surprised.

Before the engagement was officially announced Amelia and Sophia paid a courtesy call on Mrs Trevise and Selina.

As Amelia usually made some excuse not to go on visits, when Sophia mentioned that she was going to pay a call on Mrs and Miss Trevise, Amelia surprised her by saying she would go too.

The Trevise's lived in a quiet little street. The house was large, detached and hidden behind an enormous yew hedge. It looked well-cared for. Sophia was surprised when Mrs Trevise herself opened the door to their ring. She concluded that they were between servants. After all nobody who lived in that sort of house would be without at least one servant!

Mrs Trevise took their outdoor things and led them into a pleasant room. Through the window they could see a tiled terrace with steps down to a lawn. The garden was small but the judicious use of trees and shrubs made it appear larger. Sophia was sure it would look very pleasant in the summer.

The room was tastefully furnished. The furniture, although old, was of very good quality. A grand piano stood by the window. Mr Trevise must have been a wealthy man.

Sophia was curious about Mr Trevise but did not know how to broach the subject. She looked round the room to see if there was a likeness but the room was unusually bare of photographs and pictures. The only painting being a non-descript watercolour. Seeing her studying the picture Selena said complacently, "Mama will insist on having my watercolour over the mantelpiece. Do you like it?"

"It is very nice, Selina. Look Amelia, this is Selena's work."

Amelia looked. Selina preened herself waiting for Amelia's praise.

"If you say it is nice, Mama, then I am sure that it is. I know nothing about these things."

Selina, not being sure whether this was a compliment or not, seated herself on an armchair near the fire. The rest of the party seated themselves.

"You do not seem to have any pictures of Selina, Mrs Trevise." Sophia was determined to get to the bottom of the mystery.

"I do not like likenesses of people."

"But surely," Sophia persisted, "you must have some momentos of Selina growing up and of Mr Trevise. It is so nice to have them, they evoke so many memories. I have many momentos of William."

"I can keep my memories alive without such aids." Mrs Trevise's reply was crisp.

Sophia took the hint that the subject was definitely closed.

"Please play to us, Selina." her mother requested.

After some persuading Selina launched into a spirited rendering of the overture to one of Mr. Offenbach's latest operettas. She then sang a ballad.

John was right, Amelia thought, she has a sweet voice, but there was something about her rendering that she did not like but she could not put her finger on it. She was silent all the way home trying to work out what it was. By the time the cab reached No 13 she was still no nearer a solution to the puzzle.

Sophia decided to hold a very quiet dinner party to celebrate the engagement just the family and Arthur and Patience Douglass.

Mrs Coalport was in her element – she had not had so much cooking to do for years. Rose was kept busy serving the various courses. If this sort of thing happened often after they were married she would have to ask Mrs Wallace to engage another servant to help, Rose thought, as she served the soup. As if she could read her thoughts Patience enquired.

"When are you thinking of getting married, John?"

"Quite soon, I think," John replied.

"And how are the arrangements going?" Patience asked.

"Very well," Sophia replied. "The young people seem to be in such haste we are working very hard."

"That reminds me," John said, "I have a special favour to ask of you, Arthur. Selina has no male relative so we thought we would ask you to give her away." He waited for Arthur's answer as if he had asked him if he would accept a Knighthood – he would, of course, accept!

Arthur looked surprised.

"No male relatives at all? No long lost cousin lurking somewhere?"

"Unfortunately my husband was an only child, as was his father before him, so there are no cousins. I have long since lost touch with my family and don't know whether they are alive or dead." Mrs Trevise was very firm. Nobody had the courage to ask what everyone so badly wanted to know – why had she decided to disown her family?

"I have often asked Mama about her family but she will never tell me." Selina was bright as she took another helping of Mrs Coalport's excellent Quaking Pudding.

Amelia watching Mrs Trevise's face saw a look of pain and decided that there was a story behind this.

Sophia led the ladies to the drawing room and they settled down to various occupations. Selina sat down at the piano and began to play a Chopin Nocturne. It was a very competent performance but there was still something missing. Up until this evening Amelia had not known what it was but now she did – there was no emotion or sensitivity. Selina played the piano not because she enjoyed the music but because being able to play well was an accomplishment. There was no emotion in her singing and although her watercolours were good, they had no feeling for the subject matter.

"Come, Amelia, please sing something for us. A duet with Selina, perhaps." Mrs Trevise encouraged.

Amelia shook her head and Sophia came to the rescue.

"I am afraid that Amelia has no gift for music."

"I am sure there is something that you are good at!" Mrs Trevise persisted.

"I can des... draw a little." Amelia realized that she had nearly given away her secret. It was becoming harder and harder to keep it to herself, she wanted to be acknowledged as the designer for Wallace & Sons. She had asked John several times if he would do this but each time he had emphatically refused. If only father were alive, he would give her her due.

At this point the men came in and a game of cards was proposed between Selina, John, Arthur and Patience. Sophia excused herself to go and fetch a magazine which had a dress pattern she wanted to show Mrs Trevise and Amelia found herself more or less alone with Selina's mother.

"I am sorry if I embarrassed you by asking you about your accomplishments." Mrs Trevise looked upset.

On impulse Amelia decided to tell her everything. When she had finished Mrs Trevise was not shocked as Amelia half expected her to be.

"I think you should be very proud of yourself, Amelia. I am sure that I could not keep such an accomplishment to myself but I do see that John has a problem. Whether we like it or not women in our situation are not expected to do anything except run a home for the menfolk."

"I don't think it is fair! I have been reading a lot lately about The National Union of Women's Sufferage."

Mrs Trevise frowned.

"That is rather a dangerous thing to do if I may say so, my dear. I am sure your brother would not approve." Then seeing her face, "Don't worry, I am not going to tell him. You may rely on my discretion."

At this point Sophia appeared with the Magazine and there was no further opportunity for confidences.

CHAPTER TWENTY ONE

John had tried to talk to Amelia about her future. Selina had left him in no doubt that she expected to have her house to herself. He had a very exhausting afternoon trying to persuade Amelia that either she found herself a post as a Governess or she went to live with Grace. Amelia replied that she had read Miss Parkes' article in The English Woman's Journal regarding the reports of The Governors' Benevolent Institution and she then lectured an astonished John on the injustices suffered by these unfortunate women concluding passionately

"I would rather DIE than become a governess!"

John then proposed that she go with Mama to live with Grace. Amelia did not want to live with Grace – she did not like Grace and Grace did not like her. She did not like her nephews and they...

"I think I understand thank you, Amelia."

Amelia then played her trump card.

"If you send me away I will *never, never* do another design in the whole of my life!"

John threw up his hands and Amelia left the room confident that she had won the day.

On being informed by John that his mother and sister would be living with them for the foreseeable future Selina was inclined to indulge in a bout of hysterics until she realized that John was not going to be moved.

She did however express concern regarding her mother living on her own. In view of this a few weeks before the wedding John asked Mrs Trevise to go and live with them. When she refused he tried to discover why. Was it because Mrs Trevise did not like his mother? No, it was not. Was it because of Amelia? Definitely not, Mrs Trevise liked Amelia very much. Then why? Mrs Trevise explained in a quiet, reasonable voice that she liked her independence, she had sacrificed a great deal to keep it and she was not going to give it up now. She was quite happy to live on her own. John tried to persuade her but she was adamant. He did manage to get her to agree to have a servant. He was not going to have it said that his wife's mother did her own housework.

As he told Arthur, with whom he was becoming more and more intimate,

"I am surrounded by stubborn females! If only they would do as I ask but they will not!"

"Best to leave it for a while, John, and see how things develop. Things may change after your first child is born."

As Selina had no other relatives than her mother the wedding was a quiet affair with only a few guests present. Grace and Gerald came down and the house was full once more.

Mrs Coalport made sure that the wedding party came back from Church to a magnificent wedding breakfast. She had made a superb four-tier wedding cake.

Before they left for their honeymoon, a month in Venice, Selina went down into the kitchen as the new mistress. Mrs Coalport and Rose were clearing away the debris of the wedding breakfast. They stopped and stood respectfully side by side when Selina entered the room.

"Good afternoon, madam," said Rose.

Selina looked round the kitchen. She went over to the shelves containing the crockery and ran her gloved finger over the surface. She inspected her finger which was clean. Rose and Mrs Coalport stood by impassively.

"You seem to keep things in good order." Selina was reluctant in her praise. "When I return I shall require a full inventory of the contents of the pantry. While I am away I want you to give the whole house a thorough cleaning. You must move Miss Amelia to one of the upstairs attic rooms."

"Miss Amelia has been in that room since she was small, madam," Rose was shocked.

"I am here now, Rose, and you will carry out my orders if you please. I want to use Miss Amelia's room as my boudoir. It is one of the nicest rooms in the house. She will be quite happy to move I can assure you."

Rose doubted this very much but kept silent.

"That will be all, I think. When I return I will engage another servant as I expect to be entertaining a great deal. I hope you can cope with large numbers, Mrs Coalport?"

"Oh yes, madam. In my previous position..."

Selina interrupted.

"I am not interested in your previous position, Mrs Coalport, only in this one. So long as you can give satisfaction we shall get along very well," and with a frosty smile she left the kitchen.

Amelia had been silent most of the day. She found the wedding ceremony very exhausting as she had been put in charge of the youngest of Grace's four boys, the eldest at ten was not very much help in keeping his younger brothers under control. They were clearly spoilt and at one point, just as the Bride and Groom were about to go into the vestry the three-year-old had wriggled away from Amelia's restraining hand and run up the aisle towards the altar. Amelia ran after him and picked him up. In the silence just before the organ began to play while the Bride and Groom signed the register, his voice, furious, rang out "Get away from me, you ugly thing!"

Amelia was very tempted to give him a well-deserved smack. When she got back to her pew Gerald took the child away from her with a muttered apology. Back at the house the boys ran riot round the table until Gerald finally lost his temper and threatened them all with a whipping if they did not sit down and behave themselves.

Grace turned to her mother.

"Gerald is always so hard on them. They are only young, after all."

Sophia, who had a headache, could not agree and said, "Boys need discipline. They are very unruly, Grace, and also rude."

Grace flushed a very unbecoming colour and moved away from Sophia. They had always got on very well together but since father had died Mama had changed. Grace did not know what it was but she suspected Amelia had a lot to do with it. She looked over to her sister where she sat in animated conversation with Mrs Trevise. They seemed to be getting on very well and she wondered what they were talking about.

Mrs Trevise had just said to Amelia, "I shall miss Selina. It is going to be quite lonely I think. Will you come and keep me company sometimes?"

"I should like that very much." Amelia was genuinely pleased that Mrs Trevise seemed to like her company. She saw Grace looking at them.

"I must go and speak to my sister or she will think that I am neglecting her."

"I thought you handled that horrible little boy very well, my dear." Mrs Trevise had a twinkle in her eye.

"He is rather horrible, isn't he, but I don't think it is entirely his fault. He has been spoilt, that is the problem. Grace lets them do as they like. I think there are plans for them to have a governess. It was going to be me but I have managed to persuade John that I am a totally unsuitable person to have as a Governess."

Mrs Trevise laughed and watched Amelia as she went over to her sister. She was becoming very fond of her. She had certain plans in mind which she hoped would come to fruition one day in the future.

With the house in a turmoil Amelia was glad to get out and visit Mrs Trevise. They sat and chatted and sometimes they went out and shopped. Mrs Trevise engaged a servant and asked Amelia to sit in on the interviews. When Mrs Trevise asked her opinion she was quick to point out her inexperience in these matters.

"But you have a great deal of commonsense and that is very valuable in such a situation." Mrs Trevise told her.

There were several girls who were so unsuitable Amelia wondered why they even applied. She was intrigued that Mrs Trevise told each one that she expected her to be completely discreet and that there was one room which they were not allowed to enter. Mrs Trevise would clean that herself. If they were willing to take the position on those terms then she would let them know her decision in due course.

In the end they narrowed it down to two girls. Amelia favoured one above the other simply because she reminded her of Rose. After some discussion Mrs Trevise agreed with Amelia on the choice of girl. The girl was informed by telegram and began work just before John and Selina were due home.

Mrs Trevise was surprised when Amelia told her that Selina had given orders for her to be moved out of her bedroom.

"Why has she done that?" Mrs Trevise was puzzled.

"Selina said that she wanted it for her boudoir."

Amelia saw that Mrs Trevise was getting upset and hastened to reassure her.

"It doesn't really matter, Mrs Trevise. I am quite happy at the top of the house and I am near Rose. I am away from everyone and I can get on with my designs so it is very good really. I wonder I didn't think of it for myself."

Mrs Trevise had her own ideas as to Selina's reason for moving Amelia but said nothing.

When Selina and John returned there seemed to be some tension between them. Selina went early to bed and John told Sophia and Amelia that Selina had suffered on the crossing.

"She was perfectly well on the way out." He was at a loss to understand it. "The journey home was very calm."

Sophia looked up sharply from her embroidery.

"Perhaps it is all the excitement and the travelling. Travelling can be very tiring for some people." was all she said.

The next day Selina decided to stay in bed until lunchtime – and the next day and the next. Sophia ran the house as usual but she consulted Selina who was feeling very sorry for herself. In the end when this had been going on for nearly a month, Sophia told John, "You must get the Doctor in to Selina. She can't go on like this. She is hardly eating anything and she only wants to sleep all the time."

By now John was really concerned and did not have to be told twice. He was waiting anxiously when Dr. Thomas came downstairs. He was smiling broadly.

"Congratulations, John! You will be a father by your first anniversary!"

John was delighted.

"How is Selina taking it?" he enquired.

"She is not too pleased but she will come round once she gets used to the idea – they usually do." Dr. Thomas said cheerfully. "Let her get up and lie on the sofa downstairs, she needs to be with people. Also get your servant to make her some beef tea."

When Sophia was told about the baby she was not particularly surprised.

"Selina is very young, John, she will need to take care. Perhaps you should engage a nurse for her?"

John pondered this and then had what he considered to be a very good idea which he put to Selina who seemed quite in favour of it. That evening he tackled his mother

"Selina and I were wondering, Mother, whether you would take over the running of the house until she is feeling better. I don't think that hiring a nurse will be needed, do you?"

Sophia was only too willing to carry on running the house. She was surprised that Selina did not demand a full-time nurse to wait on her but she seemed to dislike the idea. Sophia put it down to her condition.

"We can try the scheme and see how well it progresses." She told John who, having made the arrangements promptly forgot all about the extra work involved.

Everyone's energies were now concentrated on Selina who was an extremely demanding patient. Sophia managed, after much persuading, to get Selina to lie on the sofa in the sitting room during the day. As soon as it was near John's time for returning home she went back to bed. John now slept in one of the spare rooms so that he did not disturb Selina who complained of difficulty in sleeping.

Dr. Thomas called regularly. He tried to get Selina to dress and go out of the house for a short walk but without success. Selina would cry and say that he was cruel and Dr. Thomas would leave wearing a resigned expression. Mrs Trevise was frequently at the house. She told Selina that it was not good for the baby if she stayed in bed all the time but nothing would persuade Selina to attempt anything other than a walk up and down the stairs twice a day. Amelia found that she was pressed into service for errands. Fetching and carrying for Selina who would want a book one minute, a drink the next, the fire made up, her bed re-made – a dozen times a day.

One day when Amelia had brought Selina a hot drink she found her looking at her over the top of the cup.

"Is anything the matter?" she asked.

Selina shook her head. That evening when John went up to sit with her after dinner as was his custom, she seemed pre-occupied.

"You are very silent this evening, Selina. Are you feeling unwell? Should I call Dr Thomas?"

"No, I am not feeling unwell John but I am worried."

"And what have you to be worried about Selina?" John was indulgent.

"I hardly like to say." Selina was coy.

"You know you can tell me anything, Selina."

It's Amelia..." Selina hesitated and looked uneasy.

"What about Amelia? Has she been rude to you, is that it?" John frowned.

"No, she has not been rude but I have been reading in The Ladies' Journal that what a pregnant woman sees could affect the child."

"What has that to do with Amelia?" John was puzzled.

"She is, well, not very good looking, is she, John. I mean, she can't help it, I know," as John frowned more than ever, "but the fact remains that she does look how she looks and I *am* pregnant ..."

"You have been filling your head with superstitious nonsense, Selina. Nothing will happen to the baby. But to put your mind at rest

I will consult Dr. Thomas on the subject. Show me this article I should like to read it."

"Oh – I think that stupid Rose has used it to light the sitting room fire."

"A pity," was all John said.

He mentioned Selina's fears to Dr Thomas and on his next visit Dr. Thomas was closeted with Selina for some time. When he came out he told Sophia, who was waiting on the landing, "Mrs John seems to have got herself into quite a state regarding your daughter Amelia. I think she is fussing unnecessarily but we must be very careful in these cases. Mrs John is not strong and if she gets too upset about anything she could lose the baby."

"Why is she worried about Amelia?"

"Well to put it bluntly, Mrs Wallace, she is afraid the baby may look like Amelia if she sees Amelia every day before the baby is born. I told her there was no medical evidence to support such an idea but she would not listen."

Sophia was distressed.

"I will speak to her about it and try and get her to see sense."

But Selina was adamant – Amelia must go.

"She can go and live with Grace until the baby is born." Selina decreed.

Amelia, when told this decision, but not the reason for it, refused to go to Grace.

"I will not be in the same room with those boys, Mama. I will not go to Grace. I do not understand why I must go away."

There was a long pause while Sophia thought of what she could say. Finally she said, "Selina is not very strong, Amelia, and pregnant women get very strange ideas into their heads. For some reason she has decided that it would be better if you were not in the house – I expect she will change her mind shortly but perhaps it would be better if, just for a few weeks until she changes her mind, you stay with Grace."

"She is afraid that the baby will look like me – that's it, isn't it, Mama?" Amelia was very matter of fact.

Sophia said nothing.

"I will not go away. This is my home. I will keep out of Selina's way. That will not be very difficult after all as she spends so much time in bed. You can tell her that I have gone and she will never know the difference."

Sophia was uneasy with this plan but it was plain that short of forcibly removing Amelia there was no way that she could be moved from the house. When John was told of the plan he readily agreed. He was having some problems at the factory and he could not be bothered with domestic trifles.

So Selina was informed that she would not see Amelia until she wanted to which she took to mean that Amelia had left the house. Rose was taken into Sophia's confidence.

"It is only until Mrs John feels better, Rose, so you will be careful not to let her know that Amelia is still in the house, won't you?"

"Yes, madam." Rose said coldly. "Will that be all, madam?"

Sophia indicated that she could go.

Amelia was only mildly upset by Selina's request. She had long grown used to the idea that she was ugly. She had once written to Cupid's Post Bag in The Englishwoman's Domestic Magazine asking if there was anything she could do to make herself more presentable. The reply was not satisfactory. She was informed that, although *she* might think she was bad looking or even ugly, perhaps she was not really so bad. She must not be so taken up with herself and should take up some work for others so that, even if she did not get married she could still be of some use in the world. She was also told not to be so vain and to be content to remain in the position in which God had seen fit to place her. Tearing the letter into small pieces she had burnt them on her bedroom fire.

CHAPTER TWENTY TWO

As everyone else was so busy pandering to Selina's every whim Amelia found it quite easy to slip out of the house to see Mrs Trevise who had been more distressed than Amelia at Selina's edict.

"It really does not matter." Amelia told her on one occasion. "I know I am ugly. It has happened to me all my life. Besides, I would not want the poor baby to look like me. It is not very nice, especially when people nudge each other and say things like 'Will you look at that poor girl's face!' or 'She shouldn't be let out looking like that.' I expect it is as Mama says – it is a cross I have been given to bear." Amelia sounded quite cheerful about it but Mrs Trevise was so distressed that the next time she visited Selina she brought up the question of Amelia.

"Don't you think you have been a little too hasty, Selina? It is not what is on the outside that is important, it is what is on the inside and Amelia is a very sweet girl. I think she is quite upset by your attitude."

"I am sorry, mother, but I am not prepared to discuss Amelia. It makes my head ache," and Selina put her hand to her forehead.

"Perhaps if you went for a walk it would clear your head. You know the Doctor said it was not good for you to spend so much time cooped up indoors."

"The Doctor does not understand, Mama. How could he? He is a man. Nobody knows what I have to suffer. Nobody cares. All I want is for Amelia to stay away until the baby is born. Surely that is not too much to ask?" Her china blue eyes filled with tears and her rosebud mouth quivered.

Mrs Trevise sighed. She knew it was hopeless to try and reason with Selina when she had made up her mind. She had a will of iron when it came to getting her own way. She just said

"I still think that it would be healthy for you to try and get some air, Selina."

"Perhaps I will" Selina said having got her own way "but not today – tomorrow."

Amelia spent much of her time sketching designs in her room. She was completely happy at these times. John was urging her to greater and greater efforts.

Late one evening when she had gone into the study to show him her latest creation she brought up yet again the question of her acknowledgement as Wallace & Son's designer. He evaded the subject as usual, but this time Amelia was persistent and in the end he said impatiently, "Because I would be the laughing stock of the city if my rivals knew that I had a girl for a designer."

"But if my work is good, and it must be, John, otherwise you would not be selling toys, why should that make it difficult? Surely they can respect a fellow designer?"

"Because commerce is a man's world. It always has been and always will be. Women have no place in it whatsoever."

"Am I then to spend the rest of my life being unacknowledged as a designer and also shut away because my looks embarrass your wife?"

"You have a good home here, Amelia. Once the baby is born I am sure that Selina will be only too pleased for you to come back and help out. There are not many brothers who would be willing to look after you. You have been fed and clothed you know." Conveniently forgetting that she was not paid for her designs.

Amelia turned and left the room closing the door very carefully behind her. She felt trapped. She had to creep about her own home in case Selina saw her; John would not acknowledge her designing ability; even Rose seemed to have deserted her. There were no more cosy chats while Rose did her hair or when Amelia went down to the kitchen. Rose was always busy fetching something for Selina or making sure that the fire was always bright. Mrs Coalport was for ever making "tempting dishes for the mistress" and her mother was always fussing over Selina. Only Amelia was not caught up in the general frenzy.

As she stood there she heard a door quietly close upstairs. She looked up and saw a figure cautiously descending the stairs. Amelia darted to the kitchen door and opened it slightly so that she could look through the crack. Who was it creeping about at this time of night? As the figure came into the hall light she could see that it was a woman muffled in a cloak. It could not be Sophia since she was in the downstairs sitting room, it had to be Selina. Where was she going? As Amelia watched Selina quietly let herself out of the house she decided to follow her. She felt behind the kitchen door for Rose's shawl on its hook and pulling it round herself she slipped out of the door after her sister-in-law.

It was a chilly September night. There was a dampness in the air but it was not raining yet. Selina walked steadily along the road in the direction of the main thoroughfare. Amelia could not think where she was going, no respectable woman went out alone at night. Perhaps she was going to Mrs Trevise's. Amelia dismissed this idea as there would be no reason for Selina to sneak out of the house in order to visit her own mother.

When Selina reached the thoroughfare she approached a cab rank and swiftly got into a cab.

Amelia watched her go. She had no way of following. Thoughtfully she retraced her steps. She would wait and see what time Selina came in. She positioned herself at the upstairs landing window. She did not have long to wait. About an hour later Selina came quietly through the gate and up the path. She seemed to be staggering – surely she was not drunk! Amelia hung over the bannisters ready to fly off to her own room as soon as Selina began to climb the stairs. She heard the door open and saw Selina stagger into the hall. She gave a moan and clutched her stomach. She was clearly in a great deal of pain. Forgetting all about her promise Amelia ran to help her. Selina was hot and sweating. She didn't seem to realize who Amelia was.

"Help me to get to my room." she gasped.

"I will call Mama."

"No!" Selina clutched Amelia's arm, "please don't. Just take me to my room. I shall be better when I can lie down."

Amelia helped her upstairs and into her room.

"Help me to undress."

"Then I shall get the Doctor." said Amelia firmly.

Once in bed Selina began to look a little better. She smiled at Amelia. "I thought you had gone away to your sister?"

"Oh no," said Amelia innocently, "I managed to persuade John to let me stay here as long as I kept out of your way. It is just as well I didn't go away isn't it, otherwise I would not have been able to help you, would I?"

"No, you are quite right. I should not have made such a fuss... Thank you, Amelia, you have been very kind. Would you get me my mirror, please? It is on the dressing table."

As Amelia went over to get the mirror Selina got out of bed and screamed. Amelia jumped and dropped the mirror which shattered on the edge of the dressing table.

Amelia began to make her way to Selina's side.

"Get away from me!" screamed Selina.

Amelia tried to get her back into bed but Selina continued to scream, apparently without taking a breath.

When John entered the room at a run closely followed by Sophia they saw Amelia apparently struggling with Selina who was screaming hysterically.

"What on earth is going on?" John had to shout to make himself heard.

"She is not supposed to be here. You promised, John. Take her away. She will do something to the baby!"

"But Selina..." Amelia began.

"She came in here and accused me of driving her away from her home. She was horrid, John. Make her go away!"

"That is not true," Amelia said hotly.

"I think you had better leave the room, Amelia." Sophia was firm. "Selina is clearly unwell and we shall have to send for Dr. Thomas. I will speak to you later."

"She hates me!" Selina was beside herself. "She will say anything! Don't believe anything she says!"

"Come now, Selina, get back into bed, you are not well." John steered her towards the bed.

Sophia took Amelia's arm and propelled her out of the room. Rose was just running upstairs.

"Take Miss Amelia to her room, Rose, and make sure that she stays there until I come."

"Yes, madam," Rose was puzzled.

When they reached Amelia's room Rose asked her what had happened. Amelia told her all she knew. Rose was thoughtful. She questioned Amelia closely on how long Selina had been gone and what she had looked like on her return.

"Why is she doing this to me, Rose? She is ill but why – it was nothing to do with me – was it?"

"No, Miss Amelia, it was not. I have an idea what has been going on but I don't think we shall ever be able to prove it."

"What can't we prove, Rose?"

"There are some things, Miss Amelia, that it is best for you not to know about. In any case we can't be sure." and try as she might Amelia could not persuade Rose to say more.

They heard the doctor come; he was in the house for the rest of the night. A nurse also arrived. Rose and Amelia sat on Amelia's bed waiting for Sophia. Finally as dawn was breaking she came wearily into the room.

"Selina has lost the baby. She says that it was your fault, Amelia. She says that she woke to find you touching things on her dressing table. Dr. Thomas says she must have complete rest. What have you to say?"

Amelia told her what she had told Rose. Sophia listened to the end. There was a long silence.

"I don't think that Selina was capable of getting out of bed and going on a journey. Also I don't think that she would tell such lies,

Amelia. I know that you and Selina do not like each other but I am sure she would not stoop to such dramatics."

"So you think that I am lying, Mama?" Amelia was very hurt.

"I think that you have been jealous of Selina and that you did not intend to upset her. It was just unfortunate that she woke up with such a start. After all she was sure that you had left the house. We should have made sure that you went away. I am afraid that John will never forgive you for this, Amelia."

"Madam," Rose could not keep silent any longer, "I am sure that Miss Amelia is telling the truth."

Shaking her head Sophia held up her hand for Rose to stop.

"That will do, Rose. It is not your place to tell me whether or not my daughter is lying. Now go downstairs and begin on the breakfast although I am sure nobody will feel like eating. You, Amelia," turning back to her, "will stay in this room until I tell you you can come out. I shall have to talk to John about what to do with you."

"But I am not lying, Mama – it did happen as I told you." Amelia was frantic – someone must believe her!

"I do not wish to discuss the matter further, Amelia. Come, Rose." She swept from the room. Rose gave Amelia a backward glance and a smile as she went.

Amelia sat on her bed with her head in her hands. She could not imagine why Selina was doing this to her. At least Rose believed her. After a time she lay down just as she was and fell into a half sleep. Nobody came near her. The light in the window faded and the room became dark but still nobody came. She knew she should feel hungry but she did not.

She must have fallen asleep at some time because suddenly the window was light. She felt stiff all over and her dress was badly crumpled. She glanced at the clock on the mantelpiece – it was still very early. Perhaps her mother had forgotten all about her. Perhaps they would never come. This was silly. She got off the bed and made her way to the door. At least it was not locked. As she put her hand out to the knob it turned. She sprang back and went back and lay down on the bed with her face to the wall.

"Amelia." It was her mother's voice. She did not move. "Come now, Amelia. this will not do. I know that you are awake."

Reluctantly Amelia opened her eyes and sat up. Her mother was standing at the foot of the bed her hands grasping the brass rail. She looked very stern.

"John and I have talked half the night. I told him that I did not think you had been deliberately cruel to Selina. In the end he agreed with me but he does not want to see you at the moment. It has been decided that you will go and stay with Grace until Selina is better.

I do not know how long that will be. She is very ill. The Doctor seems to be very puzzled by the whole thing. He had the impertinence to ask Selina if she had tried to get rid of the baby! We have had Dr Roberts for years but I think perhaps it is time we had a younger man, he is obviously too old for his job. He also says that she may never be able to have children which is absolute rubbish as she is very young still. However, that is no concern of yours.

You will pack your things and Rose will accompany you to Grace's. Once you are settled in Rose can return. There will be plenty for her to do here. I expect Grace will find you most useful especially as I understand she is pregnant again. Perhaps this time it will be a little girl."

All the time her mother had been speaking Amelia's eyes never left her face. When Sophia finished there was a pause. Amelia said nothing. Sophia came round the bed and sat down beside her. She took Amelia's hand.

"You are cold, Amelia. You must have some food before you go. Tell me that you made up what you said you saw. I will understand. It is difficult when you are expected to keep out of the way. I didn't agree with John and Selina over that. I expect you were annoyed about it and wanted to frighten Selina and you didn't realize the serious consequences that could come of such a prank. That's it isn't it, Amelia?"

Amelia knew that all she had to do was to admit that she had been lying and her mother would forgive her. But she could not.

"No, Mama. I saw what I saw. I have not told any lies. If anyone is lying it is Selina."

Sophia got up abruptly.

"I can do nothing with you, Amelia, while you persist in this attitude. What your father would have said I do not know. He would not have been very proud of you. Make sure that you are ready. I will return in an hour by which time I expect you to have changed your dress, washed your face and had your breakfast. Rose has her instructions. She is not to let you out of her sight until you reach Edinburgh."

Then she left the room without another glance.

Amelia began to pack her clothes. She felt very angry. Why should she be in disgrace when it was not her fault?

After a long time there was a tap at the door and Rose entered.

"Are you ready for your breakfast, Miss Amelia?"

Amelia nodded and together they went down to the kitchen. As it was so early Mrs Coalport had not arrived and Rose made Amelia's breakfast. Amelia had not thought she could eat but once she began she cleared the plate.

Rose watched her as she ate. She seemed very thoughtful.

"Tell me again what happened, Miss Amelia."

"Why, what is the point, nobody believes *me*."

Amelia was inclined to be sulky.

"I believe you, Miss Amelia, I told you that." Rose sounded reproachful.

Amelia was immediately contrite. She put down her knife and fork and went over to Rose where she sat in the old kitchen chair.

"I know that you do, Rose, and I am very grateful. Now we have to go to Grace's and I hate it there. Those boys are always horrid to me."

"What if we didn't go there, Miss Amelia, but went somewhere else?" Rose asked.

"Where could we go, Rose?" Amelia sounded excited "You have something in mind, haven't you?"

"Well, I did go and see someone who would be very glad to have you if you are willing to go."

"Who, Rose?"

"I am surprised you didn't think of it for yourself – Mrs Trevise of course."

Amelia frowned. "But will she be willing to have me, Rose? She may not believe me either."

"Yes she does, Miss Amelia."

"How do you know?"

"I could not bear the thought of you having to put up with those dreadful boys. Your Mama would not listen to me when I tried to suggest that Mrs Trevise would be willing to have you for a while. She was adamant that you had to go to Mrs Mitchell's. Mrs John was calling for her mother and Mr John sent me to fetch her early this morning. I told her all about it on the way back. She didn't say anything but when we got here she went in to see Mrs John and insisted that she went alone. I don't know what went on in there but when she came out she said that she believed you and that Mrs John had more or less admitted as much."

"So that's it, Rose – I don't have to go away after all. Everyone believes me."

Rose shook her head.

"When Mr John and your Mama went back into the room Mrs John denied saying anything. She accused Mrs Trevise of taking your side against her – her own daughter and said that she never wanted to see Mrs Trevise or you ever again. Mrs Trevise tried to reason with her but Mrs John began to throw herself about in the bed and the Nurse said it would be better for everyone to leave the room. Your Mama and Mrs Trevise are in the sitting room, perhaps Mrs Trevise can persuade your Mama to let you live with her for the time being."

"I do hope so, Rose."

Sophia came into the kitchen as Amelia finished speaking. Ignoring Amelia who rose from her chair, she addressed Rose.

"Go with Miss Amelia and Mrs Trevise. A cab is waiting. Make sure Miss Amelia has everything she needs. She may be away for some time. Come back as soon as Miss Amelia is settled in. There is a great deal to be done. The Nurse will be living in for a while."

"Mama." Amelia put her hand on her mother's arm.

Sophia shook off her hand and left the kitchen without a word.

Mrs Trevise joined Rose and Amelia in the hall. Rose superintended the cabby taking out Amelia's luggage and they all three left the house without speaking.

Amelia could see that Mrs Trevise had been crying. She felt like crying herself. The short journey was made in silence. No one said anything until Rose and the maid were engaged in taking Amelia's boxes and trunks upstairs. Then Mrs Trevise led the way into the drawing room where she sank down on the sofa and held her hands out to Amelia to sit down beside her.

"I am so sorry that this has happened, Amelia. Not sorry that you have come to live with me, of course, but sorry that it had to be under these circumstances."

"I really did not tell lies, Mrs Trevise. I know that Selina is your daughter but she really is not a very nice person."

"I know that you don't tell lies, Amelia. I also know that my daughter is extremely spoilt and it is my fault. I was always conscious of the fact she did not have a father and spoilt her in consequence. Now I am paying the price but it seems a little unfair that you should also."

On an impulse Amelia snuggled up to Mrs Trevise who put her arm round her. Rose found them sitting gazing into the flames of the fire.

"Excuse me, madam, but I have to go back now. Mrs Wallace will be needing me."

"Of course, Rose. Thank you very much for your help." Mrs Trevise smiled then as Rose hesitated, "Was there something else?"

"Yes, madam. Could I come and see Miss Amelia from time to time? I promise not to be a nuisance. I have known her since she was a baby and I shall miss her."

"Of course you may, Rose, come whenever you wish. You will always be welcome here."

"Goodbye, Miss Amelia, I will see you soon."

Rose went to leave the room but there was the sound of swishing skirts and Amelia put her arms round Rose and hugged her.

"I shall miss you, Rose. Please come soon."

"I promise to come whenever I can. Try not to get into any more scrapes!"

And with a watery smile she was gone.

CHAPTER TWENTY THREE

Rose and Amelia were working together in the kitchen. As Amelia chattered away Rose watched her and thought how much she had changed since she had left No.13 two years before. She seemed much happier and she had grown into a lively looking young lady. Rose was conscious that Amelia had asked her a question and was waiting for an answer.

"What was that, Amelia?"

"Wake up, Rose! I said how glad I am that Aunt Isabella took you in."

"So am I. I don't know what I would have done."

Rose shuddered when she remembered the winter's night when Selina had tried her patience once too often and Rose had taken hold of her and shaken her. Mr John had told her that he had no choice but to dismiss her without a reference. Rose sometimes felt that he was harder on her than he meant to be because he felt guilty as he had often wanted to do the same thing. She had wandered the streets for a long time wondering what to do.

A man had approached her and she realized that if she was not very careful she would take a path she had no wish to travel. She had then gone to Mrs Trevise and asked to be taken in. She offered to work for nothing, she just wanted to be where Amelia was. Mrs Trevise had been more than generous and given her a bed in return for which Rose worked as hard as she could. Mrs Trevise was between maids at the time. They never seemed to stay for very long and they all left for the same reason – they just could not contain their curiosity about the locked room.

Mrs Trevise was a pleasant woman but in this one thing she was obsessive. As soon as anyone showed the slightest sign of trying to get into the room or even if they asked about it she would become extremely angry. A few days after Rose's arrival Mrs Trevise called her into the drawing room telling her to close the door. She then asked Rose if she would like to stay and work for her until she got settled somewhere else. Rose was only too pleased to do so. Mrs Trevise then said, "I must make one thing very clear, Rose. Under no circumstances must you ever attempt to enter the locked room next to my bedroom. I will not tolerate any deviation from this rule. Amelia is happy to stay here under these circumstances – are you?"

"Of course, madam. This is your house, it is not for either Miss Amelia or me to question what you do in it."

"Thank you, Rose, I was hoping you would say that. I will pay you of course but I don't want you to think of yourself as a servant. Think of yourself more as a companion for Amelia. She needs friends just at the moment. I hope that as time goes by my daughter will relent."

Contact between the two houses was rare as Selina, after two years, was just as adamant that she would see neither Amelia nor her mother. Mrs Wallace called to see Amelia occasionally but they were not happy visits. John never came but he did send a message to say that he would give Amelia a small allowance.

Amelia sent back a terse note stating that she did not require an allowance. She no longer designed for John or anyone else. She still had the occasional idea but they were getting fewer and fewer. She did not know what John was doing about a designer and she did not really care.

"I am quite happy to have you here, of course," Mrs Trevise had told Amelia when apprised of her decision "but I cannot provide you with very much spending money. My resources are limited."

"I don't mind." Amelia was dismissive "I eat very little."

Mrs Trevise smiled sadly. She knew that one day Amelia would regret turning down John's offer.

Rose was also worried about Amelia's lack of funds. She had taken Amelia to task for refusing Mr John's offer. She pointed out that it was only what Amelia was entitled to as a dependant but Amelia would have none of it. As if she had read her thoughts, which Rose sometimes thought she did, Amelia now said

"I think I was too hasty in refusing an allowance from John, Rose."

"Well its not too late. Perhaps if you went to No. 13..."

"No, Rose. I will never set foot in that house again. I only meant that there is something I want to do and I need money for it."

Rose was intrigued.

"What is that?"

Amelia put down the lamp she was polishing.

"When I was out the other day it started to rain very heavily so I looked round for somewhere to shelter. I was very near a Hall so I decided to shelter just inside the doors. While I was there several women came in and then one asked me if I was going to the meeting. I asked her what meeting she meant and she told me that it was a meeting of the National Union of Women's Sufferage where Ann Wilton was due to speak."

"Not those Suffrigists again! I keep telling you they are dangerous."

"Let me finish, Rose. I went in with this woman whose name is Martha Ibbotson. She is a very respectable woman, Rose. I sat through the meeting. I must say that it made me think. One of the things Ann Wilton said stuck in my mind. She said she saw the home as 'an environment of stifled talents.' My designing talent has been stifled, Rose. She also said women should have professional liberty, that's what I want – professional liberty. Freedom to do the work I want to do and to be paid for it. I want to go to work and earn my own money. Money that belongs to me and that I can use however I wish."

"That's all very well, Amelia, but what can you do? You are not fitted to become a maid and Mrs Trevise would never allow you to do that."

"Martha is training to become a Typewriter and I want to do the same."

"A what?"

"A Typewriter, Rose. There are schools which teach girls how to use a typewriting machine. Then, once they are trained, they go out and work in offices. Martha says 'It's our first chance of freedom and we must take it.'"

"This Martha seems to have a great deal to say for herself," Rose said jealously.

"But it is so true, Rose. I can't expect you to understand – you are not young enough to be able to take lessons in your stride – but I am."

"Are you, Amelia," said Rose dryly remembering that she was 13 years Amelia's senior and at 31 was considered to be well and truly 'on the shelf', "What else did Martha say?"

"She said that she could introduce me to the Principal of the School where she is training. The only thing is," Amelia became despondent, "I have no money for the fees."

"Perhaps Mrs Trevise could help you," Rose suggested.

"I did think of asking her but she has been so good to us that I don't like to."

"You did say, Amelia, that it was your chance to become 'free' whatever you mean by that."

Amelia continued to polish the lamp and said no more.

That evening when they were all sitting in the drawing room at their various occupations, Amelia decided to take the plunge and before she could change her mind said

"Aunt Isabella, there is something I want to ask you."

"I thought you were quiet, Amelia. What is it?"

Amelia outlined her plan and then waited anxiously to see what Aunt Isabella would say. Rose put down the stocking she was mending to listen. Mrs Trevise was silent for a while then said, "I think I would want to go into this a bit further, Amelia. You do not really know what a typewriter is, do you? It sounds like machinery to me and that sounds like a factory. Your mother did not bring you up to become a factory girl!"

"Martha said that the Principal would be pleased to show anyone round the College," Amelia eagerly replied.

"Well, that can't do any harm. Let's say that we will look round the College and then make up our minds. If I think that it is suitable, and if you still want to train, I will finance you but," as Amelia began to smile delightedly, "the money will have to be repaid when you get a position."

"Of course, Aunt Isabella, that is understood."

"I expect you have the name of the Principal and also the address of this establishment?"

"Oh yes, Martha wrote it down for me. I can go and get it, then you can write now." Amelia jumped up.

Both Rose and Mrs Trevise laughed. Amelia looked from one to the other puzzled.

"I thought you would have." Mrs Trevise said and they all three began to laugh. Amelia realized how often they laughed in that house. It seemed to be full of laughter most of the time.

★★★★★

Mrs Trevise kept her word and wrote to the College Principal asking for details and an interview. She received a reply by return of post.

A few days later Mrs Trevise and Amelia went to keep their appointment with Miss Gaymin of Gaymin's Business College, leaving an anxious Rose.

The College was situated in Marlborough Road which, as Amelia was quick to point out, was within walking distance of Springfield Road. Marlborough Road was a quiet street off the main thoroughfare. The street was lined with detached houses, one of which displayed a discreet brass plate on the gate pillar which simply said 'Gaymin's Business College.'

Mrs Trevise was doubtful and inclined to turn back but Amelia was already marching up the path. The door was opened by a trim maid who was pushed aside by a plump middle-aged woman with a red ink smudge on her nose and hair which seemed incapable of remaining in its severe bun.

"Mrs Trevise and Miss Wallace – we have an appointment with Miss Gaymin."

"Oh yes – do come in."

They followed her into a large hall which had several solid looking wooden doors opening off it. From behind one of these doors came a clattering sound. Leading from the hall a single staircase, the wall side covered its entire length with bonnets and cloaks suspended from wooden pegs which had been driven into the wall.

"I am Miss Gaymin's assistant – Miss Crisp." As she spoke several hairpins fell to the floor from her back hair which began to fall down. She grabbed at her hair as she bent down to pick up the pins.

Amelia could feel giggles mounting. Anything less crisp than Miss Crisp she could not imagine. She was not sure whether to help Miss Crisp pick up her pins or ignore the problem. She decided to ignore it but she dared not look at Aunt Isabella.

Miss Crisp straightened up and looked at Amelia. She gave no indication of registering Amelia's unusual appearance. She smiled and announced, "Miss Gaymin will see you immediately."

As Miss Crisp led them up the stairs she thrust pins back into her hair greatly disturbing the cloaks and bonnets as she did so. At the top she stopped to catch her breath for a few seconds before knocking on one of the several doors which opened on to the minute landing. There was no reply. Miss Crisp knocked again, louder. "Come in!" the voice sounded impatient. Miss Crisp opened the door and putting her head round presented Amelia and Mrs Trevise with a vast expanse of brown back.

"Mrs Trevise and Miss Wallace, Miss Gaymin."

"Tell them to come in," was the peremptory reply.

Amelia wondered what Miss Gaymin would be like. She imagined a tall, thin lady with a very stern expression but what she saw when she entered the room was a tiny lady with a head covered in a mass of brown curls. She was to find that there was great speculation among the pupils as to whether the hair was a wig or not. Miss Gaymin surprisingly had twinkling brown eyes. Amelia could only conclude that working closely with Miss Crisp had left Miss Gaymin in a permament state of near giggles.

"Come and sit down, please." Miss Gaymin smiled and indicated two chairs placed in front of her desk. With more scattering of hairpins Miss Crisp left the room. Miss Gaymin sat with her back to the window so that the light fell on Amelia's face.

Amelia had been nervous about the interview. She need not have been. Miss Gaymin was satisfied with Amelia's explanation as to why she was now living with Mrs Trevise and not at home. Mrs Trevise explained that she needed a companion. Miss Gaymin stated the hours of attendance and then came the delicate matter of fees. Before she could go into this Amelia said, "I only want to learn to be a Typewriter. I do not want to learn either shorthand or bookkeeping. I expect it is possible to obtain a position with only typewriting?"

"Yes, of course, but you stand more chance of obtaining a better position, one more suited to a young lady, if you take the full course."

Having discussed this thoroughly with Mrs Trevise, Amelia was adamant that she did not want to spend the time learning shorthand and bookkeeping. She wanted to begin to earn money as soon as possible.

"I think I should like to learn only typewriting to begin with. I can always come back and learn the rest, can't I?"

"Well, yes, I suppose you can." Miss Gaymin was reluctant but she could see that Amelia had made up her mind.

Mrs Trevise now decided to take part in the proceedings.

"I think I should like to see where Miss Wallace will be working." She was very firm. She still thought that using a typewriting machine meant that Amelia would be working in some sort of factory.

"Certainly, I will take you to see our beginners class."

Miss Gaymin led them down the stairs and stopped outside the door where clattering noises were still audible. As she entered the room there was a rustle of skirts as all the girls in the room rose to their feet.

"Good afternoon." Miss Gaymin was brisk.

"Good afternoon, Miss Gaymin." they chorused.

"Sit down, please, and continue with your work."

The girls obediently sat. There were eighteen girls in the room. They sat on benches in front of wooden desks on which large machines were placed. A wooden rail ran along the top of the desk above and behind the machines holding books from which the girls were copying their work.

Amelia watched one girl and noticed that she would read her copy and then look for the letters on the double keyboard. When she had found the letter she wanted she pressed the key and the letter appeared as if by magic on a sheet of paper which protruded from the top of the machine.

As Amelia looked round the room she saw that some of the girls seemed to find the key they required without much hesitation but others seemed to take a long time searching. All the pupils were dressed similarly, in white blouses and navy or black skirts. No jewellery was visible except an occasional brooch at the neck of the blouse. Their hair was dressed in a severe style.

Amelia looked over one girl's shoulder to see what she was printing and saw,

Dear Sir

In reply to yours of the 16th inst

It seemed very dull.

Miss Gaymin said, "As you can see all my girls wear white blouses and dark skirts. We find that employers prefer them to be plainly dressed. They must not wear jewellery other than a single brooch and their hair must be neat. Employers will not tolerate too flamboyant a style of dress. It is considered to show a lack of efficiency."

"Do your girls have any difficulty in obtaining respectable positions?" Mrs Trevise was still not entirely convinced that working in an office with men was the right thing for a young lady to do.

Miss Gaymin drew herself up to her full five foot and said, with a touch of ice, "All my girls are respectable young ladies and as such obtain respectable positions. My College is one of the best in London."

"I am sure it is." Mrs Trevise soothed. "Are women being accepted in offices now?"

"There are still some firms that will not accept women. They make all sorts of excuses but in the end they will have to comply with the general trend or be thought old-fashioned."

Miss Gaymin then briskly led the way back to her office where she rang a small brass bell on her desk. When the maid appeared she ordered tea for three. She let Amelia and Mrs Trevise sit quietly sipping their tea and absorbing what they had seen. After some moments she asked Amelia, "Do you think you would like to come here, Miss Wallace?"

"Yes please, Miss Gaymin."

There was then only the question of the fees which Amelia thought were rather high considering she was only learning one skill but Mrs Trevise did not seem to mind so she said nothing. It was arranged that she would begin in a month's time. Miss Gaymin then said goodbye, summoned the maid who led them downstairs and soon they were back in the quiet street.

"Are you really sure this is what you want to do, Amelia? It is not too late to back out."

"I am sure, Aunt Isabella. I will be earning my own money – at last!"

CHAPTER TWENTY FOUR

Rose spent many hours sewing blouses and skirts for Amelia's entry into the world of business. Amelia was worried at the number of extras for which Aunt Isabella had to pay such as material for her clothes, books and paper. It seemed endless. She was sure she would have to work until she was a hundred before she was out of debt. Aunt Isabella told her not to worry about that just to make sure she did well.

On the first day Amelia was very apprehensive and only Rose's and Aunt Isabella's enthusiasm stopped her from changing her mind. What if she couldn't learn to type write? Rose was sure she could. What if the other students were unkind about her appearance? Rose told her to ignore them and they would soon stop. What if...she finally ran out of 'what ifs' and Rose and Mrs Trevise waved her off with cheerful smiles then spent the rest of the day reassuring each other that Amelia would manage perfectly well. By the time Amelia came home, full of enthusiasm and saying how nice the other girls were, they were both exhausted.

Once she was used to the discipline of getting up at the same time each day, Amelia began to enjoy the sensation of actually doing something herself. Mrs Trevise insisted that Rose meet her outside the College each night. Amelia thought this unnecessary but did not say so. After all Mrs Trevise was paying the fees even if she, Amelia, was going to pay them back. She did manage to persuade Rose to wait for her at the end of the road. None of the other girls had a servant to meet them and she did not want to appear in any way different.

After Martha Ibbotson had qualified and was looking for work they still met from time to time. Several times Amelia went with Martha to meetings of the National Union of Women's Sufferage. She found these meetings stimulating. She would go home and enthusiastically tell Rose all that had been said. Rose was not very impressed. She kept telling Amelia that no good could come of women being so aggressive. It was not natural.

Rose liked things to stay the same. Mrs Trevise used to wonder aloud whether or not she should forbid Amelia going but both Amelia and Mrs Trevise knew that she would do no such thing. Amelia brought home pamphlets which she devoured. Rose refused to look at them but Amelia caught Aunt Isabella reading one. "To see if it is suitable reading matter."

Then the red-letter day came when Miss Gaymin declared Amelia fully trained as a Typewriter and presented her with a handsome Certificate stating that "Miss Amelia Wallace is proficient in the operation of a Type Writing Machine at a speed of approximately 50 words per minute". Now all Amelia had to do was to find someone who would give her employment.

She had learnt from Miss Gaymin that girls usually found a position with a relative or someone that was a friend of the family. They did not go knocking on doors asking for a job as Amelia had suggested. Miss Gaymin was appalled at the idea and Miss Crisp lost all her hairpins at the same time at the very thought. Amelia discussed the problem with Martha who had found employment with her uncle. Unfortunately there was only one position available.

"What about your brother?" Martha suggested.

"I will not ask him for any favours." Amelia was adamant.

Martha tried again. "There must be someone that you know. An acquaintance of your brother's perhaps?"

Suddenly Amelia had a idea – Mr Douglass! She was annoyed with herself for not thinking of him before. She discussed the idea with Aunt Isabella who was in favour of Amelia working for someone she knew. Amelia decided to go to see Mr Douglass the next day before she could change her mind.

She took particular care with her appearance. A spotless white blouse, black skirt and her hair drawn back into a bun. Looking in the hall mirror she did not quite recognize herself in the severe girl looking back at her.

As she was critically examining herself Aunt Isabella came out into the hall with something in her hand.

"I should like you to have this," she said, placing something in Amelia's hand. Amelia glanced down to see what the object was. It was a beautiful cameo of a female head.

"I thought you would like it. It is cut from a sardonyx and set in gold. Do you think it is too smart?" she asked, anxiously

"Oh no, I am sure it is not."

"Good. Let me pin it to your blouse." After she had done so she stood back to study the effect. "That looks very elegant." she said, pleased.

Amelia hugged her. "Thank you so much, Aunt Isabella, it is beautiful." She fingered the brooch studying the reflection in the mirror.

"Time to go." Aunt Isabella handed her her hat.

Smiling her thanks Amelia left the house.

Arthur Douglass' premises were too far away for Amelia to walk. Hiring a cab was of course out of the question so she went on an omnibus. Mrs Trevise had told Rose to go with her but Amelia was unyielding – if Rose went she would not. In the end Mrs Trevise had to give in but she was certain Amelia would have her pocket picked or be accosted by an undesirable male. She warned Amelia of these hazards several times a day and made Amelia promise to go inside the omnibus – no self-respecting woman would venture upstairs.

Amelia had been on an omnibus once with Papa. She remembered that as a pleasurable experience. Travelling on the inside of an omnibus on her own she found was not so pleasurable. The omnibus was drawn by a pair of dispirited horses. Amelia was certain they were not properly fed and mentioned this to the omnibus conductor who assured her that they "Lived like princes, miss. Don't you worry about them. Now where did you want to get off?"

Amelia explained that she wanted to get to Arthur Douglass Ltd.

"We stop right outside the offices, miss – bit of luck for you, eh?" as he took her fare.

The journey was slow and the wooden seats uncomfortable. Some of the other passengers stared at her and she was glad when the conductor called to her.

"Here you are, miss." and helped her off.

She stood on the pavement and tried to get her bearings. She had never been to this part of the city before. At first she thought that the conductor had set her down in the wrong place. As she turned round trying to see where she was she was jostled by passersby who all seemed to be in a great hurry.

As she turned her back on the road she saw that she stood in front of a dark brick building of two storeys bisected by an archway the iron gates of which were wide open. Four small windows, two up, two down fitted with iron bars glowered either side of the archway over which was painted in black lettering 'Arthur Douglass & Co – Toy manfs.' It did not look very friendly. She looked through the open gates into the courtyard beyond where several men were loading wooden crates onto a wagon. Taking a deep breath she walked through the gates. The men did not notice her until she was nearly on top of them.

"Can you tell me where the offices are, please?" she asked in as businesslike a voice as she could manage.

One of the men lowered his crate into position then pointed to an iron staircase leading up to a wooden door.

"Up there, miss."

She thanked him and, followed by the curious stares of the two men, made her way up the open iron stairs to a door marked "Office". She pushed her way through.

Inside, a wooden rail cut her off from the rest of the room. Men sat on tall wooden stools at high desks ranged down each side of the room busily writing in large ledgers. The only sound pens contacting paper and the rustle of turning pages.

A young boy appeared from nowhere.

"Yes, Miss?" he squeaked.

All the heads looked up, the pens stopped moving.

Speaking firmly Amelia stated "I wish to see Mr Douglass."

An older man sitting at a desk at the end of the room rose to his feet and came towards her, as he passed each desk the man seated at it resumed his work.

"I will deal with this, Roy," he waved the boy away. Roy moved away but stood within earshot.

"I am Higgins, Mr Douglass' Chief Clerk. Do you have an appointment?"

"No, but I am sure Mr Douglass will see me – he is a friend of my family."

Higgins pondered, taking in her plain clothes. He made up his mind.

"What name is it, miss?"

"Miss Wallace."

"Come this way, Miss Wallace." He held open a gate in the rail for her to walk through. As he led her down the room past the rows of desks each occupant remained deeply engrossed in his work, once past, however, she could feel several dozen eyes staring at her back. At the end of the room Mr Higgins led her through a door into a narrow corridor. Two doors faced them, the one on the left had 'Mr Jarrett – Chief Designer' in black paint, the one on the right 'Arthur Douglass' in gold paint on which Higgins tapped, listened, opened the door and announced

"Miss Wallace to see you, Mr Douglass."

Amelia found herself in a large room. Arthur Douglas was just getting up from his desk which was placed under a large window reaching from half way up the wall to just below the ceiling. To the right of the desk was a closed door. On the opposite side of the room and facing the closed door a table covered with toys.

Arthur indicated a chair by the desk. Once she was seated he went back and sat down. Leaning on his arms he bent towards her

"This is quite a surprise, Amelia. I hope that you are well? I have not seen John for some time. I understand that you are living with Mrs Trevise now?"

"Yes, I am keeping her company." Amelia did not think it was appropriate to go into the family problems. In any case she was sure that Arthur knew about them.

"I have come to ask you for a job as a Typewriter." She plunged in.

Arthur was astounded and looked at her with his mouth open for several seconds.

"A Typewriter! My dear Amelia that is quite out of the question."

"You have type writing machines in your offices, don't you?" Amelia asked dismayed. She had never considered the possibility that Arthur would be one of those men who considered a typewritten letter to be an insult to his customers.

"No, as a matter of fact I don't but if I did I should employ a male Typewriter not a female. There is no provision for a female in these offices. It would cause all sorts of difficulties."

"What kind of difficulties?"

Arthur was embarrassed.

"Of a delicate nature," he replied feeling rather warm.

"There must be some way round that problem." Arthur was not sure whether she knew what he was talking about. "Other employers have made arrangements. I don't mind sharing a lavatory with the other clerks. Miss Gaymin told us that we could not expect to have a separate lavatory."

"Who is Miss Gaymin?" Arthur gasped. He had known that Amelia was forthright as a child but now she had grown up into a forthright woman. He would not be surprised if she did not support the feminists who were making such a fuss at the moment. He definitely could not have anyone like Amelia distracting his male employees – although, poor thing, she was not likely to arouse their passions. He must get rid of her as painlessly as possible.

"The Principal of the College where I trained to be a Typewriter." She replied in answer to his question.

"No, I am afraid that there is no opening for you here, Amelia. Why don't you ask John, I am sure he would be pleased to give you something to do." A thought struck him. "What about those designs you were doing. Why not continue with those?" That would keep her busy he thought.

Amelia was annoyed to discover that he knew about her designs but she decided to let it go.

"It is no good working on designs if nobody will acknowledge that I *can* design, Mr Douglass. I want to be known as a designer but John will not employ me. I need to be independent. I am not going to take John's money. I want to earn my own and I can if only you will give me a post as a Typewriter."

"I am sorry that you feel you have to earn your living. I am sure that John would take you back and give you a home if you only ask him. His wife could probably do with your help. You must give up this idea of being independent, Amelia. Females are not independent, they are dependent upon their menfolk, and quite right too" he sounded heated.

Amelia saw that it was no good trying to persuade him. She rose to her feet

"Will you have some tea, Amelia?" he was sorry he had been so abrupt.

"No thank you, Mr Douglass. I must get back to Aunt Isabella she will wonder what has happened to me."

"I will see you back home."

"There is no need, I came on an omnibus."

Arthur shuddered.

"I will take you home in a hansom. Just let me have a word with my clerk."

He left the room. Amelia was tempted to leave and make her own way home but he had been kind in his own way so she allowed him take her home and even endured without complaint a lecture on the place of women in society.

CHAPTER TWENTY FIVE

Although he could not imagine why, Arthur was disturbed by Amelia's visit and slept badly in consequence. Lunching at his club the next day he found himself sharing a table with a number of men with whom he had a slight acquaintance. They were all younger than himself and considered to be very modern and up-to-date. He decided to ask their opinion of female Typewriters.

Waiting for a break in the conversation he remarked, "A young lady came to me in the office yesterday asking for a job as a Typewriter."

"Did you take her on?" one asked as he signalled to the waiter for another bottle of wine.

"No, I did not. I do not have a type writing machine."

"You must keep up with the times, Arthur. I have engaged a young lady who works very hard. I find that she is more accurate than some of my junior clerks."

Arthur thought about this then asked, "Do you pay her the same as a junior clerk?"

"Good Heavens, no! That is one of the advantages of employing women, they cost much less than a man." Seeing Arthur's puzzled expression he explained "Female Typewriters are much cheaper than male Typewriters. A female Typewriter is usually paid not more than 10/- per week whereas a junior male clerk will expect at least 15/- per week. Another consideration is that a type writing machine enables the operator to work faster than a clerk using a pen."

Arthur, being a good business man, found this a very good argument.

"How do the other clerks view her?"

"There is hardly any contact with the male staff. She works in my office and I make certain that she begins work after the other clerks and leaves before them. The arrangement works very well."

"Do you find that your clients object to having a typewritten letter instead of a handwritten one?" Arthur enquired.

"Some did object at first but most of them prefer it. They say it makes life much easier especially with figures on invoices. There is no doubt what the figures are with a type writing machine. From my point of view it is better because my Typewriter has a speed of 40 words per minute which is faster than a clerk can write."

Arthur mulled this over while the other men at the table also gave their opinions. They all agreed that a type writing machine in an office was an asset provided proper provision was made for the operator's segregation from the male clerks. As he listened he noted that they all mentioned the speed of their Typewriters, in fact they seemed to boast about it.

"What sort of speeds are possible?" he asked.

There was a chorus of replies from which he gathered that the speed varied from 30 to 60 words per minute.

"Do any of you employ male Typewriters?" he enquired.

Without exception they answered in the negative.

Arthur was very thoughtful that afternoon and Higgins was uneasy for, as he said to one of the other clerks,

"The boss is thinking – that means there is going to be trouble!"

The next morning Arthur called for Higgins and told him to go out and purchase a type writing machine. Higgins frowned. He had heard about type writing machines from other Chief Clerks. He supposed one might be useful. He hoped Mr Douglass did not expect him to operate it.

"Miss Wallace, the young lady who came the other day, will be employed to operate the machine."

Arthur could see that Higgins was not happy.

"We must go along with modern ideas, Higgins, otherwise we are going to be left behind. She will work in here with me. She will come in half an hour after the other clerks and leave half an hour before them."

Higgins ventured a statement. "I never thought we would employ women in the office, Mr Douglass."

"Neither did I, Higgins, but I have discovered that they are cheaper than junior clerks and that a type writing machine will enable us to get out more letters and invoices per day. More and more firms are using type writing machines – we must not allow ourselves to be considered old-fashioned that would be very bad for business. Miss Wallace will not, of course, have access to anything of a confidential nature. We all know that women cannot keep anything confidential."

Higgins nodded in agreement. He lived with his wife, his mother-in-law and two of her sisters. From personal experience he knew women to be incapable of keeping anything to themselves.

Another thought struck him. He hesitated. Arthur Douglass did not take kindly to interference from his staff no matter how well intentioned. He tentatively asked, "What about Mr Jarrett, Sir?"

"Mr Jarrett is not in control of this firm – yet. In any case Mr Jarrett is either away seeing clients or busy on his designs so I don't think Miss Wallace and Mr Jarrett will come into contact very often. To be frank with you, Higgins, I don't think Miss Wallace will be with us for very long. No woman can stick to anything long. When she realizes she can't take a day off to go and buy a new hat she will leave I am sure. Can you think of anything we need to do?"

"You will need another desk. I could clear the table under the window?"

"That seems an excellent idea. I will tell Miss Wallace to begin work next Monday. Fortunately she will not be a distraction to the men. As you saw God has seen fit to make her extremely plain which, so far as we are concerned, is a blessing."

CHAPTER TWENTY SIX

Amelia was bitterly disappointed. She had fully expected Mr Douglass to welcome her with open arms. She now realized that it was not going to be as easy as she had thought. When they got to Springfield Road Arthur helped her from the cab. She asked him if he would like to come in but he declined.Thanking him politely she walked to the front door which was opened by an excited Rose who, seeing her arrive home in a hansom had assumed that she had secured the post.When she saw Amelia's face however her heart sank

"You don't look very happy, Amelia."

"He would not give me a position, Rose. He has not even got a type writing machine." and she went straight to her room.

Rose wanted to go and talk to her but Mrs Trevise said it was best to leave her alone.

Amelia was feeling rejected. It was something which she had felt most of her life but repetition did not make it any easier to bear. She had set her heart on this position.

Mrs Trevise was secretly rather relieved that things had turned out as they had. She could not approve of young women working in offices. She regarded it as unfeminine.

When Amelia came down to dinner Mrs Trevise merely said that she was sorry that things had not gone the way she wanted.

"I have not given up." Amelia said defiantly. "I think I may go and see John tomorrow."

"Why not leave it until the day after tomorrow? Tomorrow we could go and do some shopping.You will need more clothes if you are going to work in a dirty office."

Amelia, who was really dreading having to go to John, agreed. She would have to go to John if only to get the money to pay back Aunt Isabella. However, she *did* need some new clothes. She told herself very firmly that the day after she would definitely go and see John however unpleasant that might turn out to be.

Their shopping trip was very successful. Amelia had to restrain Aunt Isabella from buying her totally unsuitable dresses.

"But these are so *drab*!" she protested.

"Miss Gaymin said we must always dress neatly and never wear anything which calls attention to ourselves," Amelia explained.

After breakfast the next day Amelia reluctantly put on her cloak and bonnet and was just about to leave the house when a hansom drew up outside. Perhaps John had come to her! However it was not John who descended from the cab, it was Mr Douglass. Amelia's heart suddenly began to race – she dared not hope – he was here to see Aunt Isabella about something – he had rejected her – she stood in the hall, rooted to the spot, as Rose answered the bell. As soon as Amelia saw Arthur's face she knew why he had come. Before he could speak she almost shouted, "Yes, the answer is yes, Mr Douglass!"

"I have not asked you yet, Amelia!" Arthur was glad that he did not have to beg. He had been afraid that she would take advantage of the situation and make him eat humble pie but here she was excited at the prospect.

Amelia remembered her manners.

"Come in," she said as she removed her cloak and bonnet and hung them on the hallstand.

"Aunt Isabella is lying down with a headache otherwise I am sure she would be very pleased to see you."

"I am sorry that Mrs Trevise is unwell. Please give her my best wishes for her speedy recovery."

By this time they were in the sitting room. Amelia turned to Rose who had shut the front door and followed them.

"Please bring some tea, Rose."

"Yes, miss," Rose always became the discreet servant when guests were in the house.

Arthur came straight to the point.

"I have been thinking about your proposition and I have been talking to some of my business acquaintances. The firm is in danger of being left behind. The world is moving at a much faster pace than it did when I was young, Amelia, so I am offering you the position of

Typewriter with my company. Your hours will be 8.30 to 5.30 Monday to Friday, half day on Saturday from 8.30 to 12 noon and you will be paid 10/- per week. You will take lunch with me from 12-1.00 and I will arrange for a hansom to pick you up in the morning and bring you home at night. I would be uneasy if you used the omnibus especially in the winter." He leaned back in his chair feeling that he had been extremely generous.

Amelia thought about it. Then came to a decision.

"I accept everything except the lunch."

Arthur opened his mouth to protest but Amelia continued.

"When I was training I found that the new Lyons Tea Shops were very good and I do not think it would be proper for me to lunch with you every day, Mr Douglass. People might talk."

Arthur was rather pleased he would not have to sacrifice his lunches at his club. He was amused that Amelia should think it would be cause for gossip if they were seen together.

"Very well, Amelia, if that is what you want but you will allow me to hire a hansom for you, won't you? Nobody can read anything into that especially as you will be coming home alone."

"I should be quite pleased not to have to take the omnibus," Amelia confessed. "But you must take the fare out of my salary."

Arthur knew what Amelia did not, namely that he was paying her much less than she was really worth, so he could afford to be magnanimous.

"Take it as part of your salary, Amelia". He remembered something else.

"By the way how many words a minute can you typewrite?"

"I have a certificate from the Gaymin Business College stating that I have reached a speed of 50 words per minute," she said proudly.

"Would you like me to show it to you?"

"Well done, Amelia. No, I will take your word for it." Arthur was pleased he could now boast about *his* Typewriter's speed when next in the Club. He rose and Amelia rose with him.

"Can you begin work on Monday or is that too soon? And should I ask your brother's permission before you begin?" he pondered.

"I can begin on Monday morning and I am sure that John will be pleased that I am working with someone he knows."

"Perhaps it would be better if I spoke to him first." Arthur wanted everything above board.

Amelia could see her new status as an independent woman slipping away.

"I will speak to him, Mr Douglass, and if he disapproves I will tell you immediately." She did not think it necessary to mention that she had had no contact with John for many months and that she had no intention of asking his permission to do anything. She considered it to be only a small lie in a good cause. She was very glad that Aunt Isabella was not present as she was sure that she would insist that John be consulted.

"There is one other thing. I think it would be best if I addressed you as 'Miss Wallace' when we are in the office."

"Yes, I understand, Mr Douglass."

He rose.

"I think that is all then – Miss Wallace – I look forward to seeing you on Monday – eight thirty sharp."

"I will be there," Amelia promised, eyes shining.

★★★★★

Amelia was in such a state of excitement that Rose and Mrs Trevise were very glad when Monday morning came and they could wave her off in the hansom which came to collect her prompt at eight o'clock.

When she entered the building she found both Mr Douglass and Higgins waiting in the outer office. As she walked beside Mr Douglass to his office she was very conscious of the extreme concentration on their work displayed by the male clerks. As soon as she entered the room she saw the new type writing machine on the desk under the window. Someone had even put a vase of flowers on the desk. She wondered who. It could not be Higgins as he barely concealed his disapproval of the whole affair. He was slightly mollified however to see that she was respectably dressed. There was one more thing which Arthur had to do. He debated whether or not to leave it with Higgins but decided that it was his duty to deal with it himself.

"As I explained to you, Miss Wallace, there is no special provision for female staff in the offices as we have never had female staff before. You may use my lavatory. If you will come with me I will show you where it is."

He led the way out of the office and down the corridor to a stone spiral staircase.

"Be careful when you come along here, Am . . . Miss Wallace – don't slip."

At the bottom of the stairs there were two doors, one mahogany, one plain wood. He indicated the mahogany door.

"Nobody but myself and Mr Jarrett uses this lavatory. You will find a mirror in there."

He then led the way back upstairs to the office where Higgins was sorting some papers on Mr Douglass' desk. Amelia glanced at him and smiled. Before he could stop himself he smiled back then hastily left the room. She began inspecting the brand new Remington on her desk.

"Are you sure you want me to be in here with you, Mr Douglass? The machine does make quite a lot of noise."

Since he had never heard a type writing machine Arthur was quite happy to say that he was sure everything would be fine.

Amelia began by cleaning and oiling her machine. Arthur watched her for a while and then began on his post. He was soon immersed and it was only after Amelia had coughed for the fourth time that he realized she had finished her cleaning.

"How often do you have to do that?"

"Every morning before I begin work. Miss Gaymin was very strict about that. She used to say 'If you look after your machine it will look after you'".

"I am sure she was right. I have an urgent letter here which must be answered at once. Can I dictate it to you?"

On searching the desk Amelia found some headed paper which she expertly fed into the machine. She hoped she would not make a mistake.

By the end of the morning she was quite pleased with her output and Arthur was pleased to find that most of his post had been dealt with at least an hour earlier than usual.

As he signed his letters Arthur told her to take them to Roy as it was his job to copy them in the letter copying book. She found Roy in the outer office. It was the first time that she had been in the outer office as a fellow employee and wondered how the men would react. She was quite disappointed when they ignored her completely.

Roy, the office boy, was already copying letters and she watched him as he deftly inserted a letter in the Letter Copying Book between two damp tissues, took her letters and did the same to them, placed the book in the press between two metal plates then turned the screw until the book was 'pressed'. After a few minutes he loosened the screw, removed the book, opened it, took out the letter, and there was a perfect copy on the tissue sheet.

"There you are, miss." Roy was proud of his expertize. "Leave the letters with me, miss, and I will enter them in the Postages Book."

Amelia did not like to ask what a Postages Book was. Perhaps she should have taken the full course after all! She made up her mind to learn all the procedures. Roy seemed to be a good teacher so perhaps, when she got to know him better, she would ask him to teach her all he knew.

Amelia went off to lunch and Arthur went off to his Club where he boasted about his new Typewriter. The afternoon was spent by Amelia in typing invoices. At five thirty she departed in a hansom feeling very pleased with her first day's work and also very tired.

Rose and Mrs Trevise were eager to know how she got on. Amelia regaled them with her working day as she hungrily devoured two helpings of Rose's steak and kidney pie.

Very soon Amelia could not remember when she had not worked for Arthur. Her first week's wages were a great thrill and she proudly handed Aunt Isabella five shillings towards the repayment of her debt.

When Arthur saw John at the Club he told him how pleased he was with Amelia's work.

"You should have let her work for you, John. You can't have her back" he laughed.

"What are you talking about, Arthur?" John enquired.

"She said she was going to tell you – at least, I think she did. You can never tell with Amelia, you think she is agreeing to one thing when you find she had something else in mind all along."

Arthur then told John how it was that Amelia was working for him.

John was extremely angry with his sister. He went straight round to Mrs Trevise. He had another shock when Rose opened the door. Something else he had not been told. He was pleased that Rose had found a place, he had felt guilty at dismissing her. Now he just demanded to see Miss Amelia at once.

Rose took one look at his face and went into the sitting room where Amelia was telling Mrs Trevise about her day at the office.

"It's Mr John, Amelia. He looks angry."

Mrs Trevise glanced at Amelia who looked shocked.

"Ask Mr Wallace to come in," she ordered.

John strode into the room.

"Will you have some tea?" Mrs Trevise politely enquired.

"No! – er – thank you. I want to speak to Amelia – urgently."

Mrs Trevise rose at once.

"If you will excuse me I will go and speak to Rose about next week's menus." Neither John nor Amelia saw her go.

"What is all this nonsense about you working for Arthur Douglass as a Typewriter?" he demanded.

"It is not nonsense – I *am* working for Mr Douglass *and* earning money doing so."

"And where did you get the money for the training? Not from me, you refused *my* money."

"Aunt Isabella lent me the money."

"*Lent* you the money – this is worse than I thought! Do you have any idea what you are doing? First you leave home, then you take a job. How do you think that makes me look? People will think that I cannot support my own sister. What do you think *that* will do to the business? You didn't think of that did you? That's your trouble, Amelia, you have never thought of anyone but yourself! You can pack your things, you are coming home with me."

"No, I am not. I am happy here. I have a job I enjoy and I do well. It is the first time I have ever been free."

"Free! What stupid talk is that? Where do you get these ideas, Amelia?"

"I have been attending meetings of the NUWS for some time. Women should have the same rights as men to either marry or not as they please. They should also be allowed to become professional women if they wish."

"Father gave you too much freedom and this is the result." his voice rose "I have had enough of this – get your things." He strode to the door and flung it open. "Come along, hurry up. I will inform Arthur that you will not be going back to work."

"No, I will not go with you. I am not going to be Selina's servant."

"What else is there for you? We both know that you will never marry. All this business of working women will soon be a thing of the past it cannot suceed, then where will you be? Don't rely on Mrs Trevise keeping you. Much better to come home with me to Mama and make the best of it."

Rose and Mrs Trevise arrived in the hall at the same time wondering what was happening. John turned to Mrs Trevise.

"Amelia is coming home with me. Thank you for looking after her but she is obviously too much for you to handle. I will reimburse you for her fees."

Mrs Trevise's eyes flashed.

"I think I heard Amelia say that she did not want to go with you. Selina is my daughter and I love her but we both know what sort of life Amelia would have with her. This is *my* house, John, and I must ask you to leave."

Rose went and pointedly opened the front door.

John, confronted by three determined females, decided to try once more.

"Come on, Amelia – I am sorry I shouted at you. Be a good girl and come home. I will let you do some more designs for me."

"I am not coming, John. Give my love to Mama."

John lost his temper – he had tried to be understanding and this was the result – defiance! He was the head of the family after all! This could not be tolerated.

"You have not heard the last of this, Amelia. You were stubborn as a child and now you have grown into a stubborn young woman." then he added, childishly, "I will tell Mama, *then* you will be sorry!" and wondered why they burst out laughing. He could still hear their laughter as he walked briskly down the path to the gate.

John went straight home and told Selina and Sophia all that had happened. As he expected, Selina was indignant on his behalf. Perversely she now decided she needed Amelia with her. Sophia was silent. John asked her what she thought.

"I think that if Amelia is happy she should stay where she is."

John and Selina both looked at her in astonishment. Selina was the first to reply.

"Really, Mama, you do not know what you are saying. My Mama will not live for ever and then what will Amelia do? Nobody is likely to want to marry her and who could blame them? A blind man might I suppose... I am quite willing to forget her previous conduct and take her back. On certain conditions of course." She counted them off on her fingers: "1 She must always obey me. 2 She must never see Rose again. 3 She will stay in her room when we have guests. 4 She must wear a veil when she goes out. 5 She must . . .

Sophia interrupted. "I meant every word I said, Selina. I am glad Amelia is away from you. You are spoilt and selfish. I would not dream of subjecting my daughter to your 'conditions'." She turned to John and laid her hand on his arm. "I am truly sorry for you, John." then before he could speak, "I realize that after what I have said I cannot stay here. I will go and stay with Grace. She has written to ask me to go until the new baby is born. I can make myself useful there. I am not needed here since Selina has decided not to have any babies and yes I do believe Amelia's story regarding Selina's miscarriage. You are a very wicked girl, Selina, and I regret the day my son met you." She then left the room. Selina collapsed in hysterics. John was still trying to calm her down when Sophia left the house.

Before going to catch the train for Edinburgh Sophia called in at Springfield Road to see Amelia. They had a tearful reunion. Sophia told Amelia and Mrs Trevise all that had passed between herself, John and Selina. Mrs Trevise invited her to stay the night but Sophia did not want to stay in close proximity to No. 13. She gave Amelia her blessing, told her that, if necessary, she would always be welcome in Edinburgh and departed.

CHAPTER TWENTY SEVEN

Spring turned into a very hot Summer and Amelia half regretted having to stay in a hot office instead of being out in the park. She knew that Mr Douglass was pleased with her work as she had heard him telling Higgins that he did not know how they had managed before she came to work for them. From being against all forms of change Mr Douglass was becoming converted to the new technology and, like any convert, he was going over the top.

Amelia and Martha met frequently for lunch to exchange news and gossip. They still went to Meetings together although Martha did not seem to be as enthusiastic as she once was.

After Martha had made a feeble excuse for the second time in a row Amelia began to realize that something was different about her friend. Eventually, over one of their lunches, Martha finally confessed that she had a young man who apparently did not like the idea of the National Women's Movement. Amelia was inclined to be scornful until she realized that she was upsetting Martha.

"You really like him, don't you?" she stated.

Martha said that she did. In fact they were going out to Surrey to see his parents the next Sunday and she was hoping that he would ask her to marry him. Although not in regular contact the two families were acquainted and Albert was, in fact, some sort of distant cousin.

After she had left Martha and returned to work she was walking down the corridor to Mr Douglass's office and reflecting how swiftly the month had gone when she became aware of raised voices from Mr Douglass's room. She hesitated, not knowing whether to go in. Then Higgins appeared from nowhere.

"That's Mr Jarrett, the Chief Designer, in with Mr Douglass. I think you had better wait until he has gone."

"I have to go downstairs anyway, Mr Higgins. Perhaps Mr Jarrett will be gone when I come back."

She went down the spiral stairs to the lavatory and took her time putting her hair straight. When she thought she had taken sufficient time she went back upstairs. She walked along the corridor to Mr Douglass' room and listened outside the door.

She could hear nothing so she tapped on the door, Mr Douglass called "Come in." He began to speak before she was through the door.

"Ah, Higgins," as he spoke he looked up from the paper he was perusing and saw Amelia. There was another man in the room – this must be Mr Jarrett – Mr Douglass' son-in-law. She was not quite sure what to do. Should she speak first or wait for him? Mr Douglass saved her the trouble by saying, "This is the young lady I was telling you about, Simon. A very great asset she is too. This is Mr Jarrett back from his business trip as you can see, Amelia – I should say, Miss Wallace." he chuckled to himself.

Mr Jarrett looked Amelia up and down and narrowed his eyes.

"What name did you say, Arthur?" he asked without taking his eyes off her.

"Miss Wallace."

"I see. How do you do, Miss Wallace. Tell me, are you a relation of John Wallace of Wallace & Sons?"

"I am his sister," Amelia grudgingly admitted.

"I thought as much." was the enigmatic reply.

Amelia did not like this man. She did not like the way he looked at her and his voice sounded familiar but how could it be – she had never met him before.

"Will you typewrite some letters for me?" he asked.

Amelia looked at Mr Douglass, after all she was employed by him, not Mr Jarrett.

"I do not see why not. She is very fast, Simon. That machine saves us two junior clerks at the very least." Arthur sounded as if he was excusing her presence.

"I am sure it does. I will bring them in some time this afternoon, Miss Wallace."

Amelia watched him walk through the connecting door into his room. Simon – she seemed to know that name but she could not remember in what connection – anyway there must be hundreds of Simons. She put it from her mind.

Later that afternoon Mr Jarrett came back to dictate his letters. She felt unaccountably nervous and could not understand why. However she did her usual efficient job and thought no more about it.

When she went in the next morning Mr Douglass was very quiet. Before he dictated his letters he came over to her desk.

"I am very pleased with your work, Amelia," he said. The use of her christian name did not escape her notice. She thanked him.

"However, you must give other people's work the same attention that you give mine."

Amelia did not understand and looked up at him, puzzled. Arthur continued. "Mr Jarrett has complained that the work you did for him yesterday was full of errors." she opened her mouth to protest but he held up his hand.

"I can appreciate that you do not know him and that possibly that made you nervous but you must remember that you are working, not just for me, but for the firm as a whole. When I am absent Mr Jarrett is in charge. Now we will say no more about it as I am sure you will do better next time," he said kindly.

Amelia had the good sense not to reply. She was sure that her work had been correct but she had been nervous and could have missed a mistake.

Mr Douglass went out for lunch at his usual time not returning for several hours.

During the afternoon Mr Jarrett came in carrying some papers.

"I have some urgent letters here, Miss Wallace, they must go off this evening. Please check them very thoroughly. Bring them to me when you have finished and I will sign them so that Roy can take them to the post."

His handwriting was very difficult to read but at length she deciphered it. She checked each letter twice and not until she was certain they were correct did she get up and tap on the half open connecting door. There was no response. She went into the room. It was empty. She waited for twenty minutes by the large office clock on the wall. Then she went and sat at her desk where she could see through the connecting door. By 5.30 he had not come back, neither had Mr Douglass. She knew her hansom would be waiting. She did not know what to do. In the end she found Higgins and asked his advice.

"Give me the letters, Miss Wallace, Roy can copy them. I can give them to Mr Jarrett to sign when he comes back."

She was happy to leave the letters with Higgins, after all she had completed her duty by typing them. She put on her hat and went home.

The next day, being Saturday, she was looking forward to her one and a half days of freedom. She was meeting Martha that afternoon and she was eager to hear whether or not Martha's young man had asked her to marry him. Although, for Martha's sake she hoped that he had, she would be sad to lose her friend. There would be no more cosy lunches on weekdays once Martha was married since she would have to leave her employment. No married woman worked – not even widows.

Martha was at Lyons before her and from her happy smile Amelia knew the news was good. They spent an enjoyable afternoon discussing wedding arrangements.

The rest of the weekend passed swiftly and in no time at all it was Monday once more.

When she got into the office Mr Douglass dealt with his post and then said, "I am going down the factory to look at that new machine."

She smiled as he went bustling off. He was like a child with a new toy. The smile faded as the connecting door was flung open and Mr Jarrett stormed into the room.

"Those urgent letters – why did you not bring them to me yourself?"

"I thought Mr Higgins…"

"Higgins waited for me until I came in, he then took them to the post. He knew how important they were. He did your job."

"I waited until five thirty. I had a hansom waiting."

"You had a hansom waiting. Why can't you come on the omnibus like other working people? I suppose because you are John Wallace's sister you are too grand to ride in a common omnibus!"

Amelia knew that at all costs she must keep her temper.

"Mr Douglass insisted..." she began.

"Mr Douglass insisted on what?" came Arthur's familiar voice.

Before she could reply Mr Jarrett said, "Arthur, I am afraid your Miss Wallace has let herself down." He then went on to repeat his complaint. Arthur listened intently then, when Simon had finished he turned to Amelia.

"Is this correct, Amelia?"

"Yes, Mr Douglass."

"What were you about to say when I came in?"

"I was going to explain to Mr Jarrett that you had insisted on my having a cab to and from the office."

"Quite right – I don't approve of young ladies using the omnibus also, Simon, it is part of Miss Wallace's wages."

"Had I been using the omnibus I would have waited but I knew the cab would be there and I did not want to involve you in extra expense, Mr Douglass. I saw Mr Higgins before I went and I understand he made sure the letters were copied, signed and put in the mail."

"Well that's alright, then. Was there anything else, Simon?"

Simon glared at Amelia, turned to Arthur with "No, that was all," and went back into his room.

Mr Douglass settled down to dictating letters. At five thirty he looked at the wooden office clock and announced – with a twinkle "Time for you to get your fairy coach, Cinderella."

After she had gone Arthur sat looking thoughtfully into space.

Amelia was apprehensive for the rest of the week but she had no more encounters with Mr Jarrett. He was away all the following week and things went back to their old routine.

A few days after his return Simon brought her some orders to type. He was very polite and she hoped they were on a better footing after their bad start.

Again Mr Douglass was in the factory when Mr Jarrett slammed through the connecting door.

"This will not do, Miss Wallace! The print on these orders is so faint that I cannot read the figures."

She looked at the orders – true the print was a little faint but she could read it well enough.

"I think..." she began. Mr Jarrett interrupted her

"That is the trouble, you *don't* think, Miss Wallace. Now, what do you have to do to make these orders legible?"

Amelia gulped, she was close to tears but she was determined *he* would never know it.

"I change the ribbon, Mr Jarrett. I will do that straight away before I go home."

"You will indeed and you will retype the orders – they are urgent. And make sure that you wash your hands afterwards I don't want finger marks all over them!" He slammed back into his office.

As she set about the messy task she pondered. It was obvious to her that Mr Jarrett was doing everything he could to get her dismissed. Why? She turned the matter over in her mind several times during the morning but could think of no reason. She half expected Mr Jarrett to find something else wrong but he did not. Perhaps she was being too sensitive.

At twelve noon she tidied her desk ready to begin work on Monday morning. Mr Douglass had still not returned he was probably operating his new machine something which he often did much to the amusement of his workers.

She was in a hurry as she was going home to change before she met Martha. She wanted to get out of her working clothes. She had arranged to meet Martha in the park as it was still sunny and warm. She got to their particular seat early and was pleased to see that it was vacant. She sat enjoying the sun. Soon she saw her friend in the distance arm in arm with a man. As they got nearer Amelia could see that he was very dark with a small moustouche. He was considerably shorter than Martha. Surely this could not be Albert?

They had hardly got within earshot when Martha said excitedly

"This is Albert, Amelia."

Amelia was very pleased for her friend but she could not see what Martha saw in him. However she smiled and held out her hand.

"Congratulations! I am so pleased to meet you at last."

"Thank you. I have heard all about you from Martha so I feel I know you. May I call you Amelia?"

"Of course." she replied as she shook his hand.

Martha beamed. "We are going to be married in six weeks time. And I want you to be my fourth bridesmaid."

Amelia was speechless. Misunderstanding her silence Martha said, "Do say that you will, Amelia. I am sure that Mrs Trevise would allow it."

Amelia recovered herself.

"I am sure that she would and thank you, Martha, I should be proud to be your bridesmaid."

"That's settled then. You must come and meet my mother and sisters so that we can discuss dress patterns."

Martha turned back to Albert. Amelia watched them as they stood by the seat from which Amelia had risen. There were people passing by, children running about and Amelia standing by them but she could see that so far as they were concerned they were the only people in the world. For the first time she felt an emptiness. No man would ever look at her like that. She had never before felt so cursed by her plainness. Well, there it was.

Her practical side took over. She invented some work that she had to do so that she could leave them together. Martha barely managed to say goodbye. Amelia was not sure whether they realized she had gone. When she got to a bend in the path she looked back to see them sitting on the seat, heads close together.

*****

Amelia was very quiet all that weekend and Mrs Trevise was afraid that she was working too hard.

"Are you sure it is not too much for you, Amelia?" she asked her one evening after she had spoken to her for the second time without receiving a reply.

Amelia had been debating within herself whether to tell Aunt Isabella about Mr Jarrett and ask her advice but she was sure she would tell her to leave so she only said, "We are rather busy at the moment. I expect it will be better once the new machines are properly installed. Mr Douglass was so pleased with them that he insisted on being the first person to use them. I don't think the men were very pleased!"

Usually Mrs Trevise liked to hear about the goings on at the factory but now she only half listened. She was sure that there was something Amelia was not telling her. Perhaps she had a hankering after one of the men in the office. She did hope not but Amelia was growing up and sooner or later she would find out what she was missing.

By Monday morning Amelia felt better and was thankful that she had a job that required concentration. That would soon dispel her depression! It was not to be however.

Scarcely had Amelia and Mr Douglass begun on the correspondence when Mr Jarrett flung into the room.

"I am sorry, Arthur, but I have to show you these. I was hoping that Miss Wallace would improve after the talk you had with her. She is careless in her work. Just look at the mess on these letters – I told her they were urgent and I also told her to wash her hands after she had dealt with the machine but she has chosen to ignore my instructions!"

Amelia sat in frozen disbelief. She *knew* the letters were clean. At least they had been when she put them on Mr Jarrett's desk. A suspicion began to form in her mind.

"May I see them?" she asked mildly.

"I think you have done enough damage, don't you?" and Mr Jarrett held the papers away from her outstretched hand. Instead he gave them to Mr Douglass who looked at them and tutted.

"I wanted you to see them before I sent for a clerk to copy them out again."

Before she could stop herself Amelia burst into tears.

Mr Douglass looked distressed. Simon snorted.

"Now we have the usual female trick of tears when things are getting difficult. That is why women will never survive in the business world, Arthur. They just can't take the strain. They have no conception of business. They…"

"Thank you, Simon, I think you have made your point."

Amelia thought Mr Douglass sounded annoyed with Mr Jarrett. Perhaps he didn't like him either even if he was his son-in-law!

"Well, is she going to be dismissed?" Simon was sounding almost hysterical. Arthur looked at him speculatively – could it be that there was more behind this than at first appeared? Why should Simon want Amelia dismissed? She was no threat to him. A suspicion floated across his mind only to be instantly dismissed – poor Amelia was hardly the stuff that mistresses were made of!

"I have never had cause to complain about Miss Wallace's work."

Simon went red in the face with rage.

Arthur asked "Why are you so anxious to have her dismissed, Simon?"

"I will not discuss this in front of *her*." Simon shouted.

Amelia felt acutely uncomfortable.

"I think it would be better if you went home, Miss Wallace." Arthur saw her face go white and added, "This is in no way a dismissal but Mr Jarrett and I need to discuss this. I will come and see you sometime tomorrow."

Higgins was rung for and Amelia found him extremely kind. It was plain that the whole of the outer office had heard Mr Jarrett's ranting. Higgins steered her past the curious gaze of the clerks and out of the building. As they were waiting for a hansom to appear he said

"If it is any comfort to you, Miss Wallace, we all think that you are doing a very good job. I must admit that I was dismayed when Mr Douglass said he was going to employ a Typewriter but having seen your work and how conscientious you are I have changed my mind about women in the office – only some women mind who, like yourself, are willing to work hard. We don't like Mr Jarrett very much in the outer office. Don't you worry, I am sure Mr Douglass will get things sorted out for you."

It was the longest speech she had ever heard him make and certainly the longest to her. She sat back in the hansom feeling a mixture of anger at Mr Jarrett's attitude, worry about what Mr Douglass would do and pleasure that Higgins thought she was good at her work.

Mrs Trevise was very surprised to see her home so soon. When Amelia told her why Aunt Isabella's reaction was to tell her to leave immediately. Amelia tried to convince her that she enjoyed working with Mr Douglass and told her what Higgins had said. Aunt Isabella's anxieties were only slightly alleviated.

Amelia spent a sleepless night going over and over the events of the day. In the morning she was tired and headachy but no nearer a solution. She wondered how long she would have to wait before Mr Douglass came to tell her her fate.

He came early in the morning. One look at her white face and the dark rings under her eyes told him how she was suffering. He felt extremely angry with Simon. After Amelia had left there had been a scene. One thing had led to another and Arthur had more or less accused Simon of ill-treating his daughter. Arthur was sure that Higgins was listening at the door but he didn't care. Simon was beside himself with anger. Arthur began to wonder whether he was quite sane. He felt renewed anxiety for his daughter.

"You can have your precious daughter back – she is no use to me." Simon was almost incoherent with rage. "I will send her to you bag and baggage. <u>You</u> can put up with her spiteful tongue."

Arthur kept his temper with difficulty. Losing it now would do more harm than good and he wanted his daughter safe under his roof as soon as possible.

"Eleanor can come and stay with us for a while. Her mother is always asking when she will visit. We never seem to see her these days. So far as Miss Wallace is concerned, as I have never had any cause for complaint regarding her work I suggest that she works only for me and you can go back to using the male clerks. I am sure that is the best way out of the dilemma."

"I want you to dismiss her. I don't want her working for my firm" Simon spat.

Arthur decided that the time had come to remind Simon of a few things.

"It is *my* firm, Simon, and I will employ whomever I wish."

Simon had the good sense to realize that he had gone too far. He made a great effort to calm down. He even tried to smile – it was ghastly and Arthur made a mental note to get Eleanor out of his clutches permanently as soon as possible whatever it cost in money or reputation.

"Yes, I think that would be the best thing to do. I have to go to Paris next week in any case. Eleanor can come and stay with you while I am away."

Arthur was relieved to see that he was looking more composed. That afternoon Arthur went to see his solicitor and altered his will to make sure that Simon did not inherit any part of the firm.

Now he looked at Amelia and knew he had done the right thing. He explained the decision which had been made. Amelia breathed a sigh of relief – she didn't want to see Mr Jarrett again, ever, but she supposed she must. Arthur could see what was going through her mind.

"Mr Jarrett has had to go away to the Paris Exhibition at the end of the week so I suggest you take the rest of the week off. I will tell Higgins that you are ill as I shall have to use one of his clerks. I shall miss you but it is better you keep out of Simon's way. I hope he will return with some new ideas for us. Christmas will soon be here but then you know all about that, Amelia. Tell me, are you still designing?"

She shook her head.

"That is a pity. You were very good, you know."

Amelia smiled and again shook her head. She had learnt that it was a man's world and that it was no use trying to alter the system. The women at the Union of Women Meetings didn't know what they were up against.

Amelia and Martha went to no more meetings. Martha was too busy getting everything ready for her wedding and Albert did not approve of her attending them. Amelia because she now considered it a waste of time. Emancipation for women was a pipe dream which would never come true. Much better to get on with her life as best she could.

She wondered what would happen when Mr Jarrett came back from Paris but she was happy to leave that to Mr Douglass. She remembered with gratitude what he had said about her designs but she was sure she would never design anything again. She was grown up now and knew the ways of the world. When she had wanted to design she had been a child, better to forget all about it.

CHAPTER TWENTY EIGHT

During the weeks leading to Martha's wedding Amelia spent a great deal of time with Martha's family. They were nice, uncomplicated people and she felt at ease with them. Martha's father was a conductor on an omnibus and would regale them with lively descriptions of the people who rode with him. He teased Amelia about being 'a lady who always rides in a hansom'. There were always plenty of comings and goings.

There were three sisters at home and two brothers. They all seemed very happy together, unlike Amelia and her siblings. Martha's mother took a particular fancy to Amelia and made a fuss of her whenever she went for a fitting. Never at any time did any of them give even a hint that she was different to any other girl. She was still not sure about being a bridesmaid and mentioned it one day to Mrs Ibbotson, who with a mouth full of pins, was kneeling on the floor at Amelia's feet.

"Do you think it is right for me to be Martha's bridesmaid, Mrs Ibbotson?"

Mrs Ibbottson very carefully removed the pins from her mouth.

"Why ever not? You are Martha's friend and she would be so disappointed if you were not with her on her special day. Think how she would feel if you backed out now. I brought my children up to see behind the externals, Amelia."

No one in the Ibbotson household was allowed to feel sorry for themselves!

Amelia prayed that the weather would be fine for her friend and her prayers were answered. Martha looked radiant, just as a bride should, and the church service was beautiful. Amelia found that she was trying not to cry. She had remembered Mrs Ibbottson's words and taken no notice of the slight ripple as she followed Martha's sisters down the aisle.

The reception was being held at the house and it was a crush as both Martha and Albert had large families and numerous friends.

After the toasts and speeches Amelia found herself sitting in a little island of peace while she sipped her champagne and nibbled her piece of wedding cake. She watched Martha and Albert as they laughed and joked with their guests. They looked so happy. She would never have a wedding and someone to love her as Albert loved Martha. When they turned and glanced at each other she could hardly bear it.

"May I sit here?" a voice asked.

She looked up to see a tall thin man standing over her. He was against the light so it was difficult to see his features. For a moment she thought it was Mr Jarrett and she jumped, spilling some of the champagne on her dress.

"I am sorry, I didn't mean to startle you." he was contrite. He left her to go and fetch a chair which he placed next to hers. She turned to look at him. He was quite old so it would be in order for her to talk to him without an older person being present. In any case what could anyone see in *her* talking to a man!

"I work in the same office as Albert." he looked at her enquiringly.

"I am one of Martha's friends – we trained together."

"Ah yes – what a pity that training is going to waste in Martha's case. You are not married?"

Amelia laughed.

"No, my name is Amelia Wallace. I work in an office, too – Arthur Douglass & Co., do you know it?"

"I have heard of it, of course. They manufacture toys, I believe? I am in a Solicitor's office myself." He made the distinction between a mere factory office and a Solicitor's office very plain.

Amelia nodded. She didn't know what to say next. The champagne was making her feel light-headed.

"My name is Frederick Leros."

At that moment Martha's sister came for Amelia to help the other bridesmaids get Martha into her going away clothes. As Amelia was buttoning up the many little buttons on the back of her dress Martha remarked, "I noticed you speaking to Frederick Leros."

"What do you know about him?" Amelia enquired.

"Not very much, he has only just joined the firm but dear Albert did not think it was very nice to invite the others and not him."

"So you don't really know anything about him?"

"No, but I am sure he is very nice. My Albert says that he is a gentleman."

Privately Amelia was getting a little tired of the sayings of Albert but she would never dream of letting Martha know this.

Amelia was thoughtful as she went out with the other guests to wave Albert and Martha off on their honeymoon. As she turned to go back into the house, feeling rather flat, Frederick Leros approached her.,

"Can I see you home, Miss Wallace? The party seems to be breaking up now."

Amelia was not sure what to say but she could not see that there was anything wrong in being escorted home by a man who must be the same age as Arthur Douglass.

On the way they talked about the wedding. Frederick expressed the opinion that Albert was a very nice young man who would undoubtedly go a long way in his profession. Amelia murmured agreement. She was wondering whether she should ask him in. This dilemma was resolved when he said, as the cab drew up outside the house

"Forgive me if I do not take you to the door, Miss Wallace. I have a pressing engagement and I must go but I would like to see you again. May I call for you on Sunday? Perhaps we could go for a walk in the park?"

Amelia felt a little flustered but stammered that that would be very nice.

*****

When she entered the house Aunt Isabella was eager to hear all about the wedding. When Amelia mentioned Frederick Leros she became very interested. She wanted to know who he was, who his people were, where did he live. Amelia had to confess that she did not know. Aunt Isabella was disappointed but cheered up when Amelia asked if she thought it would be improper for her to go for a walk in the park with Frederick on Sunday. Aunt Isabella was delighted but said she must meet him first.

On Sunday Amelia was very nervous. She did not know what to wear and in the end Rose had to take a dress from her wardrobe and tell her that was the one she was going to wear. Then she tied her into her stays. Amelia had always hated constriction of any kind but in order to achieve the sheath-like princess style now fashionable she had to submit although not without complaint. Rose helped her into her brown dress and fluffed out the flounces at the back. A brown toque trimmed with feathers completed her ensemble. Rose looked at her critically then nodded and handed her her gloves and reticule.

"Remember not to talk too much, Amelia. And none of your clever remarks! Gentlemen do not like clever girls. After you are married you can be as clever as you like."

"Really, Rose, nobody has mentioned marriage – we are only going to walk in the park!"

"One thing leads to another, so be careful." Rose said darkly.

Promptly at two Frederick rang the bell. It was opened almost immediately by Rose who had been standing in the hall waiting for him. She was a little disappointed to see that he was older than she had imagined but as long as Amelia liked him. Everyone knew the old saying that it was 'better to be an old man's darling than a young man's slave'! She showed him into the drawing room where Mrs Trevise was, to all intents and purposes, engrossed in a book of sermons.

"Mr. Leros, madam." said Rose in her best parlour maid voice.

As they exchanged pleasantries Mrs Trevise studied him. She also was a little disappointed that he was not a handsome young man but then she supposed that poor Amelia could not pick and choose. She hoped that he saw the same things in Amelia that she did. He seemed a nice person.

"We take tea at four, Mr. Leros. Perhaps you would like to join us?"

"Thank you, no. I have to get back to my sister. She likes me to take tea with her."

"Of course, I quite understand." Here was a chance to get the information that Amelia did not seem to have.

"Do you belong to a large family?"

"No, I do not, Mrs Trevise."

She could not think that a man of his age had not been married but could not think of a polite way of asking this vital question. As she was pondering Amelia came into the room. Mrs Trevise looked at her with affection. She might not be particularly pretty but today she looked almost presentable. She did hope that something would come of it. Then Amelia could leave that dreadful factory office and have a home of her own, even children perhaps. Mrs Trevise began a daydream about the sort of house Amelia would have as she stood at the window and watched them walk down the path together.

Rose went about her duties with only half her mind on her work and Mrs Trevise gave up any pretence of reading. Rose in the kitchen and Mrs Trevise in the drawing room were both wishing the same thing – that this would be the beginning of a new chapter for Amelia.

Amelia herself was feeling much the same. She had very shyly taken Frederick's profferred arm as they strolled through the park talking of ordinary things. Thinking back afterwards she realized that she had told him all about her job with Arthur and her estrangement from John even about Grace and Gerald but he had not told her anything about his family except that he lived with his sister who was unmarried.

Amelia thought this a little strange but then she had no experience of men other than her brother. She envisaged herself telling an astonished John and Selina that she was going to be married – how amazed they would be that ugly little Amelia had managed to find herself a man! Amelia pulled herself up short – what was she thinking of, she had only been for one walk in the park! But, a little voice in her head slyly told her, he had asked if he could come again the next Sunday!

At the office things were much better. Mr Jarrett was still away but he was expected back at the end of the following week. As the weekend approached Amelia began to look forward to her walk with Frederick. Perhaps he would ask her to meet his sister this week. But he did not, not that week nor the next nor the next. By the middle of August Amelia was sure that he was not going to ask her. She still knew no more about him than she had at the beginning.

It was very hot and she felt depressed and listless when she went to work on Saturday morning. The weather was heavy and the storm that Aunt Isabella had been expecting for a month seemed about to break. She felt bad-tempered and hot in her thick skirt. Cleaning her machine was a very sticky job and she almost decided not to do it but Miss Gaymin's ghost would not be stilled. As she began the first flash of lightning followed by a crack of thunder made her sigh with relief – at least it would be cooler now. Arthur looked up from his desk.

"I think I will just go down the factory and see how things are."

Amelia smiled – she knew he was worried in case any of his precious machines got struck by lightning! She hoped that the weather would not break so that she could meet Frederick as usual in the park. She got the impression that he did not want to meet Aunt Isabella again which disappointed her as she had hoped they would become friends. Aunt Isabella had said nothing when Amelia had explained that Frederick had decided it would be best if they met in the park in future.

The weather was cooler but fine when Amelia went to meet Frederick. She would like to do something other than stroll round the park for several hours before Frederick had to go and have tea with his sister but she did not know how to approach the subject without sounding rude and ungrateful. She did not want Frederick to stop seeing her. For the first time he was late and she wondered if she had offended him in some way but then she saw him in the distance. He did not apologize when he finally reached her where she stood by the lake. He seemed pre-occupied and Amelia gave up trying to start a conversation. Finally, just before he was due to leave her, he said:

"I should like to take you to meet my sister next Sunday. I will call for you at two o'clock." Before she could answer he raised his hat and left her in the middle of the path. Amelia could not understand what was the matter with him. Surely his sister was not such an ogre that he was afraid of her? She decided not to mention this worry to Aunt Isabella as she had a suspicion that she did not approve of Frederick.

Amelia told her that Frederick had asked her to go with him to meet his sister the following Sunday. Amelia was not sure whether she wanted to meet Miss Leros or not. She was very nervous. A man did not ask an unmarried girl to meet his family unless he was thinking of proposing to her.

The week seemed to drag and Arthur asked her with concern if she was quite well. Sunday finally came and she was ready and waiting well before two. She would have opened the door and gone to the gate to meet him but Aunt Isabella would not let her.

"It is not a good idea to appear too eager, Amelia. Let him ring the bell."

Amelia impatiently waited in the drawing room while Rose let him ring twice before she answered the door although she was standing just the other side of it. She then went through the ritual of asking him whom he had come to see and that she would see if Miss Wallace was in etc., etc. Finally, when Amelia was about ready to scream she showed him into the drawing room.

"Good afternoon, Mr Leros." Mrs Trevise looked up from her book.

"Good afternoon, Mrs Trevise. Are you ready, Amelia?" He seemed impatient to be off.

"Yes, Frederick." Amelia said brightly.

"Come along then, I have a cab waiting."

Amelia kissed Mrs Trevise goodbye.

"Where does your sister live?" enquired Mrs Trevise.

"Not very far but it looks like rain so I thought a cab would be sensible."

Mrs Trevise nodded and watched them walk from the room. She felt uneasy but did not know why.

Amelia gave Rose a smile as they left the house. She did not turn back as they walked down the path but she knew that Rose was watching them.

"I am so looking forward to meeting your sister." Amelia chattered as they rode along. "I hope that she likes me." she said uncertainly. She wanted some assurance from Frederick that he loved her.

"I am sure she will." Frederick seemed dismissive. "She is anxious to meet you. I have told her all about you."

Amelia was not sure what that meant. Presumably that she was not the good-looking girl that an affectionate sister would want her brother to marry.

Suddenly she felt extremely nervous. What was she doing? Had she made up her mind to marry Frederick? She would never get another offer, she knew. He had not said that he loved her or had done anything other than let her hold his arm and even that seemed a struggle for him.

The last time she had been to visit Martha and Albert in their cosy little house Martha had told her that she was pregnant. Amelia was happy for her friend. Martha had asked her about her meetings with Frederick and Martha had been delighted for her. She was so happy in her own marriage that she wanted everyone to be married and as happy as herself. Did she love Frederick? She did not know. Perhaps it would come with marriage. She realized that Frederick was speaking to her.

"Here we are."

The cab had stopped outside a large double-fronted house protected from the road by a row of black iron railings. For some reason the railings made Amelia feel uneasy, they looked so solid and somehow threatening. The house also looked in some way unfriendly. As Frederick paid the cab driver she looked up at the windows, each one of which was covered with a thick net curtain as if the people inside were keeping everyone out. As this thought came to her she fancied she saw two little white faces peering down, only to vanish before she was sure she had seen them.

Frederick opened a tall black iron gate which he carefully shut behind him and walked up the short path to the front door. He inserted a key in the lock.

"It is the maid's day off." he explained.

"I feel very nervous, Frederick" Amelia laid her hand on his arm.

Without looking at her he said, "Don't be difficult, there's a good girl. There is nothing to worry about." and entered the house leaving Amelia to follow him.

Once Frederick had shut the door on the bright sunlight Amelia could see nothing. It was like being in a black sack. As her eyes slowly adjusted to the gloom she could see that the hall was decorated in a chocolate brown paint. There was a heavy hallstand and several pictures. The subjects appeared to be very dark and depressing landcapes. There were several tightly shut doors all in the same heavy dark paint. Frederick opened one of these. Amelia followed him into the room which was nearly as dark as the hall.

There was a fire burning in the grate but even that looked dispirited and spat from time to time. The windows were covered in a net curtain so thick that not a great deal of sunlight entered. Amelia concluded that Frederick's sister was an invalid which would explain why he had to take tea with her every afternoon. She was surprised therefore when a woman who looked only a few year older than herself rose from a chair.

Amelia thought she was extremely pretty but she would have been even prettier had her hair not been pulled back in an unbecoming bun. Her clothes were black and very severe. She was wearing a jet necklace comprising several strands which she nervously twisted in her fingers. Amelia was immediately at pains to put the poor girl at her ease and forgot her own nerves.

"This is Amelia, Maud." Frederick then waited.

Neither of them was sure what to do and in the end Maud held out her hand to Amelia

"It is so nice to meet you, Amelia, Frederick has told me all about you." She had a quiet, breathless voice.

"Would you like some tea, Miss Wallace?" Maud indicated the tea tray set ready with dainty cups and saucers and plates of thin bread and butter and a tray of cakes.

Amelia accepted a cup of tea and a thin sandwich. As Maud went to hand Frederick his cup he waved it away nearly knocking it from her hand and said, "I have some urgent work I must see to in my study. I will leave you together." He looked at Maud and said, "Remember what I told you, Maud. Do not fail me."

"No, Frederick, you can be sure that I will not." Maud replied.

Amelia listened to this exchange with some annoyance. She had expected Frederick to stay and smooth their meeting. She smiled rather grimly and said, "I will be happy to stay with Maud. We can get to know each other. I am sure we shall become great friends."

Frederick left the room without replying

There was an uneasy silence. The fire spat once more. Maud carefully put her cup and saucer down on the tray.

"I have to tell you, Amelia, that Frederick has spoken to your brother to ask for your hand in marriage. He is rather concerned that you have cut yourself off from your family. Your brother told Frederick that he is no longer prepared to be responsible for you. Frederick wonders if this shows a perverseness in your nature."

Amelia sat open mouthed.

Maud seemed to be trying to make up her mind about something.

"You are not quite what I expected, Amelia. I thought you were much older." As she paused Amelia said, "I cut myself off from my family with good reason. I have already explained this to Frederick. Why are you telling me this?"

"He finds it difficult to talk to women." Then, with a glance at the door and in a rush and a lowered voice, "Don't do anything you might regret, Amelia. You have a choice but once you are married you are married for life, remember." There was a slight noise from the door. Amelia glanced at it to see that it was on the jar – surely Frederick was not evesdropping? Maud also glanced at the door and raised her voice, "I should be pleased to welcome you as a sister, Amelia."

Amelia was not sure what to do. This seemed too much like a trap but the little voice in her head said that this was her only chance if she wanted to be married and what else was there? Aunt Isabella would not live for ever and then what would she do? She would have to go and live with John and Selina and to a life of being treated as an old spinster aunt given all the jobs that nobody else wanted.

If she married Frederick she would have a house of her own and Frederick would have to take care of her for life but she would have to give up work. She would never become a designer in her own right, it was too hard a struggle and she was tired of it. She made up her mind.

"Thank you, Maud, I am sure we will get along very well."

Right on cue Frederick came back into the room rubbing his hands.

"That's settled then." He made no attempt to disguise the fact that he had been listening at the door the whole time. Amelia expected him to show some affection towards her, his affianced, but he merely took up his cup and saucer and proceeded to drink his tea.

"It will be a very quiet wedding, of course, and I have made arrangements for us to be quietly married in three weeks time."

"In three weeks? But I have to send out invitations, get a wedding dress. I can't possibly be ready in time!"

"There will be no invitations to send as there will be no guests and as for a wedding dress that will not be necessary. No, it will be a quiet wedding and you can then come straight home and pick up your duties." He was talking to her as if he was engaging a housekeeper.

Amelia bit her lip – she was completely confused. She was not sure what she wanted to do. It all sounded so cold-blooded. Where was the romance? Seeing her set face Frederick said placatingly, "Believe me, Amelia, you will thank me for it one day."

"I cannot understand why the wedding has to be so quiet." Yes she could! Who would want to see an ugly girl married without pitying her? Frederick was doing this to spare her pain. "Yes, perhaps I do, Frederick, and I think it is very thoughtful of you."

Frederick looked puzzled but said nothing. Soon after they took their leave. Maud suddenly ran forward and kissed Amelia whereupon Frederick became impatient and said, "Come along, Amelia, we must get you back home."

She expected him to come in so that they could break their news to Aunt Isabella together but when they got to the gate he said, "I will leave you to tell Mrs Trevise."

Rose cried when Amelia told her about her impending marriage.

"I wish I could take you with me, Rose."

Aunt Isabella was very disturbed by Amelia's news. No wedding guests, no wedding breakfast and no honeymoon just a swift marriage and straight home. She said that she would go whether or not she was invited and asked Amelia which Church she was getting married in. She was even more disturbed when Amelia said she did not know.

"Are you absolutely sure you want to do this, Amelia?" she asked.

"I have given my word, Aunt Isabella." And she would say no more because she knew that Aunt Isabella was right – there was something strange about the way that Frederick had insisted on no wedding guests. He had not even kissed her. But she felt that she was in the grip of events that she could do nothing about. It went round and round in her mind all night – what was she to do? Marry a man she hardly knew or stay with Aunt Isabella and when she died live as a dependant with either John or Grace?

CHAPTER TWENTY NINE

Arthur was not pleased when she was late the next morning and was even less pleased when she announced that she would be leaving to get married. Higgins expressed the opinion that that was the trouble with employing women – no sooner did they become proficient in the job than they got married. Arthur asked her about her fiance but she could not tell him very much because she did not know very much herself. Arthur decided that he would take it upon himself to do some checking. On the Friday before Amelia was to leave he was back late from lunch. She was feeling miserable, she did not really want to leave and could not see why women were not allowed to work after they were married. She mentioned this to Arthur.

"Because, as you will find, it is a fulltime job looking after a husband and children."

"But I don't have any children."

"No, but you will have to look after Mr Leros' children, won't you?"

Amelia felt a strange sensation in the region of her stomach.

"Frederick has no children."

Arthur gave her a straight look. He didn't like what he was about to do but felt that it was his duty as a friend as well as her employer.

"I happened to run into one of the partners of the firm that Leros works for," no need to tell her that he had employed an agent "and he tells me that Frederick Leros has two children – both girls. You have never met them, I take it?"

"No, I have only met his sister who seemed a very nice person. I wonder why she never mentioned the children?"

Arthur hesitated but decided he must tell her everything he knew, however painful.

"There is also some sort of scandal about his wife. I am not sure what it is, but I think he divorced her."

"Divorced!" Amelia was aghast.

She knew about divorce of course. It had been the subject of one of the meetings that she and Martha attended. Men could now divorce their wives if the wife had committed adultery. It had always seemed unfair to her that a man could have as many mistresses as he wished and his wife could not divorce him but if she strayed from the path even once he was perfectly entitled to divorce her and make sure that she never saw her children again as she was considered to be an unfit mother.

Arthur came over to her desk and put his arm round her.

"I am sorry, Amelia. Are you very much in love with him?"

She heard herself say, "No, I am not, Mr Douglass. Thank you for taking so much trouble for me. I think I should like to go home now if you don't mind. I am not feeling very well. I will see you tomorrow."

Arthur fussed over her and personally put her into her cab. She knew he meant well but she wished he would just leave her alone.

She thought about what he had told her. It was not so bad. The children were rather a shock and she wished that Frederick had told her but he probably had his reasons. The reason for a quiet wedding was now clear, they would have to get married in one of the new register offices as he was a divorced man.

When she saw Frederick that evening she would ask him about the children. He was taking her to the house so that she could decide how she wanted to furnish her room.

She began almost as soon as they were out of the house

"Why didn't you tell me that you had two children and that you had divorced your wife?"

Frederick looked extremely angry but managed to answer.

"I did not think that it was necessary, Amelia. I was going to tell you, of course."

"When, Frederick? You were not going to wait until after we were married, surely?"

"I cannot see why you are so upset, Amelia. The children are no trouble, they live at the top of the house and have a governess. You need not see them at all if you don't want to."

"Of course I want to see them. I know what it is like to be lonely as a child. What are their names?"

"Sylvia and Mary."

"And how old are they?" Amelia persisted.

Frederick put his hand to his forehead and thought for a moment.

"Sylvia is nine and Mary is seven."

"Are they pretty?"

"Sylvia is very pretty like her mother. I want you to keep an eye on her, Amelia. I will not have her growing up like her mother. Mary is not so pretty and is more amenable to discipline."

"What do you mean – discipline?"

"Girls are inherently wicked, Amelia. They have to have the devil whipped out of them."

"You have your daughters whipped?"

"I don't have them whipped." Amelia sighed with relief. "As their father I whip them myself."

"You whip your daughters!" Amelia shrank back in the cab. What had she got herself into?

On their arrival at the house Frederick excused himself saying he had some work to do in his study.

Amelia entered the drawing room where Maud was trying to make the fire burn. She looked up as Amelia came in and paused with the poker in her hand

"What is the matter, Amelia?"

"Why didn't you tell me about the children?" Amelia was frosty. Maud flushed.

"I am sorry, Frederick told me not to. I have to be careful. There are reasons."

"Yes, there always seem to be reasons. Frederick tells me he whips his daughters, is that true?"

Maud did not answer.

Amelia flung herself into an armchair.

"Why *is* Frederick marrying me, Maud?"

"It is because," Maud began but Frederick came into the room at that point and she went back to poking the fire.

"You have too much coal on that fire, Maud. How many times must I tell you I will not have extravagance in the house?"

Maud put down the poker. "I am sorry, Frederick."

"Go and find something to do, Maud, I wish to speak to Amelia."

When Maud had left the room Frederick came and stood in front of Amelia's armchair.

"There are one or two things we must get clear before our marriage. First I will not have any extravagance, money is not for wasting. Secondly, I will not have any interference in my disciplining of my own children and finally I will not have the place cluttered up with any of your friends, and in particular Martha."

"I thought you liked Martha and Albert"

"I think that Albert is very weak the way he lets Martha do as she likes and Martha is too free."

"I don't think that I want to give up my friends, Frederick." Amelia said in a reasonable voice.

"As my wife, Amelia, you will do as I say and I say that you will discontinue your acquaintance with Martha and Albert, also Mrs Trevise. I would be quite willing for you to see your brother or your mother in my presence but since you have severed connection with them the question does not arise."

"Does Maud not have any friends?"

"Maud does as she is told. She knows that I can tell her to leave the house at any time I wish. In any case she is hoping to get married, after which we will not be seeing her at all."

"You will not see your own sister?"

"Once she is married she is no longer my sister, she knows that, Amelia."

"Now, as to your other duties. You will engage a maid servant..."

"I have already got an idea about that," Amelia interrupted.

"Never interrupt me again, Amelia. Who is this servant?"

"Rose. She has been with me ever since I was born. She came the day I was born in fact. As I already know her I think she would be an excellent choice."

"I do not. You must sever all connection with her. I cannot have my wife on familiar terms with a servant. No, it is out of the question. Possibly we could do without a servant as I have no intention of doing any entertaining and I will not pay a servant to be idle."

"If you loved me Frederick you would see that I need to have people I know around me. I need to see Rose and Martha and Aunt Isabella. Tell me that you don't mean it."

"Love! What has love to do with it? I am not marrying you for love, Amelia. I am marrying you because Maud is insisting on getting married and I need someone to look after the house and make sure my instructions are carried out. There will be no physical contact between us.

I saw you at the wedding and knew that you were what I was looking for. You will never run away with another man and you know that this is the only chance you will ever have of a home of your own. I don't intend to love anyone ever again. I was foolish once, I will not make the same mistake again. And I will make sure that Sylvia and Mary never ruin any man's life the way my wife ruined mine!"

So that was it. Now she knew everything. He had been violently in love with his wife and had smothered her and been jealous of her until she could no longer stand it. She had fled with her lover knowing that she would be ostracised from society and that she would never be allowed to see her children again. That they would be told she was dead. Her life must have been intolerable for her to take that decision. Amelia felt every sympathy for this unknown woman.

"I think I will go home, Frederick. There are things I have to do. Don't bother to come with me, I will walk. Say goodbye to your sister for me."

"You can't walk home I won't allow it."

"We are not married yet, Frederick. I wish to walk home because I have some thinking to do."

For a moment she thought he was going to forcibly restrain her but he only opened the door for her. She had a very long walk home but she needed the time to think.

*****

As she walked she thought about what she had learnt that afternoon. Frederick only wanted to marry her so that he would have an unpaid housekeeper. What could she look forward to as his wife? Being completely subjugated to his will as was his sister? There was no difference between what she would have to endure living with John and Selina and what she would have to endure being married to Frederick. In fact, being married would be worse.

When she got home she went straight to her room and wrote a letter to Frederick telling him that she was not prepared to give up her freedom and there would, therefore, be no wedding. She then went out to post the letter immediately. She felt much better having done this and, although Mrs Trevise realized that something must have happened, she didn't dare ask her as Amelia was very cheerful and every time Mrs Trevise tried to discuss the wedding Amelia turned the conversation until Mrs Trevise said, "Why don't you want to discuss the wedding, Amelia. Has something happened?"

"Yes, Aunt Isabella, I have decided not to get married to Frederick. I don't think we would have been very happy."

"Neither do I. I am sorry that you have been disappointed, Amelia, but I am sure it is for the best."

When Rose was told the news she said more or less the same thing but added, When Mr Right comes along you will know, Amelia."

Amelia smiled rather grimly.

"I don't think there is going to be a Mr Right for me, Rose. One thing I have learnt is that I don't want to get married unless it is for love on both sides. I would rather end up an old maid."

This conversation was taking place in Amelia's bedroom while Rose brushed her hair as she did every night. As Rose was saying goodnight they heard what sounded like the front door bell. They looked at each other.

"Who can that be at this time of night?" Amelia wondered.

"I will go and see. You stay here, Amelia, you can't go down in your nightdress."

Rose bustled off. Amelia went out onto the landing where she met Aunt Isabella who was also dressed for bed. They heard Rose open the front door and then a female voice asking for Amelia. Amelia recognised it.

"That's Maud!" and she ran downstairs.

"What is the matter, Maud? Has something happened to Frederick?"

"No. May I come in?"

When Maud came into the hall Amelia saw that she was carrying a small carpet bag.

"You have left Frederick!" she stated.

"Yes. When you had gone this afternoon we had a dreadful quarrel. He accused me of turning you against him. I am sorry, Amelia, but I did not know you would be so young. From what Frederick told me after he had met you I thought you were much older. You see I'm going to be married. When I told Frederick he was furious because it would mean that he would lose a housekeeper.

He tried to make me give up Henry but I refused. Soon after this he went to the wedding and when he came home he said he had found someone who would be an ideal wife and he would not therefore need to have a housekeeper. Now that you have refused him he says that I must stay, so I ran away."

Mrs Trevise had come down the stairs while Maud was speaking. Now she came up to Maud put her arm round her and saying, "Bring some tea into the drawing room, Rose." led Maud into the room while Amelia busied herself poking the fire up into a blaze.

Maud sank down gratefully into an armchair. She was clearly extremely upset. She warmed herself while Mrs Trevise watched her.

Rose brought in the tea; Mrs Trevise poured them a cup each and then sat back and waited.

"I didn't know what to do so I came here, Amelia. You have always been very nice to me and I don't know anyone else except Henry and I can't go to him at this time of night."

"What does your Henry do for a living?" Mrs Trevise asked.

"He is training to become a missionary. We are going to get married and go straight out to the Mission field."

"Do you think that your brother will come looking for you?"

"I am sure he will. I wonder if you could put me up just for tonight. I can go and see Henry tomorrow and I am sure he will find me somewhere to stay until we can be married. I can't stay here. I don't want you to be involved and I don't want to see Frederick again. Once I have left the country I need never see him again."

She did not seem particularly sorry about this, Amelia noticed.

Mrs Trevise rang for Rose and asked her to make up the bed in the spare room. While they waited for this to be done Maud told them how she had met Henry, what he was like and how much she was looking forward to helping him in his work.

Amelia let her go on talking. She was thinking how glad she was that she had had such a narrow escape. When Rose came to say that the room was ready and a fire lit they all went to bed. Amelia slept very well for the first time in days and felt ready to tackle anyone when she woke in the morning.

Soon after breakfast Rose was despatched to Henry's lodgings with a note and came back in a cab with him. Maud thanked Mrs. Trevise and Amelia and promised to write when she was settled in Africa. As they were saying their goodbyes Maud told Amelia that she was sure she would find someone better than Frederick one day soon. She then left waving from the hansom until they could no longer see her.

When Amelia went in to work and told Arthur that she was not going to be married after all he was delighted. Higgins said nothing but uncharacteristically patted her on the back. Amelia settled down to work and began doing designs in her spare time. She had several ideas for animated dolls which she diffidently showed Arthur. He seemed quite enthusiastic about them and asked if he could keep the designs. She agreed and watched him put them away carefully in a drawer.

"I may mention these to Simon after Christmas." he said "Don't worry, I won't tell him who did them. I just want his reaction."

Winter came early that year. There was frost at the end of September and snow which began in the second week of October. Amelia found that getting out of bed to go to work in the cold of winter was not as easy as it was in the summer. She was very pleased not to have to wait in the freezing cold for an omnibus.

Christmas was even quieter than usual as Amelia caught a bad chill and had to stay in bed over the festive season. She was quite happy to be able to stay in a nice warm bed and doze and read and not think about anything very much. Then Aunt Isabella went down with a very bad cold. Amelia and Rose nursed her between them. It was a tiring time but eventually Aunt Isabella began to recover. Amelia was glad that Rose was so strong – she never seemed to catch anything! When Amelia mentioned this Rose attributed it to her years in Ratcliff Court.

CHAPTER THIRTY

The New Year came in with a quick thaw which made slush of the pavements. Aunt Isabella was now allowed downstairs for part of the day and Amelia was kept busy amusing her.

On a particularly depressing day when the gas had to be lit at 3.30 in the afternoon Arthur came bustling in. He had been visiting the invalids regularly with fresh fruit and flowers sent by Patience. Now he was bursting with excitement and, hardly waiting for them to thank him for the gifts, he turned to Amelia saying

"When do you think you will be coming back to work, Amelia?"

"As soon as Aunt Isabella can spare me Mr Douglass. I am feeling quite well now."

"Good. Well, I have a surprise for you when you come in. No, I am not going to tell you what it is but it is something which I think you will like."

After he had gone Amelia and Mrs Trevise laughed over his excitement. Just like a little boy.

"I expect it is a new machine for the factory." Amelia mused. "Now Mr Douglass has decided to embrace the new technology there is no stopping him. Apparently the men in the factory have bets on what he is going to install next."

By the time Amelia felt that Aunt Isabella was really on the mend she had forgotten about Arthur's promise. When she entered his room on her first day back he was beaming and pointing to a strange-looking contraption on the wall. It was made of wood and had what appeared to be two doorbells on the top. Something that resembled a small letter box was underneath the bells and under the bells, on a hook, was a black tube. She could not think what this might be. Arthur watched her face.

"It is a telephone. I can speak to someone who is not even in this building. Let me show you." He picked up the black tube, put one end to his ear and turned a handle on the box then, speaking slowly and loudly, said, apparently to the box "Hello – London number five, please." There was a pause while Arthur stood looking important. Amelia was fascinated then Arthur said "Is that you, Patience? This is me – speak to Amelia." He turned and handed the tube to her "Speak into that hole" he instructed indicating a small hole in the box. Tentatively Amelia said "Mrs Douglass?" A tinny little voice said "This is Mrs Douglass – how are you, Amelia?" "Well, thank you." Arthur indicated that he wanted the tube back. "I am going now, Patience." He turned the handle again and after a pause said, "London two off". He then replaced the black tube beneath the bells.

"I had a telephone installed in the house so that Patience and I can talk to each other. She learnt how to use it very quickly. I wanted Simon to have one in his office but he said it would be a distraction."

Amelia was not sure how she felt about the telephone but Arthur insisted that she learn how to use it.

"They will be in every office one day." he told her. She didn't think that they would be very welcome. Higgins would go nowhere near it. Arthur wanted to have one installed by Higgin's desk but he flatly refused and said that he would leave rather than be forced to use such 'an unnatural thing.' It was a mixed blessing especially when the bells clanging to signal an incoming call made her jump.

There was a great deal of work to do that spring and orders seemed to come in thick and fast. Everyone was very busy. Arthur asked Amelia if she would mind working later in the evening to keep up with the work. Amelia didn't mind as the nights were getting lighter and Aunt Isabella seemed to be back to her old self. Due to the amount of work Arthur asked Amelia if she would consider doing some letters for Mr Jarrett. Amelia was not very happy about it but realized it was silly for Higgins and his clerks to be rushed off their feet when she could relieve them of some of the work.

On the first day of the new arrangement Mr Jarrett came to her room to dictate some letters. There had been no contact between them except in a very distant manner. Amelia was dreading the encounter but she need not have worried. Mr Jarrett was extremely businesslike and stuck to the matter in hand. After he had gone she breathed a sigh of relief.

After that first day Mr Jarrett gave Roy handwritten letters for her to type. Once the letters were finished Roy took them back to Mr Jarrett for signing. In this way they managed to avoid one another. Amelia waited for complaints but there were none. Perhaps Mr Jarrett had got over his antagonism towards her.

Toward the middle of March Arthur went to Paris for an exhibition. He would be away for several days. He had decided to take Patience with him and they would have a little holiday. Mr Jarrett was left in charge. Before he went Arthur asked Amelia how she and Mr Jarrett were getting on.

"Very well, now. We don't see much of each other. I think that is all over now, Mr Douglass. I hope that you and Mrs Douglass have a good holiday and that you see some interesting things at the exhibition."

"I will tell you all about it when I return. I am glad that you and Simon are getting on. I have an idea I want to discuss with you both when I return."

The day Arthur was due home Roy brought letter after letter to her. She was completely overwhelmed. She would have to stay late to finish. She could leave them until the next day of course but she didn't want to give Mr Jarrett the opportunity of saying that she was not capable of keeping up with the work. She sent Higgins out to the cabby telling him she would not be needing him that evening. She was extremely tired by the time she had finished the last letter.

Glancing at the office clock she saw it was past Roy's leaving time. She would have to copy the letters and take them in to Mr Jarrett's office herself. As she entered the outer office she half hoped Mr Higgins would be there but the room was deserted. For some reason she felt uneasy. Previously when she had been working late Mr Higgins had waited to see her out so that he could get her a cab and lock up.

The gas lamps were on so perhaps Mr Higgins had only popped out for a moment. She would not be a coward – she would take the letters to Mr Jarrett herself. She felt a little shiver of fear then told herself not to be so silly. She would put the letters on Mr Jarrett's desk and then take the omnibus home. She was not very happy about using the omnibus late at night but that could not be helped.

She copied the letters; thanks to Roy's tuition she was now an expert. She didn't bother to knock on Mr Jarrett's door as she was certain he had gone for the day. He was sitting at his desk apparently immersed in his work. Amelia tried not to draw attention to herself as she crossed the room to put the letters on his desk. Without looking up he said

"Sit down, Miss Wallace, I want to talk to you."

Amelia's heart sank. She could refuse and walk out of the room but then he would know that she was afraid of him and it seemed important that he did not suspect this. She supposed he had found something else to complain about. Well, she would not put up with it. When Mr Douglass came back she would tell him that she was leaving. She would be sorry to go but she could no longer put up with the situation. It was best that she went. She sat down on the chair in front of the desk.

"We are alone in the building and I think the time has come to repay you for what you have done to my life." he said matter-of-factly.

She had no idea was he was talking about.

"I think I can hear Mr Higgins in the outer office." she said brightly.

"I told Higgins that I would lock up this evening. I also told him that you had gone."

Amelia got to her feet to make for the door but Simon moved swiftly round the desk and stood in front of her. Instinctively she backed away from him and found herself moving round the room until she was pinned into a corner. The communicating door was just to her left. If only she could reach it!

"Now listen to what I have to tell you. Do you remember your sister Mary?" she nodded, speechless. "Thanks to you we never married. I loved Mary but you set her against me." She shook her head vigorously. "Yes, you did! You were always there in the way. She always had to take you home or look after you in some way. You came between us. You saw me take the designs, didn't you – didn't you?" she nodded. She did remember something. "All these years I have been wondering whether or not you would remember and when you came here as a Typewriter I knew that you had. You were only waiting for an opportunity to blackmail me, weren't you?"

Amelia shook her head again.

"No, of course not. I didn't remember you, not until you reminded me just now."

"I don't believe that. Thanks to you I am married to a woman I hate and have to do as her father tells me but he won't last for ever and once I have my hands on the business I am going to ruin your family – once I have got rid of you I will bring down your brother's firm and then I may get some peace."

Amelia had never been so frightened in her life. She had no idea what she was going to do. Her brain didn't seem to belong to her – it refused to function.

As he walked towards her he raised his hands, curling his fingers as he came. She couldn't move, watching him as he got closer. Then his hands were round her throat. She closed her eyes feeling as if it was all happening to someone else.

Suddenly the communicating door flew open. Amelia opened her eyes to see a large, rough-looking man standing in the doorway. Jarrett turned to see who was disturbing him.

"You! What are you doing here?"

In his surprise he let go of Amelia who slumped against the wall, gasping.

The intruder took in the situation.

"Up to your old tricks then, Mr Jarrett." he sneered. Walking across to Amelia he got hold of her arm and before Jarrett could move pulled her away from the wall, opened the connecting door to Arthur's office and threw her through it. He then shut the door. She heard Jarrett's voice raised in anger.

"What do you think you are doing? Don't let her get away. She knows too much. I want her."

Amelia heard Jarrett moving across the room to the door. She had no time to reach Arthur's door. She looked round for somewhere to hide and crawled under Arthur's desk.

"I am not worried about your concerns, only mine. I need enough money to get me out of the country and I want it now. I never told anyone who it was that paid me to steal the designs, now I want my reward."

"How did you escape?"

"It was all planned a very long time ago and the next step in the plan is that you give me enough money to get away before the police find me. There was a small problem. A warder got in the way. I had to kill him. The police won't rest until they get me. I shall have to go abroad. I had planned to take Rose with me but I have no time now. I shall come back for her – I always pay my debts. Now it's time for you to pay yours, Jarrett. Open the safe."

"No, Anderson, I can't."

"There must be some money in the safe and I know that you are alone. You are an important person, aren't you? Going to inherit the firm when your pa-in-law dies. You must have the key to the safe. You're not going to let me down, are you?"

"I don't care about you, Anderson." Jarrett sounded demented "Get out of my way. I'm going to find that girl and you are not going to stop me!"

Jarrett opened the door and Amelia scrunched up even smaller. She could see nothing but could hear the sound of a struggle.

"Come here!" Anderson sounded very angry. "All I want is some money then you can do what you like."

"Can't you understand – she is getting away. Let me go damn you!"

There was a gasp and then a thud. She heard someone run across the floor and out through the door. Tentatively she crawled out from under the desk. Jarrett was lying on the floor. He had a knive protruding from his chest but he was still breathing although irregularly. She must get help as soon as possible. Looking round the room for inspiration she saw the telephone apparatus. She silently thanked Arthur for his mania for new inventions.

Shakily she picked up the black tube and cranked the handle. She panicked for a moment as she tried to remember Arthur's number – something to do with fingers – she had it – No. 5. She hoped that Arthur was back and was relieved when a voice which sounded nothing like Arthur's said "Arthur Douglass – who is that?" After she had quickly told him all that had happened he instantly took charge.

"Wait there. I am coming immediately."

She breathed a sigh of relief then remembered and said "London two off", replaced the tube and sank into Arthur's chair where he found her fifteen minutes later. She was only mildly surprised to see that he was accompanied by Mr Higgins.

"I found Higgins on the doorstep, he did not believe that you had gone home so he came back."

Arthur went and leaned over Mr Jarrett then came back to Amelia.

"Go on home now. Higgins, get Miss Wallace a cab, put her in it and then come back here. I am going to use the telephone to summon the police."

Shocked though she was Amelia smiled at the excitement in his voice. One of his new toys was proving its worth!

It was late by the time Amelia got home and Mrs Trevise and Rose were getting worried. By the time she had explained what had happened and assured them both that she was unharmed it was nearly midnight.

She managed to get a few hours sleep before the Police came to interview her. Then, in spite of protests from Aunt Isabella and Rose, she went into the office and tried to work which was difficult with the Police swarming over everything.

Arthur was surprised to see her. He shut himself in Mr Jarrett's office with the police. Amelia busied herself at her type writing machine.

After the Police had gone Mr Higgins came and asked her to show him how to use the telephone.

"It seems that it could be useful after all."

Arthur came back into his office looking tired.

"It is a dreadful thing. Patience and Eleanor have been at the hospital most of the day but I don't think there is much hope. Are you sure you don't want to go home?"

"No, Mr Douglass, I feel happier working"

"Yes, work is a grand thing for taking your mind off your troubles."

Two days later Jarrett died. He did not regain consciousness. Amelia could not in all honesty feel very sorry. She had not told the Police that he had tried to kill her only that she had been in Jarrett's office when Anderson burst in and had managed to hide under Arthur's desk. She did, however, tell Arthur who was shocked. The Police had been looking for Anderson but they didn't hold out much hope of finding him. Jarrett was buried quietly and Eleanor went to live with Arthur and Patience. Arthur told Amelia that his daughter was different. Not so sharp tongued as she had once been.

On the day after the funeral Arthur said to Amelia, "As you will realize, Amelia, this means we are now without a designer but I have my eye on a very good one to whom I am going to offer the position."

"I think that is an excellent idea, Mr Douglass."

"Good. Now I want you to take a rest of about a week. Take Mrs Trevise away somewhere."

"But we are so busy, Mr Douglass."

"You will be working very hard when you come back believe me, Amelia."

CHAPTER THIRTY ONE

The weather had decided to turn into summer after all so Amelia and Mrs Trevise took themselves away to walk up and down in the bracing air of Bournemouth for a week. While they were away Rose took the opportunity to give the house a thorough spring clean. All except the locked room. When they got back Mrs Trevise exclaimed at the brightness of the house. Then she thought for a moment and summoned both Amelia and Rose upstairs. They found her outside the locked door.

"I didn't go in, madam." Rose was afraid Mrs Trevise would think she had betrayed her trust.

"I never thought that you had, Rose, but now I think it is time I opened up this room. I will pack away what I want to keep and get rid of the rest. We can use it as another spare bedroom. Will you both help me?"

"Yes, of course." Amelia and Rose glanced at each other.

Mrs Trevise took out a key which was suspended on a chain round her neck and unlocked the door.

"Come in," she invited.

It was a beautiful bedroom. There were two dressing tables and two wardrobes. Aunt Isabella strode across to one of the wardrobes and opened it. It was full of male clothing of a bygone style. Amelia looked round. On one of the dressing tables were a man's toiletries including a pair of brushes with the initials AP. She wondered why 'P' and not 'T'. On the other dressing table was a photograph in a silver frame of a nice, gentle looking man who looked vaguely familiar. She looked at Aunt Isabella who was handing suits to Rose. Aunt Isabella caught her glance.

"Yes, Amelia, that is Selina's father and no there has never been a Mr Trevise. Trevise is my maiden name. We were never married. He was already married. As he was a man much in the public eye he could not obtain a divorce without a ruinous scandal. He was quite willing to face it but I was not prepared to let him make that sacrifice. We loved each other very much and when he died I locked the room and just kept it dusted from time to time. Now I feel that I can put all these memories away. I shall never forget, of course. This is just between us three. Selina must never know, promise me."

They both promised. Amelia was very touched that Aunt Isabella had decided to share her secret with them both. She made up her mind there and then that if she could not get married for love she would never get married at all.

"There is one more thing. When I was ill last winter I did a great deal of thinking. I will not live for ever but quite a long time yet, I hope," as she saw Amelia's stricken face. "But it is inevitable that I shall die before you, Amelia. I have, therefore, made a new Will. I am leaving you the house plus a substantial sum so that you can continue to live here if you wish. I am also leaving a large sum to you, Rose, on the understanding that you will always look after Amelia."

"Yes, of course, madam," Rose managed to say.

"What about Selina?" Amelia asked. "She is your daughter."

"Selina will get her share, never fear. How like you to be worried about Selina in spite of the way she has treated you."

Amelia did not know what to reply so, smiling, she went back to sorting out the room.

★★★★★

The day she went back to work was warm and sunny. She should be feeling happy, instead she felt apprehensive about the new designer. How would he view a female Typewriter?

As she entered the outer office Roy hastened to open the wooden gate for her and stood back, grinning. As she passed him he solemnly bowed. All the clerks were standing round Mr Higgin's desk. When she reached the desk Mr Higgins presented her with a bunch of flowers.

"We are all very pleased to have you back with us, Miss Wallace."

She turned back to the room with the flowers in her hand.

"Thank you all very much." she stammered. Delighted by her blushes the men clapped.

With another smile to them all she went into Mr Douglass's room. Everyone followed.

Mr Douglass was waiting for her with yet another bunch of flowers. She went to put the flowers on her desk and then became aware of a young girl sitting there. She had never seen her before. The girl rose as Amelia approached the desk.

"That is not your desk, Amelia, that is Miss Prentice's desk."

Amelia turned back to him, puzzled. He was smiling.

"This is our new Typewriter, Amelia," he said.

She raised her eyebrows "Amelia?"

"Yes and my name is Arthur. Now come with me," and he led them all to Mr Jarrett's office but it was not Mr Jarrett's office. Amelia thought she was going to faint when she saw, in gold lettering on the door:

MISS AMELIA WALLACE

CHIEF DESIGNER

She looked at Arthur who nodded, she looked at Higgins who was rather moist about the eyes and behind him to the clerks all grinning at her. She was stunned. It was what she had always wanted.

"I take it you accept the position?" Arthur asked.

"Oh yes, please!"

The men cheered.

Mr Higgins ushered the clerks back into the outer office, saying briskly, "Everyone back to work – there is time to make up."

"I will be in my office if you want me Amelia – just come through the communicating door."

Arthur ushered Miss Prentice into his room. Amelia could hear him chuckling still.

When everyone had gone and alone in her new office she looked round with pleasure. All Mr Jarrett's furniture had been removed and she could smell new wood. The carpet was new and on the wall was her very own telephone. No wonder Arthur wanted her out of the way for a week! She sighed with pleasure then sat down at her new desk and pulled a pad towards her.

She had just had an idea...